Be Mine Baby

ANNA WHITE

Note from the author

Be Mine Baby is book one of the Be Mine Duet. This book contains triggers and makes reference to the following: sexual assault, child abuse, pregnancy, abortion, drugs misuse, violence and sexual content. Please if any of the above offends you please do not read any further.

ISBN-13: 979-8-7605-6149-7

DEDICATION

This is for you, my wonderful friends that pushed me to publish this book, without you it would still be sitting in my google docs. Thank you for giving me the confidence to ignore that niggle of self-doubt and push through.

(: - love you all, always.

CONTENTS

ACKNOWLEDGMENTS

Edited by: liji editing
Thank you, Lindsey, for making this book sparkle with
your magic!

My wonderful Beta readers

PROLOGUE
LITTLE ANGEL

CHLO

I was only small when it all started. I remembered all of the shouting and screaming and yelling that came from her mouth time and time again. Mostly, I remembered his arms wrapped around me, stale smelling clothes, and his light hum against my ear. The hum was him trying to block it out. All of it. The screaming. The shouting. The crying. All of it. Every. Single. Thing.

"It'll be alright, Coco," he whispered softly against my ear as he continued to hum a little louder this time. I simply nodded and held him closer. I pressed my head against his chest and held onto his T-shirt as he rocked us both. This was normal for a weekend when they were both in the house together. Mummy and Daddy. This is what happened. They would start off laughing and smiling with each other and then something would happen. Mummy would look at him the wrong way or say something to set him off, and then he would hit her. She would scream and then Jay would try and take us both away. Hide us for as long as possible. Like big brothers were supposed to. Or

1

that's what he said to me. Hopefully, Daddy would fall asleep before he got to us. *Before he got to me.* He'd always said he loved me, but daddies didn't hurt their little girls... *did they?* I flinched at the sound of the front door being slammed shut and felt Jay breathe outwards heavily. I knew what was coming. It was *that* time again.

"I don't want Daddy, Jay. I just want you." I choked out my little words.

"I know, Coco." Jay's words were a soft whisper as he held me tighter against his chest. My eyes were leaking again. It tasted awful. Salty. I felt Jay's chest go firm as our bedroom door was pushed open with force. "I got you." Jay squeezed me again, and I frowned as his heart beat louder. I knew what that meant. I had to go with Daddy.

"Where's my little angel?" Daddy's voice echoed around our little bedroom. I froze a little, unable to move from Jay's grip at our bedside.

"She's asleep." Jay's voice shook a little as he spoke, and silence fell between them.

"Well, then wake her, boy." Daddy was angry. *Don't provoke him, Jay, please.* I begged internally. *He'll hurt you too.* My eyes flung open and landed on Daddy's. He held out his hand and I took it. My tiny hands looked smaller in his, and they shook. I was his angel tonight. He didn't seem angry with me. "There she is." His lips thinned as he smiled. His dark eyes didn't smile like Jay's when he smiled and laughed with me. They were just always so dark. I tried to smile back and stepped closer towards him. "Mummy won't be home tonight." I closed my eyes tightly and shook my head.

"Where has she gone?" Jay asked. He sounded brave. I wished that I was brave. I wasn't. I was the weak one. I wanted to be brave, like him. Just like Jay.

"Shut up boy." Daddy raised his hand and the sound of skin landing on skin filled my ears. "Angel, will you keep Daddy company?" My eyes were leaking again. I looked down at my big brother holding his face where Daddy had hit him so hard and nodded. If he was hurting me, he wasn't hurting him. I flinched as he squeezed my hand hard in his. Daddy loved me. All daddies did this… I was being pulled towards Mummy and Daddy's room, across the dirty brown carpet, and as I glanced back at Jay, sorrow filled me. *Did Jay want me to keep him company too?* The thought of him touching me like Daddy did made me a little sick… *but why? That's how people show they love each other, isn't it?*

LITTLE WHITE LIES

I was sore. Daddy was angry and I was sore. It was a school day. Daddy must have put me back into bed last night. I shook my head and struggled to stand from my bed and wake Jay. My eyes watched my big brother sleep. He was wrapped around his favourite teddy bear, and he was breathing loudly. I smiled as I reached across the small gap between our beds and shook him. His brow furrowed deeply. The dark hair between his eyebrows disappeared as he frowned deeper and woke up.

"Coco?" His voice was shaky, and I smiled at him as his puddle-coloured eyes landed on mine.

"We have school," I reminded him. He always forgot. Sometimes, I wondered what he did most days when we weren't there. I liked our school. The teachers were nice to me. The kids not so much. Jay said kids were cruel and if he was in school with me, he'd kill them. A little laugh left my mouth, and I gripped my ribs. "Ouch." I flinched. Jay shot out of bed and was almost instantly at my side. "It's okay," I reassured him. Images from the night before flashed in my mind. Daddy's body was heavy on mine. I took another breath as my chest grew tighter and tighter.

"What happened, Coco?" Jay pushed me for information, and I shook my head.

"I can't tell you," I whispered as tears left my eyes and fell on my pyjama bottoms. "He'd kill you if you knew." He shook his head desperately.

"We should tell Mr Miller." My eyes widened, and I shook my head frantically.

"No, please don't make me tell. He loves me." I defended my daddy. Jay didn't understand. He would never understand. I gripped my T-shirt and felt his arm land around my shoulders.

"I wish you'd tell me more, Coco." His head landed on top of mine and I grimaced. I never wanted to talk about

4

it. It hurt. I was sore. So sore. "I need to borrow Mum's make up." I moved my head from his shoulder and sighed as I looked at the lovely handprint etched on his cheek. His shoulders lifted and then fell, and I touched his soft golden skin. This was a similarity we shared. Mum had said she loved that we looked like we belonged on a beach somewhere. That we were sun-kissed.

"I wish you didn't open your big mouth, puddle." I teased him. Puddle had been a nickname since I could remember. It used to be Muddy Puddle, because his eyes were the same colour as a muddy puddle. I smiled at him and watched him shake his head as he hauled himself from the bed.

"C'mon, Coco. Let's go." He pulled softly on my arms and helped me to my feet. I hadn't ached like this for a while. My legs felt heavy as I followed my big brother towards our bathroom to brush our teeth. We weren't allowed a bath until Wednesday. Wednesdays were bath nights. That's what Mummy said. Twice a week because of the water rates.

***

Every step I took today hurt. My insides hurt. It hurt to sit down. I winced as I sat next to a girl from my class. She smiled and then moved away from me. Everyone always moved. Sadness flooded my chest.

"You're not good enough for anybody but me, angel." That's what Daddy said to me. I wiped the tears from my cheeks with the back of my hand and watched as Mr Miller took a seat next to me. He looked big on the tiny chair.

"Hey, Chloe." His voice was low and soft. He looked younger than Daddy. Daddy's hair was thin. Mr Miller's was long and thick. He was tall and his cheeks were round. He always had time to talk to me.

"Hi, Sir," I muttered politely. Polite. Mummy had always said we should use our manners, speak properly and not speak a word of what happened at home. Not to a soul. Those were the rules. Not that she ever stuck to the rules. I rolled my eyes at the thought of her.

"No dinner today?" I winced as he moved on the tiny school stool of the dining room. Other children were looking at me and I felt my face fill with blood. I shrugged. I didn't want to tell him why I'd forgotten my lunch. I was hungry. My tummy ached, but Mummy had no money. The milk in my breakfast was sour and I felt sick just thinking about it. "You not talking to me today?" I couldn't look up at him. I wanted to tell him that I was hungry, that I wanted food and a warm bed and dry clothes that didn't smell funny. He had that face, the face you wanted to spill every secret to. The soft face. Mummy liked him. She had said that she wished she'd never met Daddy. That she never had us kids. I wiped my eyes again as I took a breath inward. My stomach was growling, my body aching and the sadness all-consuming.

WEDNESDAY

It was bath night. Excitement flooded me as I skipped into the lounge. Daddy was snoring and Mummy was humming a tune and swaying to a song I'd never heard before. She had a bottle in her hand which was never a good sign.

"Mummy?" I pulled on her skirt softly and watched as she turned up the radio a little. "Mummy?" I questioned a little louder. Her amber coloured eyes glared through mine. All of the hairs on my arms stood on end and Jay placed his hand against my shoulder softly.

"What do you pair of arseholes want?" she slurred. Jay's grip tightened against my shoulder, and I took a breath inwards again. I felt a mixture of emotions flood me. I was sad that she hated us. I couldn't understand why she didn't like us. All we had ever done was what they wanted us to do. All I had ever done was please them. I looked up at Jay and noticed the regretful look in his eyes.

"It's bath night, Mum," Jay reminded her calmly. Though he was only three years older than me, he was so mature. I loved him with all of my heart. He tried so hard to keep it together for me.

"Can you not run it yourself!?" she shouted. I watched his brow furrow and watched as she caught herself on the kitchen worktop before she reached for the large bottle of wine. She was a weak-looking woman, her blonde hair wasn't fake but mousey in colour, it was long and swayed wherever she did. It flowed with the bob of her drunken head. She used to be pretty. I had seen pictures of her and Daddy when they were younger, but lately, she looked tired. Small bags had appeared. "Aren't you like fourteen now?" She was swaying again, slowly, and I watched as Jay's little hand steadied her softly. So softly like he touched me. Like I was glass. Like we would break. Maybe he knew something we didn't.

"No, Mum. I'm nine," he muttered as she turned the

radio up even more. Daddy snored again, and my chest fluttered with fear. *Please don't wake up.*

"Old enough." She pushed the back of his thick dark head of hair away from her side and I watched as he tilted his head towards the stairs. I followed him, leaving the smoky, loud and scary room behind us. He was really going to run the bath. I chuckled a little. I noticed that mischievous look in his eyes.

"Jay, you can't," I whispered as I pulled on his arm. "Daddy will shout." I tried my hardest to convince him that this would all end terribly. I knew he wouldn't listen. Not now, not ever. I smiled to myself as he hopped into the bathroom and pushed the stopper into the plughole. He gave me the biggest cheesiest grin.

"Dad is asleep. We need a bath. I'm filthy." He *hated* being dirty. I felt dirty all of the time. I just nodded as he flicked the water on. First the hot and then the cold tap. I smiled at him and watched him grin at me. "You bath first. I'll wait outside. When you've finished, I'll get in." I nodded as I pulled on my T-shirt. "Okay?" he questioned me so that he knew I understood.

"Okay." I gave him a small smile and watched as he tiptoed to reach the soap.

"Use this." He placed it in my hands and kissed my head softly. We stood watching the water rise for some time. I was praying Daddy didn't wake up and Mummy fell asleep. *One bath. Just one bath.*

"You know normal kids don't live like this, Co?" He raised his eyebrow upwards as he looked towards me. He was wrapped up in his duvet. The duvet must have been as old as me because it was so thin. Somehow, we had managed to bath, with no screams from downstairs, no slaps around the face, and no shouting from either of them. Now I was cold, it was so cold in this house. I looked towards him; his sheets were Thomas the Tank Engine. The only sheets he had were those and Winnie the Pooh, and as much as he hated to admit it, he much preferred the Thomas sheets. I glanced at mine. Daddy had brought me the sheet that was wrapped around me. It was light in colour. Purple.

"What?" I asked him as he frowned deeply at me. I'd zoned out as my teeth began to chatter.

"You know, like this? Freezing, hungry and battered." I rolled my eyes and then I looked towards him. His eye had begun to bruise where Daddy had hit him only days before, when he tried to stop him from hurting me.

"Why does Daddy hit you, Jay?" I watched his eyes close briefly. I was growing curious the older I was getting. I may have been just six, but I understood that this set-up wasn't normal. Our family was wrong.

"Because he hates me." I frowned at him as he spoke.

"Is that why he hurts me?" My voice was a whisper, and my bottom lip trembled as the fear of rejection shot through my little body. His eyes shot open.

"Oh, Coco, I'll get you out of it all. I swear I will." I shook my head to try to stop imagining my daddy's sweaty face against mine, his body weight against me, and the ripping sensation when he's *there*. I muffled a scream and watched as Jay climbed into bed with me. "I'll get us out, Coco." I nodded and hugged him tighter. I wrapped my arms around him tightly and tried to breathe. He was a little bit warmer than me as he pulled my head closer to his chest. He hummed softly against my hair. This was where I was safe. With my big brother. I was always safe here.

** THREE YEARS LATER **

I was sobbing in my bed. I was oblivious of the time. Jay wasn't home. It was freezing cold. Mummy and Daddy had been screaming at each other for what seemed like forever. I'd been banned by Daddy from going to school for a week. He said he didn't mean it. *He said he'd never do it again.* I wasn't sure I believed him anymore. He always said that. There were purple marks all over my neck, face and body. I wasn't strong enough to fight him off. I never had been. I winced as the sound of bricks being thrown up against the glass of the window pulled me from my nightmare. *Jay was home.* I breathed a sigh of relief. I leapt out of bed and scrambled to undo our window. I hung my head out of it and glanced down at him smiling back up at me. His large brown eyes glistened. Our street wasn't in a bad area. Mum and Dad had said to us time and time again that we were to speak properly. There weren't many bad areas of Kensington. Kensington wasn't meant to house people like us. Kids that weren't fed. We went to school with kids whose mums and dads owned multi-million-pound homes, and who had access to whatever their little hearts desired.

"Let me in," he called up to me, and I nodded before I threw down our rope. This had been his way in and out of the house for the last year or so. He was so clever. I watched him climb the wall and reached for him before I shut the window. It didn't need to be any colder in this room. "How long have they been going at it like that?" He pointed his head towards the sound of our parents screaming at each other, and I shrugged softly. I had zoned out. I had zoned out a while ago. I had been thinking about what the kids at school were doing that week, who Olivia had been playing with in my absence, and if anybody even realised I wasn't there.

"Ages." I folded my arms. I looked up at my brother and noticed he was all dishevelled looking. I was angry at him. He hadn't been in all day or last night. I'd been scared and he wasn't there. I frowned and placed myself back on the bed.

"What's the matter, Co?" He sat next to me, and his head dipped a little as he made eye contact with me. I wasn't going to roll over and forgive him tonight. He left knowing that they would start arguing, we both sensed the tension in the atmosphere between them at dinner. I shook my head and turned over so that I was now laying down with my back facing him. I didn't have the energy to fight with anyone today. It had taken all my energy to drown out our parents screaming.

"I'm taking the fucking kids!" she screamed suddenly. I was tense. *Oh no.* Jay wrapped himself around me like a blanket and *'hid'* us under my bedclothes as Mum's footsteps became closer.

"It's all right, Co. I got you," he muttered as our bedroom door flung open, the sound of it ricocheting off the wall making me jump.

"I'll take the little slag away from you," she slurred as she pulled back the duvet and pulled me from the bed by my hair. Pain ripped through me. "Jamie Smith, get the fuck out of that bed, we're leaving." She pushed me with force out of the bedroom, and as Jay scrambled to follow, I felt my chest constricting. I couldn't breathe. Daddy was standing in the stairway, blocking us and glaring. Glaring down at me.

"I dare you, Liz." His big bellowing voice made bile hit my throat. His black eyes narrowed as he opened his arms out to me. I didn't want to jump into them. We weren't safe with either of them. I was trembling. "Take them away from me…" He spoke slowly. "I fucking dare you," he growled at Mum. My skin pricked at his low tone. Her arms were folded across her body, and I reached to grip Jay in my arms. I was petrified. They had always argued but we were never brought into it. Ever.

"Don't dare me, Jase." She was wobbling as she pulled on Jay's jacket and ushered him past Dad. Dad had me gripped in his arms. *Please don't let me go.* I was internally begging that they didn't part us. I wouldn't survive without my brother.

"Jay!" I cried after him. I could smell the whiskey on Dad's breath as he kissed my cheek. I wanted to throw up, so I wriggled and wriggled until I was free.

"Run, Co! Run!" Jay bellowed as I ran after him and Mum. I ran. I ran as fast as my legs would carry me with Jay. I ran until I physically couldn't draw on my breath anymore. Mum had caught up with us somehow, and as we hit an alleyway, she collapsed onto the floor to catch her breath. Every gasp out of my lungs felt like relief. She had really just left him. The monster. She'd left. *He was gone.* My relief vanished just as quickly as it appeared.

"Now what the fuck am I supposed to do with you?" she hissed our way and stumbled to stand to her feet. Jay offered her his hand but she pushed him away. He looked towards me like he had absolutely no idea what to do. If he didn't have a plan, then we were all screwed.

I wasn't sure where we'd spent the night, but it stunk. It was colder than the house we had called home since I was born, and I was shaking from head to toe even though I was wrapped up in Jay's arms. I was terrified. My teeth chattered and he shook his head as he breathed against my head softly.

"I'll get us out of this shit hole too." I frowned as he spoke.

"Don't swear, Jay. It's naughty." I spoke through chattering teeth. Mum had passed out on the bed in our little room. I felt him rip the duvet off her and place it around us instead.

"So are Mum and Dad." He wrapped us up in another layer of sheets as he scowled at our mum. "This is naughty, Chlo. What they're doing is bad." I closed my eyes and gripped him tighter. "We're in a hostel, Co," he added, breaking his short silence. I nodded. There was a boom-boom noise coming from above and below us, people were screaming and shouting, and I covered my ears. I couldn't deal with any more shouting and screaming today. I'd had enough.

"I wish I'd never been born," I whispered as tears dripped from my eyes.

"Don't say that," he begged as his voice wavered. "You're my baby sister, I'm not going to let anyone hurt you ever again. This is gonna get better." He spoke so softly. I wanted to believe him, but I didn't. I couldn't. Nothing ever good came from him sticking up for me or getting in the way of Dad's warpath. He just became the battering ram. I was looking into my brother's sad, wide eyes, and I jumped as the sound of the hostel door flung open. My eyes darted towards the sound, and I almost screamed as I realised it was our dad. His dark eyes burned and every hair on the back of my neck stood up.

"Get the fuck up, Liz!" he screamed at Mum as he ripped her from the bed by her hair. She screamed in pain. Just as I had when she had done the same to me.

"Get off me, Jase!" She wasn't slurring anymore. She was no longer drunk; this mum was sober mum, and this mum was okay. Not great but she was *okay*.

"Don't you dare ever try and leave me again." He raised his hand that was bunched into a fist and aimed straight for her face. Jay tried to cover my eyes with his hand, but he was too late. I'd already seen the blood from her nose splat against the duvet that was covering us. "Don't you dare try and take *MY* fucking kids away from me again." He hit her again, repeatedly. She was screaming and crying, begging him to stop, and my chest became tighter and tighter. I couldn't listen to this.

"Daddy, stop!" I screamed at him. Jay's grip on me tightened.

"Did you really think I wouldn't find you?" She was now in a ball, holding onto her legs. Blood covered the bedsheets that she was laying on. I sobbed and Jay squeezed me tighter. "You stupid fucking bitch!" I heard the thud and her scream for help.

"Daddy, please stop!" I screamed again and again, and the duvet was ripped from off where Jay and I were hiding.

"Oh, angel, don't you start now," he growled as he pulled me out of Jay's arms. Jay's grip constricted. It hurt as his fingers dug into my skin in desperation.

"Don't touch her." Jay's voice sounded strong. "I mean it, Dad, don't." I looked up at Daddy. His eyes were furious, they were black and bland. There was no other emotion peeking through but anger. I flinched as he placed a kiss against my cheek. I had always been scared to death of this man but now I was more so. I had just *seen* what he did when he was angry, and I knew he was angry with Jay.

"What are you going to do, boy?" The smell of whiskey overpowered my senses and made me dizzy. I closed my eyes. "I tell you what..." He paused as he began to take off my T-shirt. I dithered. "Why don't you watch?" His laughter echoed around the room, and it stopped. There was a sound I'd never heard before. Warmth spread against my stomach, and I held my hand out to touch it. Warm liquid. Confusion consumed me.

"I told you not to fucking touch her!" Jay's piercing cries were aimed at Daddy, whose hands were covered in red. I screamed and shook. "I warned you!" My head spun as I looked down at the pool of what I had realised now was blood on the floor and I screamed again. The room suddenly filled with people, sirens were coming from every angle, and they took him away. *My brother. My best friend.* He was still screaming at Daddy. Everything went blank. Everything went cold. I was alone.

CHAPTER ONE
COLD

THREE YEARS LATER

I would say that night was a blur but that would be a lie. Nothing about that night was a blur. I remembered every single gory detail. I was twelve and I could still feel the warmth of Dad's blood on my nine-year-old body. Bile made its way from my stomach to my throat, and I shook my head as I glanced down at my book. The book I'd been reading for the last couple of days. Harry Potter. I frowned as I closed it slowly and tried to push the image of my brother being taken away. The police had taken him to a juvenile detention centre. He was charged as a minor. He was only my age when it all happened. He was protecting his family and the courts had seen that. In fact, I thought they probably felt sorry for him. I did. He was due out in just a couple of days. He would be joining me at Aunt Lynne's. *Aunt Lynne.* I smiled to myself as I thought of her. I smiled even wider when I thought about being reunited with my big brother. It had been three years, three long years since I last felt safe. Really genuinely safe.

The police had moved me from London to Devon to

be with my Aunt Lynne when they realised that mum wasn't fit enough to look after me alone. They had tried and failed to place me in her care whilst the trial was ongoing. The courts knew that my sperm donor would be in jail for the foreseeable future, which was completely fine by me. I was now under witness protection and Jay would be too when he was released. When police realised that Mum had known about the abuse I'd suffered for years and done nothing to protect me or Jay, they charged her too. Not that this would ever be enough. None of that mattered, justice would never be brought to them because he was still alive. He still had a heartbeat. I didn't see how in any universe him being alive was justice. I could have learned to forgive my mother. Maybe. But *never him.*

Aunt Lynne was cooking. It was a Sunday; every Sunday she'd cook a roast dinner and we would watch a film. She'd done it ever since the day I was placed in her care. She was nothing like my mum—in looks or personality. There was an eight-year age gap between them, or so she had said. I was so thankful for my Aunt Lynne. She'd been as solid as a rock while Jay had been inside serving his time. She had been my consistency. My motherly figure. My home.

"I worry that your brother won't like me much." She spoke softly, and I frowned at her. Her chubby red cheeks were flushed, and she raised her dainty shoulders up and down. Aunt Lynne was in her late forties, her hair was greying at the roots, but she still had the skin of somebody so much younger than her. I envied that about her and hoped that my genetics followed hers as I grew older.

"He'll love you," I assured her. I wasn't sure what he'd love if I was being completely honest with myself. I didn't know him anymore. When he left, he was a small little boy. A scared, small, tortured little boy. I frowned as she handed me my plate of food. It steamed and I watched her walk back into the kitchen. "He gets out Tuesday, doesn't he?" I asked. She laughed and appeared with gravy in a small cooking pot before she joined me at the table.

"Yes, apparently he's bringing another lad he's spent time inside with." I raised my brow at how relaxed she was about this. The fear of God was now instilled inside me.

"Is this a home for fucked up kids?" I tried to joke and watched her smile. Her teeth were crooked, but her smile made me feel easier about the situation. It was warm and inviting and so genuine.

"Well about that, there's a man who knew your mum and dad…" She paused as she ate something from her plate. "He tried to help them out through counselling." The thought of my mum and dad made me feel sick. "He said that his son is around the same age as Jay and is schooled down this way. I was wondering if you wanted to meet him and introduce him to Jay and his friend when they get out Tuesday?" I raised my brow at her. I didn't have friends. I had one. That was Missy. She was funny, she made me laugh, and she lightened the mood when it was heavy. I didn't want any more friends. I shook my head.

"I don't like men, Aunt Lynne," I reminded her softly.

"Oh, sweetheart, I know, I didn't mean that… I just thought that he would be a good influence." I shook my head. I wasn't convinced. "That's fine. You don't ever have to do anything you don't want to." I nodded as she smiled warmly at me and reached for my hand that was resting against the table. I really liked Aunt Lynne.

RELIEF

None of the people I'd met at school knew my background. They didn't even know my **real** name. Aunt Lynne wanted to keep our first names but witness protection had made us change our surnames to Conway. I would never be known as Smith again. I wasn't even sure when it clicked that what Dad was doing to me was wrong. I was certain I'd always known deep down that dads shouldn't touch their daughters there. My skin stood on end, and I felt sick the more I thought about it. I didn't do that much anymore, but today I was thinking about it more and more because I knew my brother was coming home. Jay was back tonight. Missy nudged me softly, and I was grateful as she'd just pulled me from an internal battle with myself over my past.

"Did you hear a word Miss just said?" I shook my head and frowned at her.

"No. Sorry," I said honestly. Missy giggled and pulled on my arm as she jumped off the high stool in Miss Bentley's science class. Her dyed purple hair was long and curly today, her make-up was caked on, and she smiled at me. She was a pretty little thing with sharp features and lovely warm eyes.

"You're hopeless, you know?" She tilted her head as she smiled at me. Her eyes were light amber in colour. They almost looked fake, like contacts. I frowned at her and placed my bag on my shoulder as I followed her towards the lunch hall and down the metal staircase from the science blocks. "When does your brother get out?" she quizzed, and I rolled my eyes. I'd shown her photos of him that Aunt Lynne had taken when she went to visit him. I wasn't allowed to visit. They had told her it would jeopardise witness protection. They had also said they thought it would send him back to a *bad* place, whatever that meant in prison terms. Lately though, he'd been doing okay.

18

"Tomorrow," I whispered. She was one of three people who knew about Jay being locked up. She instantly grew red in colour as she tucked her arm in mine whilst we walked. My hair had grown lighter throughout this year. I'd found bleach. It was so light and long. She moved it from out of her way and huffed. It was so damaged.

"Are you excited?" I smiled and nodded at her as my emotions twisted in my tummy.

"I am, yeah," I admitted as we made our way into the dining room. "It's just been such a long time." She had no idea what he was in for. I was sure I'd told her drug possession when I'd gotten as high as a kite on Aunt Lynne's sofa last year. I couldn't quite remember, but she knew. I frowned to myself and shook my head as we made our way through the crowds of students and huddled at our table where we were quickly joined by our other friends.

"Hey, Ma." Jamane hopped over the back of the plastic seats to join us. He nodded at me; his dark golden skin tone matched his eyes. I got lost in them for a split second. My mouth grew dry. He was hot. He was a few years above me. I liked him. He was friendly, he was nice, and he was always dancing. He'd tried to get me into it once or twice before. "You coming to class later?" he asked, and I shook my head, trying to stop myself from blushing.

"I can't dance," I reminded him. Marley laughed a little and sat down next to Jamane. His eyes lit up as he examined him. Marley was as gay as they came. He didn't try to hide it either, which I absolutely loved. I laughed aloud.

"I wish you'd call me Ma." Marley wriggled his thick dark brows at Jamane, who in turn rolled his eyes. Missy giggled and shook her head.

"Unreal you are." She laughed at Marley who frowned at her and then ushered her away with his hands.

"He's hot. Why are you turning him down? He clearly wants to get to know you better." He winked at me. "If you know what I mean." I was sure Jamane flushed but I couldn't really tell. I knew all too well what he meant. Which was so unbelievably fucked up.

"Marley"–Jamane spoke softly–"sometimes you know you've really gotta learn to shut up." He patted his shoulder with some force as he stood from the dining chair and laughed as he ran to catch up with his mates from his own year group.

"Honestly though, Chlo. Why?" Marl begged in a whining tone. "I've gotta know why you keep shooting him down!" I winced and shook my head.

"My brother is coming home tomorrow." I changed the subject swiftly. There was no way I was bringing up the fact I was fucked by my dad as a kid and that's why I was petrified of men.

"Oh, the fit drug dealer?" I reached to punch him and frowned.

"Shut the fuck up, Marley." I groaned and placed my head in my hands against the table.

HOME

For a kid who was barely fifteen, he was buff, tall too. He seemed so much older than his age, but then he always had. He winked at me, and my heart stopped. His face warmed the second he realised it was me who was waiting for him once he climbed off the bus. His arms stretched out either side of him and I ran. I ran towards him as quickly as I could and threw myself in them before sobbing. My legs were wrapped around him like a baby monkey clinging to its mum, and I squeezed him tightly. *I was home. This was real. He was out. He was home. He was back.* Fuck, I'd missed him. His arms wrapped around me as he spun me around and laughed a little. It was deep and barely recognisable.

"Hey, Coco." He breathed into my hair. His voice seemed lower than what I remembered it being and I half laughed, half sobbed.

"Hey, Jay," I muttered back as he planted a soft kiss against the side of my head.

"Are you crying?" he teased me. I smiled a little and shrugged. I realised I was still wrapped around him tightly. He was trying to make me smile, something he'd always been so good at, and it was working.

"Maybe," I admitted as I pulled away from him. His eyes examined my face. "You look so old," I blurted. He laughed and dropped me to my feet softly.

"I was just thinking the same about you." He raised his brow and I chuckled. I'd thought about how I would feel often but I wasn't prepared to feel so safe again. I wasn't prepared to feel as though he was never taken away from me. I wasn't prepared for feeling anything.

"Oh, Puddle." I pushed his arm back with my hands and laughed before hearing a cough and a groan from behind me. Jay's eyes widened and mine darted towards the sound. My stomach churned with fear.

"Sorry, bro, this is my baby sister, Chlo." Jay's voice

was strong, and I felt weak. The lad that stood there was bloody brilliant. I knew my brother was a good looking lad. Many of my friends had told me, time and time again, but this lad was something else. My chest became tight as I stared at him. Jay walked beside him and shrugged as they both looked my way. He was taller than my brother, maybe by an inch, and he was just as broad too. I didn't think that was possible. He must have been older... seventeen, or maybe even older than that. I was quiet for a while just examining him. "She's usually a lot more talkative than this." He was making up for my lack of words, and I frowned at him. The tall God-like lad's eyes darted towards mine and I held my breath. They were the biggest bluest things I'd ever seen in my entire life. Like lagoons. I froze as his lips curled into a smirk. His heart-shaped lips curled upwards at the corners and my stomach flipped.

"Nice to meet you, Chlo," he muttered as his eyes dropped towards my white school shirt, which was probably showing a little too much cleavage.

"Fuck's sake, H, pack it in. She's my sister." Jay shoved his new friend with a force that made him unsteady on his feet. I couldn't help but blush. My twelve-year-old heart fluttered.

"You didn't tell me she looked like that though, mate." I suddenly felt flustered, and I knew the colour of my face would be giving me away. I was embarrassed.

"Honestly, you're treading on thin ice, *mate*." There was a growl that left Jay's lips. "Really fucking thin ice." I smiled to myself as I tried to hide my embarrassment. "Also, do I have to remind you of her age?" he snapped. Despite the fact we hadn't seen each other for three years, nothing had changed. He was still as protective as ever. Even more so now.

"Anyway, where are we staying?" This H didn't seem bothered by my brother's angry tone at all. He seemed used to it. I raised my brow at the possibility of him being used to my brother's angry side and crossed my arms across my chest.

"My Aunt Lynne's," I whispered. "Our Aunt Lynne's." I corrected myself before I pointed towards the alley behind the back of the houses, not far from where we were standing by the bus stop.

"So, what's your story then, H?" I raised my brow and walked towards the gully. My strides were smaller than theirs and I found myself struggling to keep up. I wanted to know why my brother had taken a liking to this lad of all lads.

"I stole my dad's BMW and got done for driving without a license." He just shrugged as my mouth twisted upwards into a small smile. Something so minor compared to my brother.

"And you got three years?" He was next to me as we walked.

"Fifteen months in the end." He grinned and I was nearly blinded by his white, wide, perfect smile. I liked him. He was hot and funny, and *bad*. So bad.

"You're a minor then?" I asked innocently, and Jay laughed. It wasn't genuine laughter.

"He's my age, Chlo, don't get any ideas." Jay's arm was draped around my shoulders as we walked, and I smiled widely up at him. He was home and I finally felt safe again.

Aunt Lynne had cooked us all dinner. She seemed to like Jay's friend. So did I. She wasn't one for passing judgement, after all, she'd lived with my mum. I helped her wash up and looked on at the boys. My heart twisted whenever I looked at them. They were laughing. I hadn't laughed with anybody like that for a while. Aunt Lynne kissed my cheek and squeezed my arm.

"I'm heading up to bed now. You should get some rest ready for tomorrow." I groaned and closed my eyes. Tomorrow my school would find out all about my brother and his new mate. I'd be bombarded with questions, and I didn't want any of that. I wanted a simple life. I was happy here, in Aunt Lynne's little cottage.

"Okay." I offered her a false smile and made my way over towards the living room after I'd watched her depart. He was laying down on the sofa, watching the television with Jay. I didn't watch much tele. It was always rubbish. I liked reading. I sat next to him and ushered him out the way. His eyes were watching me. I could feel them. The sofa wasn't big enough for the two of us, but I refused to sit on the floor.

"How long are you here for before you have to go back up to your parents?" Jay questioned him intently. I shifted under his watchful eyes.

"I dunno, it depends when Dad forgives me." He laughed a little. "Are we going to meet with that lad tonight?" He flung a question back towards Jay who frowned and tilted his head my way.

"Jay, I can see you, I'm not blind or stupid," I snapped at him. There was laughter from H's mouth and my stomach twisted.

"I like her." He grinned at my brother who tensed.

"Well, like her from a distance. You touch her, I'll kill you." His brow was still furrowed, and I smirked at his mate a little. I loved how much he wanted to protect me. He'd been the same since I could remember. His eyes softened as he glanced at me.

"So, what's his actual name then?" I questioned my brother who laughed.

"Harry." I watched his friend freeze as I chuckled.

"Well, that's a very posh name," I teased as I bobbed my tongue out at him. He rolled his beautiful blue eyes my way.

"It's after my dad. I hate it. You can call me Haz, sweetheart." I scoffed at his comment and pushed him so that I was now spread out on the sofa too. He budged over and shook his head. "You know, you're just like your brother." I laughed as I watched him prop his head on his arm. His eyes traced my face. This was the first time I'd seen him this close up. He was pretty much a man. Well, not a man, but he was close. He'd already got better facial hair than most men I'd seen in their early twenties. I laughed a little as I looked at him in greater detail. His skin was smooth.

"I bet that takes some upkeep..." I realised I was touching the hair on his face and moved almost instantly away from him.

"I shave every other day, yeah." He swallowed and sat upright before he looked back towards Jay who was watching the television. *Thank fuck.* An awkward silence fell between us all and I closed my eyes tightly. I one hundred percent had a crush on this guy.

THE BIG BOYS

I pushed my bleached blonde hair from my face and back up into a bun. It had been a year since they were released and now the whole school knew who Harry and Jay were. They were in their last year. Not that either of them ever spent much time in school. Harry didn't end up going back home either. He had stayed with me, Jay and Aunt Lynne. Until Aunt Lynne dropped down dead last year out of nowhere. My heart twisted at the memory of it. We all went to bed, and she just didn't wake up. I frowned deeply as I tried to pull myself from my memories. We had been shipped to stay with a friend of Harry's dad–Larry–so that we could finish school without too much upheaval. That was the plan. I placed my hand over the necklace that was once Aunt Lynne's that rested against my neck and smiled as Haz placed his hands on my hips from behind. He kissed my cheek, and I pressed my arse into him. It had always been sneaky flirts and quick kisses until recently. I no longer had the burning desire for him like I used to. I'd had him and it was fun because if my brother found out, shit would hit the fan. My feelings for him were strange. They confused me.

"Don't do that," he growled, and I chucked.

"I thought you'd be dancing?" He nodded as he clicked his fingers and pointed towards me, releasing his heavy grip.

"Heading there now." He beamed as he jogged down the corridor of the school. Jay legged it after him and I smiled widely. Missy nudged me.

"Does your brother know you've been shagging?" she questioned as she pushed open the double doors into the dining hall.

"Nah." I smirked and joined our table full of friends. Jamane and Marley were sitting down eating already.

"I'm so jealous of you. I wish I was getting some." She sighed and I frowned. I was still only a baby myself.

Thirteen. Thirteen-year-old school girls shouldn't even know what a dick looks like. I placed my head in my hands and shook it softly.

"Chlo is getting some?" Marley squealed as he caught the back end of our conversation.

"Marl!" I spat venom his way and watched him grin.

"I wish I was fucking your brother." He spluttered. I laughed loudly.

"Name one person who doesn't wish they were in Jamie Conway's bed." Missy laughed with Marley and Jamane. Holly smirked at me and shrugged. She was really pretty, and she had naturally blonde hair that fell over her shoulders. She was sweet and one of Jamane's best friends.

"Me," she admitted. "I don't want to be in his bed." Her voice was strong but soft, and she bit down on her lip. I frowned a little at her admission. "Rather be in Vens's." She spoke quietly and my stomach dropped. I had known she'd fancied him for a while, and I was almost certain his feelings were reciprocated, but this stirred up jealous feelings from deep within. "Just friends though." I couldn't help but clear my throat. Missy nudged me and I frowned at her a little, her over bronzed cheeks looked full as she smiled a devilish smile my way.

"No," I mouthed and watched as she nodded.

"I'm gonna go watch them dance." She took another bite of her sandwich before she stood and walked off. Jamane followed her and then we all followed. If there was one thing I could admit to it was that he looked fucking amazing when he danced. I laughed as we went into the dance hall.

I watched wonder fill Holly's eyes as she watched him dance with Jamane and some of the older girls in the school. The sixth form kids. It made sense that he and Jamane were used as props for them. None of the older lads danced but now I bet they wished they had. Holly was smiling widely, and her dirty long blonde hair flowed down her back. She was unusually pretty. Her chin was pointed but her cheeks were full like a hamster. I'd never noticed until now. She was the same age as him. Apparently, she'd transferred here last year sometime because of her dad. I'd heard her talk about him once or twice. It didn't seem like she was fond of him. I frowned as Haz smiled at her a little once he'd stopped dancing. He offered his hand out to her and she flushed a pink shade as she shook her head. *He was such a fucking flirt.* His hair was lighter than brown but still fell into that category, it was mousy. His jaw was chiselled out perfectly and he looked older, so much older than he was. I shook away my thoughts and glanced at my brother, who was being chatted up by some girl in the year above him. He too seemed relaxed and at ease with their conversation. I suddenly felt inferior. I'd always been the pretty one. I'd always been the girl they were bothered by. Now I wasn't.

CHAPTER TWO
FRAGILE

JUVE

Life for me wasn't straightforward. I was just seventeen but felt like I had the weight of the world laying on my shoulders. Family ties were binding–or apparently, they should be–but since I'd point blank refused to do my dad's dirty work or join him on his criminal empire journey as his eldest son, everything had changed, and now Haz was being punished. My little brother. Well, one of them. Our family was huge. Absolutely huge. My brothers and sisters were all a few years apart, but it was my little brother Haz who had always caused the most trouble. He'd gone away to juvie because he'd stolen my dad's car. At fifteen. Stealing cars. I wanted to laugh at it, but I fought it off, and instead, there was a slight smile turning my lips upwards. He'd got himself into gangs, or so that's what Mum and Dad had been talking about last night. Dad knew all about that line of work, he'd spent the last three years trying to talk me into joining him, trying to mould me into him.

***

My head was leaning against the door to the snug. It was my mum's favourite place to relax. I wasn't brave enough to let them know that I was listening.

"Henry, he's going to end up dead if you don't do something!" my mum slurred his way, she'd had a little too much to drink this evening whilst they were out, dining with the high and mighty. I fought the urge to roll my eyes and listened closer.

"Carol," he breathed. It was a pathetic effort to settle her. He sounded pulled. "He will not get himself killed, beaten up maybe, but not killed. He's a Vens." I heard the pride in my dad's voice when I heard him say our surname. Vens. I shrugged my shoulders at his statement. How would he know how he'd end up? My mum scoffed at him.

"You…" There was a shuffling against the floor. "You wouldn't know. Larry drip feeds you information. Your little rat." She spat Dad's wingman's name. His dearest friend. She hated him. "That poor girl." My ears pricked up at this. A girl? My brother was many things, but a girl? No. I shook my head and pressed my ear closer to the door, listening harder.

"Carol," he breathed. "We cannot bring him home," he growled at her.

"What if that girl was Aimee?" There was silence. Aimee was my dad's world. His little girl. His baby. "What if Aimee needed stability? What if that was our baby?"

"Chloe Conway is not our baby, Carol." The air in his voice was dark. "Don't bring my relationship with Aimee into this, this is about your son." There was a scuffle of feet again against the floor.

"When did he become my son?"

"When he turned his back on me!" he bellowed. "When he joined that bastard over me." He was speaking through gritted teeth. My heart was pounding. This conversation was one I definitely should know nothing about.

"Diego Bandoni has used your son against you. Don't let him fucking win, Henry." My stomach dropped. Nobody ever spoke his first name. Mob boss. Italian mob boss. My brother was involved up to his neck and beyond. He had joined my dad's fucking worst enemy *to spite him. My chest fluttered uncomfortably. Please don't drown. My heart was heavy.*

***

I was pulled from my memory; I wasn't sure how Mum had talked Dad into having him live with Larry for a while but she had. She looked triumphant in the way she moved today. I knew they were with Larry now, whoever *they* were. I knew my brother was caught up in some illegal shit, it wasn't so much that it was illegal that bothered me really, the worst that he would get in England was a prison sentence if he got caught, but in Dad's world, in Diego Bandoni's world… it would be death. I shivered on that thought. I frowned deeply and examined my face as I finished washing it. I ran my hand against my jaw and pushed my hair to one side. It was darker when it was wet. Almost brown. I'd made my decision. I wanted to join the army. I wanted to get away from the constraints and pressure of joining my dad in his empire. That wasn't a life I wanted. I wanted to be strait-laced. I didn't want to have to lie to my own kids about where my money came from. I looked around my ensuite bathroom that was bright white in design and sighed loudly. So much extra money to spare. I rolled my eyes and skipped across the hallway to find my baby sister Aimee. It was Saturday and I'd promised I would take her to her dance class. She would love that. Mum and Channa took her more often than not, but today, Channa was busy. *Busy seeing her boyfriend.* I tensed at the thought of my sixteen-year-old sister having a boyfriend and frowned as I knocked on Aimee's door. I knew all too well what seventeen-year-old lads wanted to do with their girlfriends. I shuddered and opened Aimee's door.

"Princess?" I called out innocently. A small giggle came from the lump underneath her baby pink bed sheets. I smiled as I called out again. "Where are you?" My tone was childish, and I caught her infectious giggles.

"I'm here!" She jumped out, platinum blonde hair flailing around her face as she bounced on the bed towards me. I smiled softly as she threw herself around my neck and slapped me in the face with her hair. She was the baby of us all. She was just seven. I wrapped my arms around her and picked her up. She squeezed my face between her little fingers and grinned, her front tooth missing. I kissed her chubby cheek.

"Are you ready to go?" I quizzed enthusiastically.

"Yeah!" She beamed, pushed herself out of my arms, and then ran off down the hallway and down the stairs. I couldn't help but laugh.

I walked her across the fields and then through town to the little dance studio, all the time she was gripping my hand in hers. It was warm this summer and she was full of excitement as she skipped, holding my hand tightly up the stairs towards her dance studio. I smiled widely as she kissed my cheek and grabbed her bag and began to get changed into her pink tutu and ballet pumps. Her dance teacher smiled at me and flushed a little. Her pale skin turned pink for a split second. I smiled back politely. She was pretty with dark auburn hair that dangled behind her shoulders and lively blue eyes that mimicked mine. She stood staring before Aimee grinned and pushed me softly.

"Are you going to watch, Juve?" Her bright blue eyes sparkled as she smiled up at me.

"I always do." I gasped. She rolled her eyes before looking towards the redhead.

"He doesn't." She paused. "He looks at you." She skipped off as the redhead laughed awkwardly. I shook my head and ran my hand over the back of my neck in an attempt to ease my discomfort with the situation. She simply blushed again as she joined her and all the other little kids in the class. I'd never introduced myself to her. I wasn't sure if she thought I was her stepdad, brother or actual dad. I shook my head and frowned. It wasn't unusual for people to look at me. I looked older than I actually was. This was a Vens trait. We all did, except for her. Little Aimee. She looked like a baby. Our little ray of light. We had our dad's genes, so did Haz. I hoped that he was okay. I was pulled into a childhood memory of my own for a short time as I thought about him.

CHLO

I was still struggling with the sudden loss of Aunt Lynne. She was a consistent figure in my already messed up life and I craved some normality. I placed my head against Haz's shoulder and held his arm in mine. He kissed the top of my head softly in his best attempt to comfort me. This was about as close as we got anymore. His red-rimmed eyes looked down towards me and I smiled softly up at him. He winked at me, and my heart fluttered. I had always been a little confused about how he made me feel when I was around him. He was such a cocksure of himself idiot, but when that was all stripped back, he had such a good, kind heart. I moved my head and held his hand in mine, playing with his fingers.

"So, this will be home until when?" I asked him. His broad shoulders rose upwards and then fell as he shrugged. We'd been shipped here pretty quickly after Aunt Lynne died. Larry was Harry's dad's best friend, or so that's what I'd been drip-fed.

"Think my mum and dad are on about us going back up there for a while... not sure yet though." I nodded slowly. His mum and dad. I still had never met them, but I was so fucking thankful for them placing us in Larry's care. Larry was a greying, hard-faced looking, scary mother fucker but he was nice enough. I glanced at the expensive watch that was wrapped around Harry's wrist. "Where did that come from?" I quizzed him. Both he and my brother had changed since they had left school, they were hardly ever around and then there was the fact they came home with expensive things like this. I touched the watch again and watched his brow crease.

"A friend." His heart-shaped lips pursed together, and I watched as his shoulders rose and fell again.

"Haz, are you and Jay stealing shit?" He shrugged and pulled me on his lap. My heart rate spiked from fear. I was scared that they'd be taken away and I'd be left alone.

Again. Only this time, I wouldn't have Aunt Lynne.

"Not stealing things, no." He spoke quietly. I pushed his shoulder softly and relaxed as he held me closer to him. "Your brother will be home soon." He kissed the bottom of my neck in-between my collar bones, and I rolled my eyes. I didn't ache for him like I once did.

"Don't start," I warned in a low whisper. "You have Holly." I felt him grin against my skin as I reminded him of his girlfriend.

"She wouldn't know." I couldn't help but chuckle.

"Thanks for making me feel like a dirty secret, H." I paused as his head shot up at my words. "Love that for me," I teased him again. His eyes widened.

"I didn't mean…" He began to fumble on his words and a sinking feeling appeared in my stomach. It's all I'd ever been to somebody. A dirty secret.

"Nah, you know what, Haz, it's fine. I've got used to it." I moved off his lap and felt his grip tighten as I tried to escape his clutches.

"You know I didn't mean it like that, Co. I love you… you know that." I was lost in the sincerity of his tone. I nodded a little. *I was weak.* All he had to do was tell me he loved me, and I'd stay. I wouldn't be mad at him.

"Sure." I choked as I sat back next to him on the sofa, my hair tangled behind the back of it. We sat in awkward silence. I wasn't sure he knew what love was. I sure as hell didn't. My warped idea of love was completely and utterly fucked. I did know that I really cared for him though. Enough to want to take his hand back in mine and squeeze. He gave me a small smile as his eyes dropped back towards the tele.

TIME TICKED ON

The same mundane scenario played out–day in, day out. Jay and Harry left the house, and I went to school. School was tedious now and I was just ready for it to be over. Missy's arm linked through mine and I smiled softly in her direction. Her amber eyes warmed.

"How are you feeling today?" she asked as she pulled herself up onto the science high stool. I shrugged and then glanced down at my book against the table.

"Fine, yeah, I can't come around yours tonight, I promised I'd have a night in with Jay," I lied. I had been sworn to a schedule. I had to be back at Larry's by four p.m. at the latest, for my own safety, apparently. My brother knew something I didn't.

"Oh, okay. Well, I'll let Jamane know." She didn't seem overly fussed by my confession. "I wish I could come round yours." She nudged my arm and wriggled her overly plucked brows. "I wish it was me staying in with your brother and his hotter than fucking life best mate." I laughed to myself and shook my head from side to side.

"Be careful what you wish for." I smiled back at her and heard her giggle as our science teacher walked into the room. The backs of many students went straight but I continued to draw scribbled love hearts and stars on my paper as I was transported back in time to the day we realised *Daddy* was out.

***

My brother walked in through the door of Larry's home and offered me a small, closed smile. Something was wrong. I forced a smile back at him and then patted the stool next to me. We didn't speak all that much anymore. He was still fuming over the fact Haz and I had slept together, and that he had been kept in the dark about it for years. I remembered vividly the beating he gave Haz. I almost thought he was going to kill him. I shuddered next to him. That Jay was scary, that Jay was similar to our dad. I gulped. He sighed as he placed his bag next to the seat before he slumped on the stool.

"Find anything out?" I questioned him and watched him shrug as he spun a coin on the kitchen island and placed his hand against his cheek. All of the care in his face had gone.

"Nothing interesting, heard our sperm donor is out though." He said it like it was nothing. I gripped onto his arm as every fibre of my being tingled and froze to ice.

"When?" I croaked, still frozen in my seat. My world had stopped as every memory of his hands on me flooded my subconscious, every dirty word he ever spoke being replayed like a tape recorder over and over in my mind. I fought the urge to throw up as my hand shook.

"Four weeks ago, apparently." My gut twisted and noise from the door made a scream escape my mouth. I had assumed we were safe; I was under the illusion he was gone now, but he wasn't. Terror consumed me. My eyes didn't leave the doorway. It was Haz's face at the door, but my heart rate still hadn't registered his face. He was dripping, he'd clearly been caught in the rain. He slammed the door shut behind him as he placed his hood down.

"Why all the screaming, Co?" He frowned as he shrugged off his coat, my heart unable to contain its erratic pace. I felt tears appear in the corners of my eyes. "What's going on with her, Jay?" He tilted his head towards me, and I opened my mouth to try and speak but not a word came out. I simply continued to shake violently.

"Dad is out." Jay spoke softly now and Haz's face dropped to the floor, it was full of horror. I imagined that was the look on my face. He made his way over towards where we were sitting to offer me some comfort. I pushed away from it.

"Does Larry know?" he asked, and Jay shrugged.

"I didn't know until fifteen minutes ago." Haz took his place next to me and draped his arm across me slowly. He pecked my cheek and ran his nose over it. I didn't want his touch. My skin was still standing on edge. I refused to close my eyes.

"It'll be okay, Co. You've got us." I shook my head at him slowly and flinched away from his affection.

"It won't be enough." My hands were trembling as the whisper *left my mouth. I closed my eyes and a flash of nine-year-old me played over in my brain. My stomach churned as I reached for it, remembering the blood on my T-shirt. The memory of Jay being ripped from me. A gasp left my mouth. "It was never enough." I gulped out my whisper. My eyes opened and I glanced up at Jay whose dark eyes were suddenly sad. I hadn't seen that emotion on his face for a long time. He was solid muscle now and older beyond his time, but dad was strong. I remembered how strong. I could never forget.*

"Co, he won't find us." Jay spoke softly as he moved my hair from my face in the most delicate way. "We have different names." He spoke again, trying to assure me that we were okay, that we were safe. "We aren't even in the area, how would he find us?" His words made sense. He was talking complete sense. This should have offered me some solace, but it didn't. I was still absolutely terrified. I just nodded as he pulled me to his chest like I was six again. Like I was that broken little girl he so desperately wanted to save. I breathed him in as I wrapped my arms around him and squeezed.

"Somebody would tell him." Haz broke the silence. He paused for a while. My gut twisted. "For a price, if we fucked up." His tone was low, and I released the tears that were threatening to escape.

***

I was pulled back into the land of the living with a thump to the shin.

"Ouch, shit, Miss!" I cursed and heard her chuckle. It took me a while to register that Mr Lakin was now glaring at me. His dark hair was all neatly pushed to one side of his head.

"Have you quite finished, Chloe?" He folded his arms across his chest. He was too young to be our science teacher. He was way too enthusiastic about such a boring topic. He was too hot.

"Sorry, Sir." I placed my hair behind my ear and smiled politely at him, batting my eyelashes as I did so. "Would you repeat the question?" He simply shook his head as he wandered off in the opposite direction. I glared at Missy. She was giggling as she shook her head from side to side, her faded purple hair following her head movements.

"Honestly." She sighed aloud. "Where the fuck do you go?" I watched her shake her head at me again "I would love to know where you disappear to in that head of yours," she mumbled as I retaliated and kicked her shin under the desk. *Payback.*

"Trust me, you don't." She rubbed her shin as she rolled her eyes at me. *Hurts, doesn't it? My* subconscious sniggered.

I had kept my promise to the boys, and I didn't stay out past my curfew. I did as I always did and went back to Larry's house. I had placed my tea in the microwave, caught up on schoolwork, and then had my shower all before the boys had even walked through the door. They weren't so great at keeping their side of the deal. The sound of a guitar being strummed distracted me. It was now being played softly. I recognised the tune from one of the shitty games that we played together on the PlayStation. I followed the scent of weed, along with the wonderfully soft sound of the guitar into the lads' bedroom. I knew that it wasn't my brother who was playing the instrument. He had as much rhythm as a cat with three legs. No, it was Haz. I peeked my head around the bedroom door and watched him play for a few short moments. It was a peaceful song. I'd never heard him play before; this was a first. He jumped as he realised I was watching him. He offered me a closed smile and then reached for my hand to pull me in. I slammed the door shut with my foot and laughed as I landed next to him with a thud.

"I didn't know you played?" I raised my brow and watched his lips twist into a smile before he took another puff of the spliff in his hand.

"Man of many talents." I laughed louder this time.

"Boy." I nudged him. "Boy of many talents." I watched as he passed the blunt my way. I took a hit and then a deep breath out. Every bone in my body relaxed. "Overheard

Larry talking to your dad the other day." I began to blab as he started to play the song again.

"What's he been saying?" He spoke softly. I took another hit and shrugged as I lay back on his bed, the drugs in my system clouding my senses.

"That I need a stable place to stay out of trouble." I giggled and heard him join me in my drug-fuelled laughter.

"Hm. I agree with him." He said. I chuckled a little more as I listened to him hum.

"I know the song you're playing?" My tone was questioning. He nodded in response.

"Yeah, it's *The Last of Us* theme song." I nodded in response and took one more drag before I handed it back to him. I knew my eyes would be red–so red–but I didn't care so much now that I had joined him on the high road.

"You know I love you, don't you, Vens?" I watched him roll his eyes and nod before he placed down the guitar next to his bed. I wasn't sure where this out-pour of emotion had come from, but it was true. I did sort of love him.

"I love you too, Conway." He leant forwards and kissed my lips softly. My heart didn't flutter. "Even if you are the most annoying thing I've ever been around." I pushed him backwards and laughed a sincere laugh. I did love him, but I wasn't *in love* with him. Whatever *in love* meant.

BURN

Larry had gone away for a week on 'business'. Which left three teens alone. We'd been given strict instructions to do as we were told and no trouble. I'd tried to do just that. I didn't stay out late; I was always the first home and first in bed. The boys would stroll in not long after. I stepped from the shower and yawned as I wrapped the towel around my body. I was tired tonight. I was tired of just struggling my way through life. The front door clicked but there was no shout out from either Haz or Jay. Goosebumps filled my arms and I frowned deeply at my reflection. *It was fine. Everything was fine.* I stepped onto the landing and called out. The sound of the front door being opened again happened, and soon, I heard them.

"Back, Co!" Jay's voice echoed around the house. I held my towel and began to climb down the stairs. My heart thudded and banged against my rib cage. "Traffic was a pig!" Haz's voice was now being carried throughout the hallways too, but I still felt *wrong*. My gut said something was off. I reached the bottom of the stairs and the smell hit me before anything else. *It was him.* Every part of me wanted to scream but I was like stone. Like frozen ice. "Co?" Haz called out again. "Where the fuck is she?" he called out to Jay from down the stairs. My eyes met my dad's pools of black, and I stopped breathing. The monster that I was just about getting over was standing in front of me. His facial expression was hard. He didn't even flinch as his eyes wandered over my face and body. I gripped my towel tightly. *Did this man have no mercy?*

"Don't move, angel." His lips twisted upwards into a small smile. A secret smile. A fucking cruel smile. His hand lifted to my cheek and then my chin. Internally, I was crumbling, but I refused to let him see I was still weak. He was so much more fragile than I remembered him. He'd aged. His hair was no longer thick and dark but thin and greying. "My, haven't you grown." I gripped the towel in my fingers tighter. There was no way in hell I was about to give in to him. Not now. Not ever. Not again.

"So has your son," I whispered back at him. "Jay!" I screamed as loud as my lungs would physically let me before he grabbed me, stopping the breath from leaving my lungs by squeezing his hand over my mouth. His hand seemed bigger now than my memory recalled. I was still as a rock, gripping my towel tightly in my hands. I didn't struggle. I could live with him killing me, part of me hoped that this would be it. That I wouldn't be subject to him ripping me apart again. I would cope if this was how it all ended. If he killed me now, that was fine, but he wasn't ever going to get to see me stripped bare again.

CHAPTER THREE
FAMILY TIES

JUVE

Apparently nothing much had changed. Haz was still just the same troublesome soul he had always been. I hadn't got myself involved with that side of Dad's empire. I had stayed well away. I'd been around when Mum and Dad spoke about him, his friend, and the girl. The best friend was locked up again, I didn't quite catch why or what had happened, but Mum was insisting that they stay here for the six weeks school holidays. Dad had finally caved. Apparently, the young girl needed stability and Larry wasn't providing that for them anymore. Something must have happened. *'He'd only made it worse'* or so that's what Mum had said. I shook my head as I thought a little too hard on it. I wasn't sure what had happened to them all whilst they had been living down there. Mum wouldn't fill me in. She said it had nothing to do with me and shouldn't be of my concern. My baby brother had always been, and would always be, a fucking menace and one of my biggest concerns. Dad had hoped that by him spending time in the nick he'd grow up a bit, stop pissing about, and come around to the idea of siding with Dad, but he didn't. He seemed to have gotten worse. I knew that from the conversation he had with Mum all those years ago. *Diego Bandoni.* I shuddered at the thought of him. The sad thing was I could picture my brother running around with men from gangs with knives and guns. I didn't want that for him. He was a bright kid. Really bright and talented. He could have a future–of sorts. My thoughts were invaded by the chime in my mum's tone. He must have arrived home. That or Amber had knocked on the door for me, though I hadn't invited her round tonight. I frowned a little as I jumped off the kitchen counter to see what had caused all of the commotion. Dad had been to fetch them both, Mum had insisted he did it and not his dog, Larry. I followed the sound of my mum's voice down the stairs and froze the second my eyes landed on her. *The girl.* My eyes wandered over her expression, she was all sweet and little and young. She looked fragile. So fragile. I wasn't judging the small girl in front of me but something about her screamed, 'fix me.' Her dark ashy blonde hair didn't make any sense against her darker skin colour. Her skin was olive, like she'd been sat in the sun for too long. Her eyes hadn't left the ground yet. She hadn't looked up. There were just two years between Haz and me. I wondered how old she was. Haz was resting his eighteen-year-old body against the door frame. He was hench. Clearly, he'd had time to spare down in the nick to work out. I glanced at myself out of insecurity and bit down on my bottom lip. I wasn't the jealous type, not really, but I had two years on the fucker and army training, and I still wasn't as buff as him. *Steroids.* Mum's voice broke the silence between us as she spoke. Her voice was soft towards the girl as though she was talking to a child. She placed her hand against her tiny shoulder as she ushered her inside out of the rain.

"Come through, Chloe dear." Her tone soothed even me. "They don't bite." I watched as the girl flinched at her words. *How old was she? Haz's age? Older? Younger?* I had no idea. Haz was rolling his eyes as he made his way towards me. He thumped my shoulder with his fist and a wicked grin appeared across his lips.

"Mum's gonna have a hard time breaking her walls down after what she's seen in her lifetime." Haz smirked and I frowned deeply at his lack of empathy towards her.

"What?" My interest in the girl peaked.

"Chloe. She's had a rough start and the reason Jay is where he is is because of their dad." I couldn't wrap my head around it. *What was he talking about?* I shook my head as I made my way down the hallway and followed them into the living room. Dad was carrying in the bags and had pulled Haz to help. *I would love to be a fly on the wall listening to that conversation.* My eyes landed on the fragile girl again. I was just a kid myself; a twenty-year-old hormonal bloke and I pitied the girl in front of me. On my sofa. All broken looking. *Broken but sodding beautiful.*

"Fancy a drink?" My mouth was dry as I spoke. It grew drier when she looked up from her lap. *Shit.* Her eyes were beautiful, I smiled at her then. They were mud brown in colour and warm in the middle, tiny little flecks of gold scattered throughout them. Her warm eyes weren't what I was expecting. She seemed like she'd be a bitch. But she just smiled a little as she looked at me. Her perfectly white teeth flashed.

"I'd like a glass of water, please." She spoke softly in a strange accent, it wasn't quite Southern, not considering that's where they had lived all of their lives. It was more of a well-spoken London accent. A little too well-spoken. I frowned a little as I desperately tried to wrap my head around her. Was she a spy for Bandoni? Was this all some sort of set up? I fought with myself over this question, at how dark my own thoughts had gotten. She was nothing like I'd pictured her to be. I nodded as her mouth hung

46

open a little before her lips pressed together again.

"Coming right up." I smiled to myself as I walked into the kitchen. The kid seemed all out of sorts being here. It was clear that my mum was fond of her already. She joined me not long after. "She seems shy." I raised my brow at my mum who was now faffing about next to me, trying to find a glass herself.

"She's only fifteen so don't be so judgemental." *Fuck. Fifteen.* My gut dropped to the floor almost instantly. I'd been wrong in my guesses of her age. *She was fifteen.* I could have sworn she was older than that. I shrugged as I pictured her face again.

"Hey, I'm not judging." My voice croaked out a response. I held the glass of water up to my mum and watched her brow furrow. She had a serious look etched across her normally playful expression. Her blonde hair was like silk down to her shoulders and her green eyes glistened as she huffed. Her sun-damaged skin was wrinkled around her eyes.

"Good, be nice to her." She pushed my arm softly as I moved to take the water to the tiny fragile girl. She didn't look directly at me but took the water from my hands.

"Thanks," she muttered quietly. I had noticed she had only looked up at me once and now her eyes couldn't even make it past my nose as she spoke.

"No worries." I smiled to myself as I spoke back to her. Pink spread across her cheeks as she moved her hair behind her ear. There was a weird silence between us for a little while. She didn't speak, just sipped her water and stared down at her glass. Haz interrupted my thoughts about the girl by throwing himself next to her and kissing her cheek. She pushed him softly as water trickled out from the glass onto her lap. She was scowling.

"Fuck you," she whispered towards him. He flashed his teeth as he kissed her cheek again. I frowned deeply and watched her look at him, just glaring. I was shocked that this sweet looking angel had a potty mouth.

47

"Oh stop pretending that you don't love me." She pushed him again and stood to her feet as she huffed and walked away. It seemed like she'd had enough of my brother's antics already and they'd been here for less than an hour.

"Prick." She continued to mutter as she sauntered off. Haz was laughing as he lay back on the sofa. I wanted to ask what was going on between them both. Haz was shifting his longer than normal mousey coloured hair from his eyes. His bicep flexed as he did so.

"I thought you'd got a girl down there?" I could hear the hostile tone in my voice.

"Her name is Holly." My gut wrenched as I recognised the name.

"As in Holly from ages ago? Dad's mate's daughter Holly?" He flushed a little as I spoke about her. "The fit Holly?" I pushed him again. I wondered how much he cared for her.

"Shut up." It was evident to me now that he felt uncomfortable talking about her, which made me want to push the subject again.

"So why are you pushing the girl?" He raised his brow again.

"The girl?" he quizzed with intent. I wanted to reach and throttle him. *Yes, the girl.* She was a girl; it didn't matter if she looked older. She was a fucking kid. "I'm leaving in a bit to sort some shit out with Rava. I need you to look after her." The thought of looking out for her made me laugh a little. I couldn't imagine she'd want anybody to look after her. I had a busy diary this weekend and she hadn't exactly been in my plans.

"Does she need looking after?" I questioned and watched his expression twist. He cared about her, that much was evident.

"Yes." I smiled a little. I recognised that my brother had a soft spot for the young girl, but he wasn't in love with her. He had saved that for Holly. Or at least that's what I had taken away from our rather short conversation.

"Then I'll keep my eyes on her," I promised without knowing why.

CHLO

Haz had explained where he was going and why. I didn't really understand much of it at all, though I'd tried to wrap my head around it. I knew now that Larry had finally had enough of trying to keep us safe and that's why I'd been dragged to stay here. To the middle of nowhere in the Shropshire hills. It was a far cry from home. The sea. I kind of missed it. Jay was facing another stay in prison for grievous bodily harm, only this time, he'd been charged as an adult and not a minor. I prayed that their friends in high places could afford a damn good fucking lawyer. I crossed my arms against my chest.

"I've stayed longer than I wanted to, Co." I frowned as Haz's voice echoed around the room I had been staying in and his head appeared in the doorway. "I'm off." I shrugged. We had been here for a few days; I hadn't left the room I was in often. Only to grab a drink, food or to use the bath. This house was like the Ritz. I'd always had a feeling his folks were rich.

"Can't believe you're leaving me with strangers." He laughed a little, and his eyes sparkled as he looked at me.

"Hey, I promised Jay I'd keep you out of trouble." He paused as he made his way towards me before he placed my hair from my face to behind my ear in the most delicate way. "You're out of trouble here." He smiled again and my heart fluttered.

"Thank you," I murmured. He squeezed me in a big hug, and I closed my eyes. I breathed him in. The scent of his expensive aftershave hit me in the face, and I squeezed him harder. "You'll be back soon though? You just have to go and settle something with Rava?" He nodded. I'd learnt now that Rava wasn't just a friend. He was involved in the gang Harry and Jay were in. Their ring leader's son. He kissed my hair as he released me and nodded.

"Promise you, I'll be back real soon." I nodded. I owed this young kid my life. He was the reason I was standing here alive. He smiled softly and kissed the backs of my hands. "You're all right here, Co." He released my hands and then bowed as he backed out of the room he'd placed me in. I suddenly felt really sad. I shook my head and threw myself backwards on the bed after groaning. I covered my face with the pillow and screamed into it.

It had taken me a while to adjust to being in such a normal home environment. His youngest sister Aimee was the sweetest little thing I'd ever seen. She reminded me of Haz a little. She was so highly strung for a nine-year-old. So innocent and sassy. His mum doted on her, and so did his dad. She was clearly their favourite. We were all gathered around the dining room table and Aimee was sitting next to me, her legs dangling from the chair, and I couldn't help but watch her. Her baby blonde hair was all wrapped up in a high bun. She was so full of innocence. *How could anybody ever want to hurt a child?* A lump grew in my throat as I thought about it, the threatening sensation of being dragged back into a bad memory lingered. I shook my head softly as his mum handed out the plates. Harry's eldest brother was staring at me again and I blushed instantly before I looked down at my plate. *He was so fucking hot.* My stomach clenched whenever I looked at him. *Juve.*

"Mind the plate, Chloe. It's hot," his mum–Carol–reminded me, and I nodded. The smell of her perfume mixed in with the cooking.

"Don't speak much, do you?" Juve threw a question my way. My eyes darted up to his and mine narrowed. *C'mon, Chlo, you can look him in the eye.* I got lost in them. The big deep dark pools of blue. He was handsome, painfully, classically handsome. Handsome to the point that Brad Pitt had nothing on him.

"I have nothing interesting to say." I watched his lips twist into a smile and couldn't help but smile too. He rolled his eyes as he placed the fork in his hand.

"I'm sure you have some stories to tell." His mum and

dad were lost in another conversation as they tucked into dinner. I had zoned them out and my attention was on him. I tilted my head to one side as I examined what he had said.

"What's Haz actually told you?" I raised my brow at him. He shrugged and my stomach churned. He better not have said anything, or I was in so much shit. I'd fucking kill him.

"Not much," he admitted, and I laughed with relief a little as I placed a potato in my mouth. He frowned at me and then began to eat too. "When are Warren and Buddy home, Mum?" he asked her, his attention away from me. Her eye contact moved from his dad to him. She looked at him fondly, and her eyes were full of love for her son.

"They are spending the summer at school this year. What with Chloe being here, I thought it would be best." She offered me a small smile. Her green eyes glistened under the lights in the kitchen, she didn't look old enough to have had so many children. "You know what hormonal teenage boys are like." She chuckled and shook her head slowly as she cut her carrot in half. "I wanted to save you from that." I smiled at her as I flushed red, embarrassed that she'd suggested it. We continued to eat dinner in this way. Awkward conversations and looks shared between Juve and I.

I NEED TIME

I couldn't be in the house anymore. I couldn't look at the same walls, wallpaper or furniture, as lovely as it all was. I sighed and made my way down the stairs to see if Carol was around. I wanted to take a walk, but I wasn't sure where I was walking to. Everywhere around here looked the same. Long winding roads that led to nowhere. I was hoping she would show me some routes or even just point me in the right direction. Juve was standing by the front door with a girl. A really, really pretty girl. Her dark hair– that was almost black–was tousled around her face. She had a tiny frame. She was slim. I was the opposite. I had grown curvier and curvier the older I'd gotten, and Carol's cooking hadn't done me any favours. My boobs were now an uncomfortable D cup. I cleared my throat a little and watched as he leant against his door frame. I could feel my heart pound as I watched him. He was pretty spectacular to look at. I'd stolen looks between conversations he was having with his family in front of me or whilst we'd awkwardly eaten our dinners together. My mouth hung open slightly and I flushed as I thought more about him. His broad shoulders blocked out some of the light from the front door. It felt almost as though I knew him. I'd heard Haz talk about him so often and I'd been here for a few weeks now, so I'd had plenty of awkward conversations with him. I'd never called out his name though. Not out loud.

"Juve?" I said his name quietly. I liked the way it sounded coming out of my mouth. It was unusual. His head turned almost instantly and the girl at his front door scoffed.

"Who's the princess?" Her eyes gouged into my face, and I instantly looked away from her. *A princess?* I was a little confused by her hostility.

"I can hear you, you know? My name is Chloe." I forced my eyes back to her face and noticed she was shocked by my direct approach and my cool tone. Her mouth hung open in shock. She looked like a bitch. Juve was trying his very best–and failing–to hide his smirk. My heart became uneven again and I flushed as I watched him. *Get a grip.* "Juve?" I called him again and watched as he nodded and leant to kiss the girl's cheek. Jealousy ripped through me as I watched his warm action towards her. I really missed being hugged. I missed my best friend. I missed my brother. I missed my Aunt Lynne. I rolled my eyes as I stood awkwardly watching them exchange goodbyes.

"I'll speak to you later." She was too bewildered to argue with him. It was clear she was shocked. Why? I didn't know. He placed the door shut and turned to face me, folding his arms as he did.

"Can I help you?" He cocked his full brow in a sexy manner, and I shook my head. I knew he was just being playful, but it seemed everything this bloke did made me feel all sorts of funny.

"Do you ever say no to her?" I asked as I tilted my head, pulling my eyes away from the door. "Or do you just give in to her every time?" He scoffed a burst of small laughter and I smirked.

"Can I help you, Chloe?" he asked again. His voice was steady and level and deep as he spoke. I folded my arms again.

"Yeah," I stumbled. "No… I don't know," I admitted. "I wanted to walk… go out for a walk," I added and watched his lips turn upwards. *God, he was beautiful.* Even though his lips were thinned they were still plump.

"We can go for a walk. That's not an issue." I nodded awkwardly as I reached for my coat by the front door.

"Thank you." My eyes lowered and I peeked up at him to see him grabbing a coat too. It was colder here at night, even in the summer months, and it had been known to drizzle on a night like tonight. It had been pretty overcast all day.

"Where do you wanna go?" he asked.

"Anywhere." I looked up at him under my lashes and felt myself blushing. He looked just like Haz, but rougher. Older. He looked like a man; his jaw was sharp, almost rectangular in shape, but his cheeks were almost chubby enough to want to squeeze. I shook my head slowly as I forced my eyes from him. He cleared his throat a little and nodded before he shrugged on a coat off the rack by the front door. It was padded and made him look even broader.

"I know just the place." I followed him out of the house and up the long driveway of his parents' home. There was an awkward silence that fell between us. I caught up with him quickly by walking an extra two steps to every one of his. "So…" He whistled.

"So…" I mimicked him as I cocked my head to one side.

"What's the deal with you and my brother?" I scoffed back an uncomfortable laugh and shrugged softly as I examined his expression. *Why was this his first question?* I wanted to wind him up, to tell him I was fucking him. I ached for a reaction from him, and I wasn't sure why.

"Not a lot, why?" I raised my brow at him and bit down on my bottom lip to stop myself from laughing. What I wanted to say and what actually left my mouth were two totally different things.

"No reason." He paused as he grinned at me. It was the most refreshing sight. His teeth were whiter than white and straight. "I just know what he's like." I wanted to laugh again. I knew what he was like too. He was a prick. A class A bellend. But he was my very best friend. I'd grown to get used to his mannerisms, his sarcasm, and I sort of enjoyed it. "I don't know where he gets it from." There was softer laughter leaving Juve's mouth now. It was a magical sound.

"He's my best friend," I added softly. Juve glanced down at me pacing next to him and flashed his smile my way, almost dazzling me. "I mean, he's shielded me from some pretty rough shit this last year." I cringed as I spoke. I didn't want to bring up what had happened and the reason we were staying here, but the smallest part of me did. That part of me wondered if it would help to talk about it. To get it all off my chest, but I was never sure how that would go down. I wasn't even sure if it was something I was supposed to talk about.

"Haz?" His tone sounded shocked as he spoke his brother's name. Like he wouldn't have done that for somebody. I nodded automatically to hearing his name, and we walked in sync up the incline of the hill. He sounded shocked when he spoke his brother's name and he slowed his pace down a little more so that I could keep up with him. "Haz is your best friend?" His one eyebrow was raised as he glanced towards me. My smile widened the more he looked at me in the most disbelieving manner.

"Yeah," I muttered. We were now close to the gates of his mum and dad's house, and we made our exit through them. Juve held the gate for me to slip through. *What a gentleman.*

"What shit has he helped with then?" I knew this was coming but I wasn't sure how I was going to answer it. *Truthfully? Or just lie?* I could feel the colour disappearing from my skin. My shoulders rose and fell as I looked at his friendly face. His face screamed, *tell me.* My gut twisted in response.

"He stopped Jay from getting sent down for longer." My voice was a whisper. "He stopped my dad from ripping me apart again." As much as I didn't want to think about it, it didn't matter, memories came back from that night. He'd got out and found us. All three of us.

"Your dad?" He raised his brow and glanced down at me. I didn't nod or acknowledge him speaking. My heart was beating fast, too fast. "So that's why you're here? So we can keep you safe?" He sounded confused as he spoke again, his brow twisted with confusion, and I nodded.

"I suppose that's what Larry wanted, yeah." I watched his face tense. His jaw locked a little in place. He looked older now that his expression was hostile.

"I can't imagine living with Larry was great." He was trying to keep his tone level, but he was failing. *What was so bad about Larry?*

"We stayed with him for about a year after my Aunt Lynne died." I held my arm with my hand, and I watched him frown again. "Can we stop talking about me? What about you?" I gestured towards him as we wandered towards the forest clearing. He shrugged and cleared his throat.

"I'm in the army, being deployed soon, I hope." I smiled widely at him. I could picture this being his path in life. It dawned on me that this was the first time I'd smiled so genuinely since I'd been here.

"Wow." I whistled. "When?" He smirked a little and then shrugged.

"As soon as possible." I nodded slowly. I couldn't imagine why he wanted to leave this family. I trudged along the path set out in front of us and I suddenly felt comfortable in his company.

"Why didn't I know you were in the army?" I questioned him light-heartedly. His beautiful face softened as he shook his head.

"I suppose I don't boast about my achievements." He grinned as we continued to walk at a steady pace on the path. I kept walking forwards as the hill trailed upwards. Other people were walking too. The trail thinned, which meant we were closer. I didn't mind that so much.

"So Haz said you're an old man…" I broke the silence with a shitty comment and watched his lips curl upwards into a smirk and then a smile. He tilted his head towards me, and I laughed a little as our eyes met. My breathing stopped as I looked into his dark pools of blue.

"I am, I suppose." He spoke clearly and then I frowned slightly. He certainly didn't look old. "Twenty is old, right?" he teased himself. I ran my hand over my chin and let myself grin at him. I was sort of expecting him to be in his twenties from my conversations with Haz, but I was a little gutted too. He really was a man. Not an immature little shite like his brother.

"Very." I watched him roll his eyes and smiled to myself as he jogged ahead a little. I found myself beginning to like Juve. He was easy to be around. He laughed and then we were climbing a bigger hill. This wasn't an easy walk; it was more of a hike, and it made sense that he wasn't even a little bit out of breath. I frowned to myself and continued to follow him. This trail was sodding awful, I didn't have his stamina or level of fitness.

"So where is Jay?" He was back to quizzing me. I liked that he didn't really let things just lie.

"Serving a sentence." I rolled my eyes thinking about what he was getting himself into whilst he was behind bars. I just hoped it didn't make his sentence longer. He was wiser beyond his years with the temper to match, the temper that had landed him back behind bars. "They both said I needed the stability of being in a family environment." I half scoffed, half laughed. "By both, I mean my brother and Haz." A soft chuckle left his mouth. It was a delightful sound and his expression warmed.

"Well, I don't think my family is the one that's going to make you feel like a unit. We're just as dysfunctional." I frowned at his teasing tone and pushed his arm slightly.

"Juve?" I frowned at him and watched his big blue eyes land on mine. "I don't think you realise how fucked my *family* is." I spat the word family and laughed as pity filled his face.

"Think I'm starting to get a picture," he mumbled at me. I frowned and shrugged softly. This wasn't the conversation I wanted to have with him. He was cool and clueless and that's how I wanted it to stay. I didn't really want him to know all of my gory life details. I was happy that he didn't have any pity for me. Glad he didn't see me as weak. The clearing in the trees opened and the hills rolled out in front of us. The sky was orange and I breathed outwards. *This* was on his doorstep.

"Bloody hell, this is stunning." I gasped and watched him nod before he threw himself down on the floor and hugged his knees. The gust of wind made the tall grass wave.

"It sure is." I watched him looking out over the hills and smiled to myself. The view from where I was standing was like no other, countryside swarmed one side and cityscapes the other. I tore my eyes away from the city below and looked back at Juve. The orange sun beamed down on his mousey, slightly curly hair, and I felt my chest flutter. I *liked* him. He seemed so normal, and normal was what I desperately needed, what I craved more than anything. I laughed a little to myself before I sat next to him and crossed my arms. "This is the safest and easiest route to walk if you ever want to get out of the house." He didn't look my way. He just watched the sun in the sky. I nodded and placed my head against my knees too. I liked this green scenery. It made a change from concrete or the sea. We sat in silence, a comforting silence listening to other people's conversations about work, their dogs and their plans for the rest of the evening. "Your accent isn't a Southern accent, Chloe?" He broke the silence after a while, though he wasn't looking at me, and from the tone in his voice, I knew he wanted to engage in a conversation. I sighed and stayed quiet for a while. "I know accents change over time, but you sound posh. Almost London posh." I frowned at him. I'd hoped that being in Devon would have been enough to change it, but it hadn't budged. My mum had drilled our accent into us. I may have been dragged up, but you would never have known.

"I was born in London." I breathed and cringed all at once. It hurt to admit it out loud. "Near Kensington." I rolled my eyes as he whistled. I hated talking about my past. It was difficult to bring up. *So why did I want to tell him?*

"How the hell did you end up in Devon then?" His head was now off his knees, and he was watching me intently for a reaction and a response.

"I don't really..." I stumbled on my words as I shook my head. "I feel really uncomfortable talking about it." My throat grew dry, and I tilted my head on my knees, so I was looking at him now too. His eyes darted over my face.

"Just spill, Chloe." His brow furrowed. "Who am I gonna tell?" His face warmed and I shrugged. It was true. Who was he going to spill my life to? Everyone I had ever known was dead or in jail. I was alone. I was alone with him. I took a deep breath in and gulped down my pride. I would give in to the curiosity of how it felt to tell an outsider my tale. My life. My trauma.

"I landed up in Devon after the courts placed me with my aunt." I frowned at him for making me bring all of this up. "My dad sexually abused me as a kid and my mum was a piss-head." I didn't wait to watch sorrow and pity fall across his handsome face, but I was certain I heard him take in a breath. I just continued. "We were placed under witness protection but that didn't really work. My dad got out and found us before we came here." I half laughed at how wild my life sounded. "My sperm donor," I added. "That's why I'm here and Jay is in prison. He found me." My mind replayed the night my sperm donor found us at Larry's. Juve didn't speak and I didn't look at him either. "I've never seen Jay so angry, and I don't think I'll ever see him in that state again. Larry came home just in the nick of time, and unfortunately, so did the cops." I frowned as I tried to push the memory of that night away.

"So that's why your brother is in the nick?" He pushed me for an answer softly, and I nodded.

"Yeah, my dad was in a pretty bad way." I closed my eyes briefly and remembered screaming at both Jay and Haz to stop hitting him. A shiver ran through my body. "They stopped when Larry got home." I gulped and opened my eyes. His were now drowned with pity. "I lived with my Aunt Lynne in Thorverton for a little while. She was my mum's elder sister. Thank God they were nothing alike." I dropped the story of Jay and Haz beating my dad to a pulp and tried to side-track him. The memory of my Aunt Lynne was a much better, sweeter memory. I liked talking about her. I placed my hand over the necklace that was resting at the nape of my neck and felt my eyes brim with tears. "I was hoping my accent would disappear with time, but it hasn't." I frowned. "My mum and dad liked to keep up appearances, so we spoke properly." I shook my head. "You wouldn't ever have known what went on behind closed doors." He stopped my train of thought when his hand covered mine. My eyebrows raised upwards, and my eyes widened with shock—or fear. I wasn't entirely sure which emotion was the strongest out of the two.

"I think I've heard enough." I didn't look up at his eyes. I just nodded. I'd said enough. Of course I'd said enough, and now my curiosity was satisfied. Talking didn't help. Talking made me weak. Talking made me fragile.

JUVE

As soon as she'd opened up I realised why she was so guarded, and also possibly why Haz felt like she needed to be looked after. My world stopped pretty quickly when she spoke her truth. I had only asked why she sounded so posh and now I felt awful for asking, partly because I had forced her to bring up something traumatic. She didn't look at me for a while after that walk. In fact, she didn't talk to me for ages either. My big brotherly instincts ate away at me for a time, and I just felt sick thinking about how anybody could ever hurt somebody so lovely. She put on a brave face all of the time in front of my family. My mum especially. It was as though she was desperate for her approval, but my mum already loved her. I wondered how much my mum and dad actually knew about the tortured soul that was residing in our home. She was sprawled out on my mum's new cream fabric sofa. Mum had gone to a yoga class, Dad was out on business, and Aimee was at her friend's house for the day, which left us all alone. The weather was rough today and she'd obviously decided that it wasn't the weather for a walk. She'd made it a ritual that she went for a walk at least once a day. Sometimes she was gone for an hour, sometimes two, but it was always at dusk. I hadn't quite wrapped my head around her; I'd spent much of my time over the last few days trying to work her out. I watched her head tilt at something that was playing on the television. She seemed interested in whatever it was.

"Good film?" I questioned her and watched her eyes land on me briefly before she shrugged softly. Her dainty shoulders fell.

"I'm not really watching it." A peal of soft laughter left my mouth at her honesty. She smiled before she looked my way, her lips didn't thin but they lifted in the corners. She had a great smile. Her eyes seemed warmer today. She pulled her knees up towards her chest and placed her face against them. She suddenly looked her age. I found myself staring at her, examining her and how my view of her had taken a complete turn. She was an attractive girl, but now all I wanted to do was protect her. "What?" she asked the more I looked her way. I shook my head slowly.

"Just thinking how young you look today." I laughed again and raised my brow at her.

"You look old," she teased, and I grinned widely before I threw myself back on the sofa next to her.

"I know. It's because I am old, Chloe." I watched her flush pink in colour and smiled to myself.

"Please call me, Chlo." Her eyes met mine for the first time in days, and a feeling of warmth overcame me. "Chloe seems so formal." I laughed a little and nodded.

"Okay." She smiled politely back at me and looked back towards the television that was mounted on the wall. "What's the deal with you walking?" I desperately wanted to get inside her head, to understand the way her brain dealt with everything she had ever been through.

"It gives me something to do." Her voice was soft and clear. "Saves me moping around, staring at you." I scoffed back a laugh as she poked my ribs. That part of me was sensitive, ticklish. Not even my closest friends touched me there. I held her hand in mine and watched her struggle to hold in laughter of her own. I had no response to what had just left her mouth. I was frozen, holding her hand, frightened to let it go in the fear that she'd poke me again. I felt the blood rising in my face and shook my head from side to side.

"Well, that's put me straight, hey?" I gulped out my words. She just rolled her eyes, putting her attention back on the television and I cleared my throat, my hand still in hers.

"What's with that girl that keeps calling here for you?" She was asking her own protruding questions now. Her eyes didn't break from the television as she asked her own prying questions. She didn't struggle with me to move her hand, and in fact, she moved it so that her fingers wrapped around mine. I liked her, she was outspoken and direct. I wondered if this was all a facade. A bravado?

"She's my girlfriend." I spoke honestly. *Amber.* She was talking about Amber. I glanced down at our hands and felt my chest twist.

"So you date bitchy women?" She raised her brow my way. My eyes widened, and I fought off a chuckle. Amber was a bitch. Her perception of Amber was spot on. She was hot. Really fucking hot, but she was such a bitch. I simply shrugged.

"I suppose so, yeah. Wouldn't really call her a woman though." I bit down on my bottom lip to stop myself from smirking and relaxed back a little. Chlo's expression softened, and I found myself staring at her again. I examined her side profile now, her nose slightly upturned and her chin a little sharp.

"Is she younger than you?" she questioned again, and I nodded. I had no reason to lie. Amber had always been a year below me in school.

"Why'd you ask?" She shrugged softly and placed her head against my shoulder. My initial reaction was to pull away from her touch, but I couldn't. Instead, I sat with her head against my arm and her hand in mine. She rearranged her legs so that they were out straight in front of her, and she yawned before she opened her mouth to respond to me again.

"I could tell she was a bitch." She spoke in a low tone— it was teasing. "By the way she looked at me the first time I saw her." I smirked as I drew on the memory. "She was the green-eyed monster." I laughed and nodded as I pulled on the blanket from the back of the sofa with my free hand.

"Yeah, she gets like that," I admitted and kicked the blanket over our legs. I looked at the film that was playing in the background and rolled my eyes. It was my mum's favourite. Billy Elliott. "Mum loves this film." Chlo sighed, and I smiled to myself.

"I need a chick flick, possibly a cry and a hot chocolate and then I'll feel better." I laughed at her admission and nodded.

"I can sort the hot chocolate but I'm out if you're gonna watch a chick flick." She laughed a loud laugh and then shrugged her shoulders, her head lifted from my shoulder.

"Don't be a spoilsport." Her brown eyes narrowed, and I rolled my own eyes.

"Fine, pick one and I'll be back." I stood up and headed towards the kitchen to pour the hot chocolate. If this would make her feel better, then I would spare some of my time this afternoon to help her out. She was clearly missing Haz. I imagined this behaviour with him was normal, with me it should have felt wrong, but it didn't. It was comfortable. *What the hell was she doing to me?*

It was another shit day for weather in the Shropshire countryside today, so I'd decided on staying in. Chlo hadn't left either. I closed my eyes briefly and listened to the rain pouring outside, the window cracked slightly, and it was warm. *British weather.* I rolled my eyes subconsciously when I was hit by the familiar smell of Chlo's perfume. She was almost silent before she placed herself on the sofa next to me. The warmth of her skin against my arm made my eyes open. Her huge dark muddy pools with golden flakes stared back at me. She was just looking at me.

"Can I help you?" I croaked. A small shy smile appeared on her face. She shrugged softly.

"I wanted to apologise." She spoke quietly and I sat up.

"What on earth for?" I frowned at her. She wasn't looking at me again, this was a habit of hers, I'd gathered she did it when she was uncomfortable.

"For spilling my guts to you." Her face twisted and she huffed. "You're really easy to talk to apparently." I crossed my arms and held in laughter. "I don't think witness protection would be happy if they knew it was that easy to get information from me." I smiled at her softly and moved her chin up a little bit. She flinched a little away from me. I held in my sigh; I didn't want her to look at me like she was shit scared of me. She moved my hand away from her chin.

"Don't apologise." I spoke softly, and she cleared her throat as I dropped my hand from her face. "Can you start looking at me now?" I asked and watched her flinch as I dropped my hand and nudged her a little. "I don't bite, I swear." I wanted this kid to feel comfortable around me, I wanted to help her overcome her fears, and in the weirdest way, I wanted to be there for her if she needed somebody. I wanted to be *her* person. Nobody should ever have to go through life struggling alone. I stood by that. I vowed she wouldn't have to be alone as long as I was around.

CHLO

I'd felt more at home with Haz's family than I'd felt in a long time. Here felt like home. I'd only got three weeks left before we went back to Devon. Part of me felt sick when I thought about it. I'd overheard Henry talking to Larry and his wife about me and my wellbeing. I didn't want to keep moving around. I had a year left at school. *Surely to God, they would let me finish the year?* I was sick of dropping everything. I was sprawled out on the sofa in the family snug. The snug was a dark room, one wall was painted a deep red colour, and there were bookshelves on either side of the log burner. I loved this room. Juve appeared from nowhere at the entrance. I smiled at him and patted the sofa next to me. We had grown closer over the last couple of weeks, we'd spent days just watching crappy television and I'd loved every bit of having somebody so bothered about my wellbeing. He waltzed over and placed himself so that my head was in his lap. He reminded me of Haz in some ways. It was his warmth; they shared that similarity. It was so easy to just *be* with him. I wasn't sure why I felt this way about him, but I did. My chest fluttered and then my stomach as he ran his fingers through my hair that was against his lap. The smell of his aftershave surrounded me. I opened my eyes and watched him smile down at me. It was so big and wide, his cheeks looked chubbier when he smiled.

"So, is your brain doing overtime again?" he teased, and I laughed a little. He'd grown to know me more clearly. I bobbed my tongue out at him and watched him grin.

"I'm going home in three weeks, and I've never felt more at home than I do here." My heart broke a little admitting that. He sighed outwards and nodded his head. His hair swished with the movement of his head.

"Well, I'm being deployed too. First tour in a month." I sat up quickly, my eyes wide and my mouth slightly open. I was *not* ready for this.

"Where to?" I asked. I didn't want to alarm him, but I was worried. Everyone good I had ever come across had been ripped away from me.

"Afghanistan." He didn't say anything else, but my stomach filled with dread and my chest tightened.

"Juve, that's a war zone." His lips turned upwards into a smile as I spoke. I knew that this wasn't for his benefit but for mine. I knew that he'd be scared. I knew he was hiding his feelings.

"I'm in the army, Chloe." He rolled his eyes and flicked my forehead softly. "It's kinda what I signed up for." I shook my head and pushed his chest. He held my hand against it and his smile became wider.

"I know." I frowned and shook my head. "Just come back," I pleaded. "You're kinda my person." I flushed a little as I looked towards him. His facial expression changed then. He was no longer smiling. He just nodded. His deep dark blue eyes saddened as he squeezed my hand in his.

"I'll be back, baby Chlo, don't you worry." He patted my shoulder softly, squeezed the hand that was against his chest again and pulled me in for a little cuddle. I forced away my tears. I wouldn't worry anymore. I couldn't worry about anyone else. I had no more room in my heart for it. If I was being honest with myself, I couldn't make any more room in my heart for anybody else. I feared if I did, I would shatter completely when that went wrong.

CHAPTER FOUR
CHANGE

TWO YEARS LATER

CHLO

I'd grown sick and tired of being dragged into their meetings, their drug deals and Haz's constant battles. The years of being back in Devon hadn't been easy for any of us. I'd watch my brother and best friend be dragged deeper and deeper into a mess they had no way out of. I ran my hand over my arm as I hugged myself on the hostel bed. The boom of the base from the room above reverberated around us and I growled. I didn't think life could get much rougher but fuck me was I wrong. I was seventeen. I'd seen my birthday in high as a kite in this shitty room—a hostel room, a grubby hotel room in Torquay. *What a dream.* I rolled my eyes. I was just grateful I was sitting on a hostel bed though and wasn't in Holly's position. I remembered clearly how blissfully happy Haz and her were until Rava ruined it all. Until that went tits up. I flinched at the memories that came flooding back.

***

Jay gripped my hand in his. His face was paled, his usual mahogany colouring gone, along with all of his bravado.

"You've gotta stay quiet, Chlo." I nodded at him. "Promise me?" he begged. I squeezed his fingers and nodded again.

"I promise," I muttered towards him. My eyes glanced over his smart black suit, and I gulped. It had been a while since Holly was taken into Rava's clutches. He was supposed to be their friend. I fought the anger away and glanced up at Haz. He was placing his blazer over his broad shoulders in the front of the car.

"Ready?" He looked at my brother who was just nodding whilst his eyes never left mine. I pulled his arm back as I looked on at the warehouse in front of us.

"What are we doing here?" I asked him. I watched him swallow his Adam's apple and force a smile. It offered me no comfort.

"Bandoni wants to see you." I fought the sick rising in my stomach.

"You swore you'd never put me in harm's way, Jay." I'd lost my faith in my brother a little now that he'd been dragged into the underworld. He frantically shook his head.

"You think I'm gonna give you over to him?" He scoffed. "He wants to meet you to see if you can join us. He can offer us a better life than this, Chlo." I folded my arms as I examined the pleading look in my brother's eyes. My heart twisted.

"What if he wants something in return?" I gave him my ultimate thought and watched his face twist.

"Then he can fuck off and I'll shoot him myself." He flashed a wicked grin at me which made me smile too. I shook my head slowly. "I won't let anything happen to you ever again." He pulled on my hand, and I followed him out of the car. "I promise." I nodded and followed him and Haz towards the warehouse. Two huge men were standing outside, one of them had a scar across his lip, it was large and deep. He nodded at the boys and then the older man's mouth twisted upwards as he looked at me. His eyes wandered over my chest, and I squeezed my brother.

"Put your eyes back in your fucking head," he barked at the

*man guarding the doors. "I'll blow your bastard bollocks off myself."
He spoke through gritted teeth as the guard got closer to his face, and
Haz stepped between them.*

*"Steady on, dog." He teased the guard. "Go tell your boss we're
here, yeah?" Haz patted his shoulder in a patronising manner, and I
could breathe again. I was lost in my own bubble for a while whilst
they argued amongst themselves. The scar-faced older man gestured
towards us, and we followed. The sound of my shoes clicked against
the concrete floor and then there was a groaning noise. My heart
stopped as my eyes landed on a guy bound and gagged on a chair. His
face was unrecognisable from the bruising and blood–a pool of blood
at his feet.*

*"Fuck," I breathed out and felt Jay squeeze me. There was a
knife against the table along with other tools–household DIY tools.
A loud booming voice came from behind us.*

*"Is this your sister, Mr Conway?" He had an accent. It was
Italian. I spun around as my heart pounded again in my chest. Jay
was nodding now. The older greying man stepped towards me and
touched my cheek, every hair on my arms stood up. His eyes I was
not expecting, they were bright green, not black in colour like I'd
expected. Black eyes just like Dad's. I felt a lump grow in my throat
and tried my best to swallow it. I wasn't weak anymore. "You have
the most wonderful eyes, Miss Conway." He breathed as he offered
me an almost friendly smile. "It's a pity they have witnessed the
trauma they have." Jay tensed next to me.*

*"Please stop touching her," he begged and laughter erupted from
around the empty warehouse.*

*"I'm sure she would tell me if she wasn't comfortable." I felt sick,
the smell of blood was making its way up my nostrils that were
flaring with fear. "Don't tell me what to do." The older man reached
to grab my brother and I instantly gripped his arm with my hand.*

*"Don't fucking touch him," I growled. Bandoni's face lit up and
he dropped his hand. "He might be scared of you but I'm not." I was
bluffing and I had absolutely no idea what I was doing. I was going
to get us all killed.*

*"She speaks." He grinned widely at me and offered out his arm
to me. "Come, walk with me." My brother's eyes were wide now.*

"Let these lovely boys finish their task for the night." There was a scream from behind me and I knew they were torturing the man in the chair. I couldn't witness that. I wouldn't listen to that. I would walk with Bandoni and I would leave this warehouse in the company of a mafia boss. I placed my arm in his and walked away from my brother and Haz. Fear rippled through me as I fought the urge to look back.

"I will need your help, Chloe." He spoke softly as he wandered further away from the empty warehouse and into the back of a limo parked out the front. We were alone. A man held open my door open and I slipped into it. I should have been shaking from fear, but I was still. I was calm. My eyes landed on Bandoni's.

"I haven't forgiven your son," I admitted. I would never forgive him for the way he treated Holly to get his revenge on Haz. I gulped and pushed a memory from my head.

"I don't expect you to, however, I do want you to keep your eye on the boy's interaction with him. He is not to be harmed by either of them." My eyes widened as I opened my mouth to protest. *"If they do"*—he paused—*"see Mr Smith in that chair?"* My stomach dropped.

"Mr Smith?" I muttered his name. Smith. I couldn't make out his facial features, but I went rigid. Smith. *"Your brother and Harry will end up like him, and you wouldn't want that, would you, my dear?"* I shook my head slowly.

"Mr Smith?" I asked quietly again. He simply nodded. His green eyes landed on mine and he offered me a closed smile.

"I may be a heartless man, Chloe…" He spoke softly as though he was talking to a child. *"But I am not a monster. I would give anything to have my Natalia back."* The expression on his ageing face didn't falter as he spoke. *"He deserves everything he is getting tonight and a lifetime more."* My blood ran cold as the realisation hit me full force in the gut. That Mr Smith was my father. Sick rose in my throat as the image of his blood pouring from his broken, tore up skin appeared in my head. They had ripped him apart. I pushed open the door and threw up all over the pavement and down the side of the limo, barely missing the doorman's shoes. I heard a groan from behind me.

"You are safe from him now. I hope your brother enjoys his

revenge." I spat out the remaining bits of phlegm and sick and slumped back against the leather of the limo's seat. He was dead. He would die here alone in a warehouse. My heart burst with relief, but it still wasn't enough.

***

I hadn't seen the worst of what had happened to Holly, but I'd seen enough. I now knew that if I didn't do as I was told, I would end up like her. Battered, drugged, and forced into doing things I had no interest in doing. These men weren't men you wanted to get on the wrong side of. I had no intention of getting on their bad side.

I rolled over and heard him screaming her name again. **Holly.** I'd heard her name being screamed over and over again when he writhed and tossed and turned in his sleep. There wasn't much that triggered him whilst he was high, but when he was sleeping, that's when the demons came to get him. There was something about him in his sleep that screamed for help. I ran my hand over his face in an effort to comfort him. His stubble carved out the shape of his face almost perfectly. I moved his mousey fluffy hair that was now darker and dripping with sweat. I hated seeing him in pain. Physical or mental. I understood why he had turned to harder drugs. It numbed him. It just didn't make seeing him ruin himself any easier. I shook my head and turned to look at my brother. His eyes were red-rimmed too from his earlier spliff.

"I'm in court tomorrow, Co." I nodded.

"I know," I whispered as we looked towards our best mate tossing and turning in the bed. "When is this going to stop, Jay?" He shrugged softly and patted his chest as he held his arms out to me. "Like when are you going to stop going to prison?" I gulped down my tears and squeezed him softly as I placed my head on his chest. This was possibly one of my favourite places to be. He just stroked my hair.

"Last time," he breathed against my head. "I promise."

I closed my eyes and nodded.

"Promise me, Puddle?" I looked up towards him and watched him nod.

"Promise, Coco." I smiled and snuggled him. "I think you may need to stay with Carol and Henry though." I groaned at the thought. Since I was last there, too much had changed. I'd seen too much to fit into what they remembered. The damaged little fragile girl no longer existed. I was tougher now, stronger and colder. I'd seen too much for *that* Chloe to ever return.

JUVE

Time didn't stand still for any man. Deployment was still fresh. As in, I had landed back on UK soil this morning and I'd already got the joys of having a house full. According to Mum, Haz was home and bringing Miss Conway along for the ride. Just the two of them. I shook my head from side to side and thought how little and fragile she'd been once upon a time. I wondered how much she'd changed over the years we'd been apart. I'd remembered her telling me to just come back. I'd made it home. I was back. For how long, I didn't know. If there was one thing I was dreading, it was seeing Haz again. He'd been through a bit since I'd left. I wasn't even sure if he'd speak to me or whether he'd think I'd abandoned him. I clenched my teeth together and held my dog tags close to my chest. I took a breath and made my way down the stairs to falsely place a smile on my face when secretly I was hearing the sound of gunshots in my mind.

CHLO

I hated that I'd been dragged up here again. Only this time, Haz was in a worse state than last time and Jay was nowhere to be seen. He was finishing up his sentence for drug possession. I groaned inwardly as I looked at Haz in the car. He just shrugged my way as he drove. Our relationship had grown more volatile and dependant on sex just lately. We were both alone and sad and just as fucked up as one another, and I suppose we both sought some sort of solace from that.

"Should you even be driving?" I raised my brow at him, acknowledging the way he slumped in his chair, and he held out for my hand. The car he was driving was expensive. More than likely stolen and we had been doing a minimum of ninety miles an hour on the motorway. I frowned as I glared at his hand.

"I should never be driving." His tone was mellow. "I'm always high." I frowned and slapped his chest. This wasn't a shock anymore. It was the norm. Seeing him high was normal. "Juve has just got back though, so don't drop it out." I shook my head at him. The sound of his name being said aloud made my chest flutter. I hadn't heard his name in a long time. My memory didn't recall much of his features, but I remembered his kindness and warmth above anything else. I'd found myself Facebook stalking him from time to time. There was the odd photo uploaded of him in his uniform, but his face was almost always covered. I thanked him for that. One thing I never quite got over were his eyes. Wonderful dark blue ocean eyes that I had been lost in time and time again when he spoke.

"When did he get home?" I asked him, completely ignoring his demand. He smiled and shrugged as we pulled up to the driveway of the house.

"This morning, apparently." My heart thudded as a reaction to his statement, and I shook my head.

"Oh," I breathed. "Right, okay." I loosened my grip of

his hand and stared at the wonderful old house that was set back off the road up the long driveway. The house that never seemed to change. After two years, I was back here, and I was actually going to see the lad I'd crushed on so hard once upon a time. The kindest soul I'd ever had the pleasure of meeting. Two years of seeing more shit and adding to the damage. I wondered if he'd changed as much as I had. I wondered if we were both fucked now, and it wouldn't just be me who was a wreck.

Haz slouched against the wall, and I reached to knock on the front door. Carol opened it swiftly and beamed at me. She pushed my hair from my face. It was much shorter than it once had been and was now almost silver in colour. It hit her shoulders comfortably. Her greenish in colour eyes lingered on mine and she smiled widely. She hadn't aged. Not one bit.

"My, haven't you changed." She was now cupping my face softly. It had been a long time since I'd felt such a warm motherly touch. Tears brimmed in my eyes. I felt as though I barely recognised who I was as I looked at my reflection in her eyes. She released my face, and the sound of heavy boots thudded down the stairs which made me step backwards from her. There was a whistle from the direction of the footsteps, and I frowned deeply.

"My lord." The gruff voice echoed around the hallway. "Is that you, Miss Conway?" My eyes widened as I looked towards him. *Holy shit.* He was still dressed in a military uniform, combat boots, and silver dog tags that dangled around his neck. I wanted to reach for him. I almost wanted to touch his dog tags, to read them, and I closed my eyes before I bit down on my lip to stop myself from smiling like a Cheshire cat. His mousey coloured hair was longer than I'd remembered it being. It was slightly curlier too. He almost looked adolescent in comparison to his younger brother, only the faint lines in his skin gave him away. There was nothing sweet about this hunk of a man anymore. I'd always remembered him as sweet and funny.

It must have been my age. He had always been hot, but fuck, he was even hotter now. I hadn't spoken yet. He flashed a wide smile that nearly knocked me over, flicking his hair to one side before he ruffled it with his hand and then placed it on the back of his neck. His shoulders were broad as they flexed. I could have sworn a tiny groan left my mouth as he grinned.

"Indeed, that's her." Haz laughed and reached for his older brother. He pulled him into an embrace, the sound of slapping could have been heard from outside. They were so similar in their appearance. I started to look for the similarities in them. Juve's face was shaven and Haz had a shaped stubble. They could have passed as twins. His eyes landed on mine again and he smiled softly at me. It was their eyes that were different. Juve's were dark blue like the deepest depths of the ocean and Harry's were crystal blue like ice.

"Well, haven't you changed. You're all grown up." He reached for me, wrapping me up in his large arms, the smell of him consumed my nostrils and I cleared my throat as my heart pounded against my chest. He smelt the same. Just like clean laundry. *Breathe, Chlo, breathe. Jesus Christ.* His grip was tight, and I was beginning to wish I'd have had time to wrap my head around the fact that he'd be here before I got here. I wished I'd had the time to prepare myself for feeling this goddamn attracted to him. He had bowled me over.

"Sure." I swallowed. This was the only word that slid from my mouth. *Get a grip.* I felt utterly ridiculous. My little teenage crush was back with a vengeance. He was resting his arm over my shoulder, and I smiled as I shook my head slowly. I knew I was blushing.

"So…" He turned his head towards my ear. "Who are you gonna share a room with? Him or me?" He pointed at his brother, and I couldn't help but laugh as Carol reached to slap his chest. I'd always loved his humour.

"Juve! That's disgusting!" she squealed. "She's a baby!"

He flinched away from her strikes as we all laughed. I crossed my arms and leant against the hallway wall.

"Are those the only options I have?" I raised my brow at him and watched him shrug his shoulders as his mum walked off cursing into the kitchen. His eyes wandered over my face.

"Behave, Chloe," Haz warned from next to me. I pursed my lips together as I stared at him. He was ruining my fun already. "You have your own room." He glared at me as he tilted his head towards the living room. "The usual." He grinned at me, and I rolled my eyes at him. He was on a comedown. Or at least I thought he was heading that way. He was sombre and irritable. More so than normal. He was probably due a fix soon.

"You're really rude, Haz, you know that?" I reminded him as I placed my bag back on my back. He laughed his signature belly laugh and my heart warmed slightly.

"You love it." He gave me a cheeky wink and I placed my fingers down my throat in a gagging motion. There was a time I'd loved it. Almost thought I loved him. But now, not so much. That ship had long sailed.

JUVE

She's seventeen. She's seventeen. She's seventeen, I repeated to myself over and over again as she placed her fingers in the back of her throat, so far in. I gulped as I followed her up the stairs with my eyes. My younger dickhead of a brother was laughing. I knew he could read what I was thinking because he must have been attracted to her too. She was absolutely beautiful.

"What?" I questioned him innocently.

"You." He began to speak as he continued to watch the television. "You look like you're gonna explode." I scoffed at his remark and shook my head. "Was the eye candy that bad over there?" I frowned again. Since the second I laid my eyes on her, I'd had a soft spot for her. But the girl that had just climbed my stairs was not the same girl I'd said goodbye to two years ago. She had always been witty and sure of herself, but now she just seemed cold. It was clear the life she had been living with Haz and her brother had not been kind to her. It was evident the path that my brother had taken as I looked into his red-rimmed eyes. I was just finding it hard to picture her involved with all that too. I thought about her again, she'd always been such a pretty thing, even when she was younger, and the olive undertone in her skin was more obvious now. My memory had not served her smile well at all. Her teeth were the straightest teeth I'd ever seen. I remembered teasing her about that big cheesy grin all of the time when we were younger. My brain was now reminiscing on our short time together when we were much younger, and I fought my smile. *I hadn't felt like this then, surely? There* was an awkward silence between us now. I was still in my uniform, and I perched next to him on the sofa as I looked at him. I barely recognised the brute.

"So, Jay is still locked up?" I asked as I placed my foot on my leg stretched across my lap. "Dad said he was busted with drugs again." I watched his brow furrow.

80

"You taking everything he says for gospel now?" he snapped back at me, his tone full of hostility.

"Jesus, Haz." He shook his head from side to side.

"Yeah, he's inside. He's doing a month and then he's out again." I frowned at how easy this seemed to leave his mouth. It was clear that this was something they were getting used to.

"You been back in?" He shook his head.

"Not since Holly, no." I shuddered at that. Dad had said she was pregnant when it had all kicked off, though I didn't know what to believe anymore, and definitely not now they were in opposite gangs. "I ain't been caught yet." He rolled his eyes and I watched him sprawl out on Mum's sofa. If she knew he was laying around on her furniture like that she'd kill him. He looked tired or stressed, or something else entirely. It had been such a long time since I'd been in a room with him that I couldn't read him anymore. It had been so long since we had held any sort of conversation. I'd left him when he needed me the most. I examined the way the red spread in his eyes and how his pupils seemed tiny. I knew drugs were a possibility.

"What are you on, H?" I questioned him again.

"What's it matter to you?" He didn't look at me. His eyes were closed. "I deal with losing her my own way. You fucking left." My gut twisted at his admission. *There it was.* I'd known for some time he felt this way, but I didn't expect to feel so fucking guilty for leaving him.

"I left because I didn't want to be dragged into that shit, Haz." My tone was steady. "I didn't want to be involved in Dad's way of life. I didn't know you would fuck up that much that they would take her away from you." I frowned deeply, struggling to fight my anger. He sat up poker straight and his jaw clenched as he looked me dead in the eyes.

"They didn't just take her from me, Juve! I watched them rip that poor fucking kid from her stomach." I flinched as he spoke about it so easily. "I was there when she screamed for me and there was literally fuck all I could do about any of it. I just had to watch." He shook his head and turned his face away from me. "I know I fucked up, but she didn't deserve to have that butchered from her body and face a lifetime of abuse." He ran his hand through the front of his hair and growled. "As I said, I chose to deal with that loss in my own way, now fuck off." He had made it quite clear that he didn't want to talk about it. My stomach was twisting at his admission, and I wasn't quite sure I was ready for any more of our discussion. The short snippets of what Dad and he had said were enough. I'd seen my fair share of bloodshed. I'd killed people, probably many of them innocent people, but I'd never had blood on my hands. Not like him. Mine was through the barrel of a gun. Not like any of them. Firing a gun was my talent. I placed my hands on my knees and pushed myself up. I looked down at my brother who was rigid and staring into the abyss. I walked away from him. I was too tired for this argument.

I showered, changed into something more normal and nonmilitary, and ruffled my hair dry with a towel. It was fluffy–it was nice that I didn't have to make it neat. I folded my uniform up without thinking about what I was doing and shook my head slowly. I pressed down on the door handle and Chlo was standing awkwardly outside. My eyes wandered over her face and then her figure. She was hourglass all right. I cleared my throat as my eyes met hers. I was certain she flushed in colour. I smiled a weak smile at her and then moved from her way.

"I don't have an ensuite." She was justifying being outside the bathroom whilst I had been in there. Her big mud-brown eyes grew wider now. I laughed a little and shrugged. *Would now be a bad time to tease?*

"I think you were trying to see me naked in the shower," I teased her. It was now that colour rose in her cheeks again. She reached to thump me, and I laughed. I liked the way she'd cut her hair shorter. It was almost a baby blonde now. She really did look older, but then she always had.

"Oh shut it, Juve. You wish." She rolled her eyes, disappeared into the bathroom and slammed the door behind her. I grinned and heard the taps go on. I wanted to catch up with her. I wanted to see if she had changed much or if she was still that sweet fragile flower underneath her harder bravado. I wanted to know what was going on with my brother, what the real story with Jay was. I felt my brow furrowing and leant against the wall opposite the bathroom as my curiosity got more and more intense. I *needed* to get this girl alone. The sound of the taps running flooded my ears and I pictured her undressing. *Jesus, what was I doing?* I pushed my thoughts of her getting naked away and cleared my throat.

"I'm gonna play The Last of Us if you wanna join me?" I smirked to myself as I spoke. She had loved the first game from when she was here two years ago. The bathroom door handle went down, and she appeared again. Just her head–to my disappointment her body was hidden. Her brown eyes were narrowed, and her brow was furrowed slightly.

"Number two?" I simply nodded and she grinned a wide, wonderful smile. "I'm in." I laughed a little and watched her smile more softly at me, her eyes lingered on me for longer than they should have, and I nodded.

"I'll be in my room." I saluted her and watched her pull her eyes away from my mouth.

"Plan," she murmured before she closed the door again. My heart was throbbing. There was a zing in the air. I was sure of it. I wandered down the hallway towards my room. I knew Warren had a copy of the game downloaded, he'd already played it through with Buddy, my two younger brothers forever acting their age. I padded my way towards my empty room and turned on the television.

I'd loaded it up and now I was waiting, patiently waiting. I ran my hand over my arm as I placed my head back on the pillow. I listened to the guitar from the trailer being played in the background and smiled to myself. Haz played, and I wondered if he'd had a go at this yet. There wasn't much he couldn't play. There was a knock at the door and my eyes shot open.

"Did I wake you?" She was looking at me which made a change from the first time we met. She was actually looking me in the eyes without struggling. *She had changed.* I smiled to myself as her eyes wandered over my body again. *Was she checking me out?* I was possibly checking her out. Her large, toned thighs were only covered with pretty grey pyjama shorts which matched the cropped grey shirt that was barely covering her abs.

"I was just listening to the theme music." I patted the bed and watched as she skipped without hesitation towards me. I smiled as I shook my head slowly. I loved that it didn't matter how long we'd been separated, she still felt completely comfortable to skip into my room and play video games with me.

"Haz played the theme from the first one loads when we lived with Aunt Lynne." Her skin looked dewy, her face was bare, and I watched as she ran her hand up her arm to hold it against her as she shrugged. Her eyes were on my tattoos, and I cleared my throat. I suddenly felt exposed.

"I was thinking about that," I muttered before I examined her. Her eyes hadn't moved off my arm. Her fingers moved from her arm and to mine. As her fingertips touched my skin, there was a spark. My skin tingled under her touch; they trailed the picture of the angel on my arm amongst the others that created my sleeve. I smiled at her delicate touch and watched her snap back into reality. "I got it over in Afghan." I spoke softly and watched her smile to herself. Only a tiny one but it was there. "There was a guy called Mark who was really good at it." I thought about Mark and then looked back down at the tattoo. "The majority of them appeared while I was on tour." Her fingers ran across the wings that were on my forearm.

"I like her." She cleared her throat and moved her hand. "You're much more tattooed than I remember." Her brow furrowed and I smirked at her as I tilted my head.

"Don't you like them?" I quizzed her innocently. Her smile twisted as she looked up at me.

"I *love* them." She ran her thumb over my arm again as she emphasised the word love and I watched her eyes light with fire. I fought a groan from within my throat. *You haven't been laid in a while.*

"How do you remember me?" I teased her again. She rolled her eyes at my question before she pointed towards the television.

"Annoying." She smirked and bit her own lip. *Fuck's sake.* She was testing my self-control. I reminded myself of her age. "Forever asking too many questions." I gasped falsely and laughed all at once as I covered my heart with my hand. "Please start the game." She plonked herself back on my bed and held a pillow against her stomach that was exposed. I laughed at her and shook my head all at once.

"Yes, baby Chlo." I saluted her and pressed the start button. I'd been sort of looking forward to playing this game. Tonight would be fun.

CHLO

I couldn't even remember falling asleep. We had spent hours playing through the storyline of the game. The air in the room had been heavy and hot. It was charged between us. I hated video games, but this was one I was really looking forward to playing. I'd watched Haz and Jay play the first one numerous times back home. I'd even watched Juve play it here when I'd stayed years ago. I stretched out and yawned as I flexed. The room was still dark. It wasn't my room. The controller was still placed between his hands, his thumbs still on top of the controller, and he was still sitting upright. I chuckled quietly and frowned all at once. It was now I had a chance to actually look at him. He was such a good looking human. His face looked almost childlike with no stubble on it. His lips were full and parted slightly as he breathed softly. I wanted to reach for him and stroke his cheek, but I refrained from doing so. His face didn't look peaceful. He had deep frown lines that were set. He was mumbling. I knew these signs. I placed my head against the pillow I was holding and reached for his hand. It dawned on me that this was his first night back home. In a normal bed. Not in a war zone. I placed his hand in mine and squeezed it softly.

"It's alright, Juve," I whispered. "You're home." I ran my thumb over his hand and watched his frown iron itself out. I took a breath and closed my eyes. Rational parts of me knew I had absolutely no right touching him whilst he was unconscious, but it seemed to be that that part of my brain had given up working. I held it and watched him settle before I settled back off myself.

JUVE

Gunshots. *Gunshots everywhere. Large explosions were surrounding the base we were camped out in. Mark was signalling me to move forward. I was frozen. I gripped my gun and looked him dead in the face, his blues twisted with fear as I watched my own emotion mimic his. The old 'out of use' high rise in Iraq's main city was a prime spot for us. I was a fucking good sniper. I nodded, gulped, and ran in front, clearing the path for Mark and the rest of the platoon. I wouldn't let what happened to Green happen to them.*

I awoke from my memory; my light grey T-shirt was soaked through with sweat. It was now nearly black. I knew that I'd have a nightmare. This was regular. Some were worse than others. It was part of PTSD. Flashbacks. I shook my head as I came around to where I was. I looked towards the television that was still on the game we were playing last night. Which meant... *Oh God...* I groaned internally as I looked to my side. Chlo was holding my hand in hers. She looked peaceful in her sleep as she cuddled the pillow. I went to move her perfect blonde bob away from her eyes and stopped myself, reminding myself of her age and of our relationship. I didn't remember holding her hand before we fell asleep. *Oh God, what else did I do in my sleep?* I moved her fingers from mine and sighed. *How could I have let her fall asleep there?* Her eyes flung open before I could move. Her mud-brown eyes that were almost gold in the middle stopped me in my tracks. They moved down to look at my darker in colour T-shirt and then back at my face, but she didn't move.

"We fell asleep then?" She offered me a small smile and my chest fluttered at the look etched across her sleepy face.

"Looks that way." I spoke softly, my voice giving out halfway through, making me clear my throat. I watched as she sat up a little and stretched upwards. Her shirt didn't leave much to the imagination. I reached towards her and pulled the T-shirt back down, so she didn't expose any more of herself. I'd already seen her midriff that was perfectly toned and her under-boob. I closed my eyes at that sight to try and push it out of my brain. I wouldn't cope if I saw any more of her. I'd spent two years in a war zone, and now I was lying next to a semi-dressed Miss Conway, with raging morning glory. A guttural growl left my lips, and a small gasp left her mouth. "You were flashing." I tried to keep my tone steady as I moved away from her quickly and felt her arms rest on mine, holding me in place. My hands were now resting on her thighs, and they weren't covered or hidden. Shorts. Short fucking shorts. *For God's sake, Chloe.*

"Why are you wet?" She trailed her hand down the damp T-shirt that was against my chest and I closed my eyes to try and control my urge to touch her. My jaw clenched together. I couldn't answer her, our faces were close, so close, almost too close. She placed her cheek against mine and I held my breath. Every feeling that consumed me should have been wrong. I should have been moving away from her. My eyes stayed closed as I fought with myself to do the right thing. "You talk in your sleep." Her voice was almost an angelic whisper against my ear. I wondered what I'd let slip. My mind was worrying about that now more than where my hands were on her. They were still pressed against her thighs, my grip hard on them. She smelt like a soft perfume, it wasn't too strong but maybe it had worn off a little and had just stained her hair. I took a long breath inward and savoured the feeling of her warm cheek against mine. I moved a hand slowly from her thigh and let that same hand touch her face. I moved the hair that was draped in her face and tucked it behind her ear slowly. Her breathing stopped. I pulled away from her slowly and cleared my throat.

"I tend to have nightmares," I added before she could speak. I stood to my feet and watched as she continued to look at her lap. Even now, playing with her hair, she didn't look juvenile, and I found myself becoming increasingly frustrated with myself. "Should probably stop playing zombie games before bed." I forced a false chuckle and watched the corners of her mouth twist upwards.

"That's probably best." She too stood from my bed now, placing the pillow she had cuddled all night back in its position and then the duvet. Her eyes looked through me before she nodded my way. "See you later." She turned and walked from my room. My eyes landed on her arse, and I growled. She was my little brother's best friend's baby sister, but there was nothing adolescent about her. *Fuck's sake!*

CHAPTER FIVE
BE MY MISTAKE

CHLO

It went on for days, me doing everything I possibly could to ignore him. He was avoiding me too. I was kicking myself for falling asleep with him. I kicked myself for getting too close to him, but surely, he felt that spark too? I bit down on my lip as I watched Henry appear in the kitchen doorway. His boys were the image of him. He was slumped against the door frame of the kitchen; his shoulder was resting against it. Carol had taken Aimee to school, so it was just me in. Or at least that's what I thought until he wandered in.

"How are you finding the country life?" he joked. I really liked Henry. He was a kind man. A kind man with a lot of money from a highly illegal and inappropriate lifestyle. To many, he was not kind. To many, he was a thug, but to me, he was wonderful. He had saved me when I needed saving from awful situations. He had done his best to keep us safe. He had provided a home for me when I had no home. I guessed this was where Haz and Juve got their kindness from. Their soft side.

"I really enjoy being here, Henry," I admitted as I bit into the last of my Nutella covered toast.

"Why don't you go out for a walk? It's been days since you left the house." He was now making a coffee; the one Carol had left had now gone cold, so he'd poured it out and started again. "You used to love walking." He was stirring the coffee in his cup... I was taken back that he had remembered how I'd spent my time here wandering the Shropshire hills. "You're as bad as my son." He chuckled and I frowned.

"Harry hasn't been in the house." I was still pissed off with him leaving me here alone with Juve and his family. I knew Carol didn't really want him here anyway, but nonetheless, it had pissed me off when he had disappeared up to Manchester without any warning. I wasn't even sure when he'd be back.

"I meant Juve." I flushed at the mention of his name and my stomach fluttered.

"Oh," I began before the sound of laughter came from the hallway. It was Juve's big booming laughter. My eyes landed on his and he stopped laughing almost instantly. His younger brothers–Buddy and Warren–stopped in their tracks and Warren whistled.

"Well, well, well..." I wanted to roll my eyes, and though I had looked at him, I wasn't paying any attention to him. Juve had all of my attention. "Who is this?" Warren wolf-whistled again.

"Have some respect, Warren," Juve barked. I flushed and looked back at my empty plate.

"I'm Chlo and I'm leaving to go for a walk." I hopped down off the barstool and placed my plate in the sink before I squeezed past them all in the doorway. I was sure Juve went to reach for my hand, but I was climbing the stairs before I could stop myself. I couldn't let myself be around him. I'd cross a line. I was sure of that.

Family quiz night. Friday night. Game night. I liked Friday nights in this house. I'd gotten to know Warren and

Buddy a little better over the weeks. Warren was a crowd pleaser and nothing like Buddy who was a free spirit. They were absolutely nothing alike in looks either. Warren looked more like Carol, with strong pointed features, and Buddy like Haz, Henry and Juve. Chubby cheeked, friendly, and a jawline that would cut somebody, but such warm kind eyes. I winced as the bottle landed on me. Warren laughed and I frowned at him.

"I don't know the answer." I spoke quietly. If I'd have been listening to the question that was asked forty-five seconds earlier, I'd have known the answer. "Another one?" Warren growled as he pulled another card from the deck and grinned at me.

"What was the name of the old man in the Disney movie Up's wife?" He read off the card in front of him and I grinned widely.

"Ellie!" I smirked and heard Buddy laugh as he offered me his hand in a high five. I knew Disney.

"Nice!" He smiled widely at me. Juve was smiling too.

"So you don't know what the most famous dish in Italy is but you know that?" His lips curled into a smirk and my heart stopped. I just nodded.

"I love that movie." My eyes left him the second he looked at me. I was too scared to look him in the eyes in case I gave myself away. That zing would still be there for me, and I needed to find an off button. Quickly.

"Why don't you two go and pick up some pizza or something? I'm hungry," Buddy suggested as he pointed towards myself and Juve. His mum was nodding. My stomach growled as it agreed with him.

"That's a good idea, poor darling hasn't left the house in a week." She was fussing over me now, and I shook my head at her. I adored the woman, but she could be a little too much sometimes.

"It's fine, I'll stay here, Juve can go." I watched him smirk again.

"I'm not going on my own. You're coming with me,"

he protested as he stood to his feet, and I frowned deeply as he offered me his hand. "Come on." I groaned and took his hand in mine; a pulse ran through my whole body. I flinched and released his hand quickly. "I don't bite, you know?" I laughed as he spoke the words just out of his family's earshot. I was grabbing my coat.

"Oh, I know," I teased and raised my brow at him. He shook his head softly and I smirked as I walked out of his parents' house and towards his car. "I wish you did," I murmured as I opened his car door and watched him freeze. *Surely, he had got to have heard that?* I was certain I saw his head tilt to one side, and I smiled awkwardly as I got into his black Range Rover. The engine started and he placed his seat belt on.

"I'm not waiting for pizza when it's minus four outside," he declared as he turned down the radio. I rolled my eyes at his exaggeration of the British weather.

"It's zero. Probably one." He smirked and shrugged softly. We could see our breath in the car as he started the engine and rubbed his large hands together.

"Well, I ain't doing it. Mum likes the share boxes from the pub down the road. Call them and ask them for like four. That will keep them happy." I saluted him, partly to take the mickey out of his military career and then partly because he was being so bloody bossy.

"Yes, sir." I watched the corners of his mouth lift upwards and he shook his head.

"I wish you wouldn't say that." I laughed as he spoke the words and flicked the radio up again.

"Why?" I watched him drive and he shrugged as he began to sing the song playing on the radio quietly. "Actually, scrap that question, I want to know what your job was in the army." He tensed and then relaxed when he changed gear.

"I was a sniper." My eyes widened a little, I couldn't picture him aiming and shooting just one person. A target. "One of the best, apparently." He cleared his throat and then looked at me. His gaze turned soft. "I'd disagree with that though." I smiled at him and nodded.

"Can't imagine you being a very good shot." He scoffed back a laugh, and I grinned. I loved hearing him laugh. I always had.

"No?" He raised his brow and moved his hair from his face, still slightly fluffy and curly. "I'll show you one day, if you like?" *Was he flirting?* I chuckled and rolled my eyes as we stopped at the quaint little pub just two miles from his home. His hand was resting against my thigh, stopping me from getting out of the car, and I froze. My heart was in my throat, and I held in a gasp. "You know you're going to get me into so much trouble one day…" His expression was playful, but his tone was so serious.

"I can't imagine why." I spoke back in a low tone so as not to offend him. Our faces were close, close enough that I could feel his breath against my lips. He smiled at me and then shrugged, releasing my leg and letting me go from the car. I followed him in through the entrance and watched as he was greeted warmly by two of the fairly young women behind the bar.

"Oh my God, he's back!" they exclaimed as they ran towards him and threw their arms around him, showering him in such love and affection. Juve was laughing and I moved slightly further back so that they had the space to cuddle him. "Your mum said you were back." I smiled at their friendly exchange and just watched on in awe. He really was the kindest man I'd ever come across. People just loved him.

Turns out, they were the owner's daughters. Well, one of them was, the other was her wife. She'd served in the army too, only she'd retired when the pair wanted to start a family. She had told us that they were trying to adopt. It warmed me that people like them existed. Apparently, the food was going to be a while. I stood from my seat and glanced at the drink's menu.

"Do you want a drink?" I asked him as I pointed at it.

He shrugged.

"What you having?" Pink-coloured his cheeks as he realised I wasn't old enough to legally drink with him. Not that this had ever stopped me before. I bit down on my lip and shrugged. The sad thing was that I'd probably out drink him. Willow, one of the daughters, bounced her way over towards us with a small glass of house wine and a pint of Carling. I watched his nose wrinkle. I guessed from that reaction he wasn't a fan either.

"So, who's the lovely blonde lady by your side this evening?" she asked innocently. I had to catch my laughter at the expression on his face. "Your mum didn't mention a girlfriend…" He was really red in the face now and I closed my eyes, so I didn't have to look at him.

"She's my little brother's friend." He paused.

"Harry? Oh, how is he now?" I rolled my eyes internally at Willow's response to hearing about him. Not many people actually knew what had happened to Holly, so I wondered what bullshit story they had fed her about him. I bit down on my lip as my eyes met the sharp-featured beauty with wispy blonde hair. She smirked at me and tilted her head towards Juve.

"If I was straight, I know which brother I'd have." She nudged my arm and laughed before she slapped the table, stood, and skipped back towards the kitchen.

"I'm sorry, Chlo." He groaned and I laughed a little as I shrugged and took a sip on my wine.

"Don't be. All part of coming to local places." He nodded and shrugged all at the same time.

"Suppose you're right." He was quiet again then, just gorping into his pint glass as I sipped slowly on mine. There was tension between us. It always seemed to be there when we were alone. I cleared my throat and excused myself.

"I just need to pop to the bathroom." I rose to my feet and walked towards the toilets when I was distracted by the outside of the pub. I opened the door and walked further out. I hadn't realised this was here when we had pulled up. It was silent, no road noise but the sound of birds in the dark sky and the sound of hooves moving in the grass paddocks a stone's throw away from where I was standing.

"Wow." I took in a breath of the wonderful countryside air and wanted to wrap my hands around myself. It was refreshing. There was something I'd always loved about being here. Two warm hands placed themselves on my shoulders and I smiled.

"Boo." He placed his chin on my shoulder and I froze at the close proximity between us.

"What did you mean earlier when you said I was going to get you into trouble one day?" I asked in a whisper as I turned to face him. His shoulders rose and fell. It had been bugging me since he said it.

"You're underage." There was space between us again and he flushed crimson. I watched as his breath made the air look like smoke.

"Since when has my age ever stopped anyone from doing what they wanted to do?" I crossed my arms across my body, and his face twisted as sorrow filled me. It was the truth. He ran his hand down my arm.

"Jesus, Chlo." He frowned a little. "Low blow." I shook my head and then moved my arm from his hand.

"I didn't mean to offend you." I glanced back at him and watched him pull me closer. His head was slightly tilted as he looked into my eyes for a while like he was really trying to read me. "Why do you look scared, Juve?" I paused as I watched him. "Like I'm going to bite you." He stepped closer.

"Because you're a baby." He shook his head as he examined my face and touched my cheek a little.

"I'm seventeen. You're twenty-two." I paused. "I'm not a baby." I was watching him now. He frowned.

"You are to me." He spoke softly, and I tilted my head slowly to one side.

"It's five years," I mumbled.

"It just can't happen." His eyes examined mine and he smiled. "Anybody ever told you how beautiful your eyes are?" I laughed at how quickly he changed the topic of conversation.

"They're poo brown, Juve."

"Is that what you think?" He tilted his head as he placed my hand in his.

"I know." I raised my brow and watched him shake his head.

"They're muddy like a puddle." Laughter exploded from my mouth. He frowned and I smiled as I played with his large fingers in mine awkwardly.

"I used to call Jay puddle because of that." I opened up to him a little. I'd guarded so much from everyone, but with him, it seemed so easy to open up. It had always been so easy.

"Puddle, huh?" I nodded and felt his finger trace the back of my hand. My heart stopped and I glanced at us holding hands.

"Puddle," I whispered and squeezed his hand in mine. It felt *right*. He just smiled and I closed my eyes as the wind blew between us. "Ready?" I questioned him as I opened my eyes again. His eyes were on the fields opposite us, and he nodded as I reluctantly let go of his fingers.

"Yeah, let's get back." I just nodded and followed him inside the country pub again. My mind was a puddle too now.

His mum, dad and Buddy had all left and gone to bed. Warren was heading that way too. They had demolished the food. I was washing up the plates in the kitchen sink. Juve and I were alone. Again. His fluffy mousey hair was pushed out from his face in the most delightful way. He stretched as he rose to his feet, and his black fitted T-shirt lifted up to reveal his stomach. Deep V lines distracted my thoughts. *Holy fucking shit.* I pictured running my hands over them. My eyes closed involuntarily and then I turned away from him.

"Did you play any more of the game?" I croaked to try and keep him around for a little longer. I bent to pick up my glass from the table and then straightened out again. His eyes wandered over my physic, and I smiled to myself as he shook his head, almost as if he was telling himself off. I knew he was looking.

"Wanna have a go?" I nodded automatically and watched him step towards me. The smell of having him so close again made my heart flutter.

"I'd like to get to playing as Abi," I breathed and watched his lips turn upwards.

"Yeah, me too." He walked past me, disturbing the air around me, and I followed him towards his room. I knew this was a bad idea, I knew I wouldn't have the self-control to stop myself from doing something ridiculous, but I didn't really want to either. I had never felt a pull as strong as this. I watched as he walked into his room, turned on the PlayStation, and then sat cross-legged on his bed. It was perfectly made.

"Do you make your bed every day?" He just nodded at my question as I sat next to him. The bed didn't dip under my weight. It stayed firm. I frowned as I watched him play. He wasn't talking much. "Didn't realise that it took so much concentration to play a video game," I teased him and watched the corners of his mouth turn upwards into a sexy smirk. He shot me a look and I caught his smile.

"Play the game, Chlo." I smiled at him as I pulled on his arm so that he was now sitting comfortably on the bed and not perched on the edge. He raised his brow at me, and I shook my head. "So forceful." He tilted his head as he spoke. *Tease.* I growled to myself. I glanced down at the controller in his hands, his thumbs moved over the sticks softly as he pulled and pushed them to control the figure on the screen. I closed my eyes for a split second, imagining them moving like that between my legs. His eyes moved from me and back to the screen. It had now dawned on me that I wasn't too bothered about the storyline of the video game. I was more interested in him. I took a little breath and reached to press the pause button. His face turned to me, and he raised his brows upwards. I tried to suppress my blush as I placed myself on his lap. A gasp left his mouth as he moved backwards, attempting to put space between us.

"Chlo?" The way he called my name sounded like a question and a warning all at once. He was confused, shocked or dazed. Hell, it could have been all of the above. I gulped softly and traced the dog tags that were dangling against his chest. I was reading them before long. His blood group, his name, service number and his religion—which was blank.

"When are you being deployed again?" I asked softly, the whole time his eyes had been closed and he was still. He didn't touch me. He was just inhumanly still.

"Probably soon." His voice was stable as he spoke. There was a pull, a draw I had towards him. Gone were any innocent feelings I had. I wanted him. Silence fell between us again. "You're seventeen." He spoke again. "A baby," he whispered. My heart flurried. *So he did feel it too.* I found myself running my lips over his jaw and he instantly went rigid.

"You're twenty-two, not thirty." I kissed closer towards his mouth and stopped as I reached the corner of his lips. "Tell me to stop, Juve," I whispered softly, praying internally that he wouldn't do as I asked. For once in my entire life, I wanted somebody to go against me.

"Don't hate me for this." He paused for a second. "But I think I'm gonna be your worst mistake," he whispered against my mouth as his hands finally wrapped themselves around my waist, holding me closer to the skin of his body, his other moving the hair from my face. My heart thudded loudly as his breath lingered on my lips. I ached for him. His soft lips pressed themselves against mine hesitantly as he cradled me in his arms. The hand that had moved my hair was now holding my face as he kissed me softly like I was glass, and I was breakable. He ran his thumb over my cheek, and I parted his mouth with my tongue. I could taste him on my own tongue now and my southern region clenched. I was lost for a split second in our gentle kiss. I bit down on my lip as we parted and watched his eyes slide open. He was flushed with colour.

"I'm terrified now, Miss Conway," he whispered as he moved beneath me. I couldn't help but smile at his admission. His lips traced mine again and I pushed him back slightly onto the bed.

"That makes both of us." I'd never wanted to be ravished by anybody as much as I wanted him now. I was certain of that. My heart was pounding as his eyes glazed over my face. He was pinned beneath me, and I flushed softly. He just smiled. "You won't be a mistake." I spoke softly and watched him smile as he ran his fingers down my neck towards my chest. I held my breath as my eyes fluttered closed and then opened again. He knocked the shoulders of my T-shirt off, and I helped him remove it slowly over my head. My hair wasn't anywhere near long enough to cover anything. He propped himself up on his arms as I leant down to kiss his lips. He was smiling and shaking his head all at the same time.

"What'd you want, Chlo?" My heart fluttered in my chest. I'd never been asked that before. I ran my nose over his cheek and placed my lips against his ear.

"You." His breathing stopped momentarily as he kissed my jaw softly and traced his hands up my back.

"Are you one hundred percent sure of that?" I just nodded.

"Stop ruining the mood," I whispered against his lips. He chuckled softly as we kissed, and I was flipped beneath him. His kiss was deep and gentle.

JUVE

There was a fumbling of clothes, but no real rush attached to it. I could feel my dick in my boxers being held down by the constraints of my joggers and her partial body weight, but now all of that was gone and it was standing to attention. Every inch of me was nervous. My mouth found her nipple and I teased it slowly with my tongue. I was in awe of her. It had shocked me how strong-minded she was. Her hand fell on my shoulder as she squeezed it the more I teased it with my mouth. I trailed kisses from her chest to her chin before I kissed her softly. She wrapped her fingers around mine as I savoured our slow kisses. She guided my hand between her legs and my chest thudded. She was clean-shaven, moisture escaping her slit as I circled her clit with my thumb over and over again. I groaned as I flicked between lathing her nipples with my tongue and kissing her soft mouth over and over again. Her legs were ridged for a split second before she shook her head and moved my hand. I stopped instantly.

"What's wrong?" I asked breathlessly. She simply shook her head again before she half-smiled, turning the sweetest shade of pink.

"Nothing is wrong." She spoke breathlessly as she planted soft kisses against my mouth. My hand trailed between her legs and over her thighs, but I stopped as I reached just above the line where her knickers should have been resting. Her warm eyes burned through me as she stared down at me. I wasn't entirely sure what I was waiting for, but she nodded as though she understood exactly what I was thinking.

"Where do you want me, Miss Conway?" I didn't recognise my voice as I peppered kisses against the nape of her neck. I felt like a shy kid again that had only just found out what that part of his body did.

"Inside me." She breathed as she placed my bottom lip between her teeth. I groaned as a shiver ran the length of

101

my spine. We shared a frenzied kiss as I placed my fingers between her moist slit. I knew that there wasn't any going back once we'd done this. I was terrified I'd want her over and over again and that I'd never get enough of her. "Only if you want to," she added shyly. I ran my nose over hers and kissed her again. *Oh, I fucking wanted to.* If I was being completely honest with myself, I suppose I'd always wanted this very scenario to play out.

"Are you sure?" She just nodded and pulled my hair to force her lips against mine. I groaned as our mouths collided–sloppy wet kisses. I nudged myself between her legs and pushed into her slowly, softly, sort of like she'd break. I was savouring this feeling, the sensation of being inside her–pulsing around me–made it difficult not to cum on the spot. My hips moved softly with her rhythm for a few minutes, slowly, deeply, and then quickly, caressing every inch of her exposed skin with my mouth.

"Juve." She moaned my name as her legs went rigid and every muscle around my cock inside her went hard. *It was the way she said my name.* If I could have been any harder, I would have been. This was unlike anything I'd ever had before her.

"Baby," I groaned as I placed my mouth around her neck and released myself inside of her. I could hear her breathing heavily from next to me. We lay there in silence for a long time, just catching our breath. Her fingers caught mine after a while. I was reluctant to move an inch. I wanted that feeling to happen every day. I'd had sex. Multiple times. But that. That wasn't *just* sex.

I placed her leg over mine and traced my fingers over her thigh. Her muddy brown eyes were now golden in colour as she peeked up at me from between her thick lashes. I smiled to myself and moved her hair from her cheek, I pushed it behind her ear and kissed her nose softly. She caught my hand in hers and stopped me. I was scared shitless she'd wake in the morning and freak out completely.

"I think I'll be your mistake," she whispered, breaking the silence. I frowned at her and shook my head.

"I don't think so." I tried to reassure her that this wouldn't be the case. Her hand dropped from mine towards my dog tags. I watched her stare at them for a while.

"Why do you still wear them?" *Why all of the sudden questions? Was she feeling awkward?* My shoulders rose and fell as I acknowledged her question.

"Habit." I thought back to my time in Afghanistan. I remembered the brutal telling off my squad had for forgetting to wear them vividly after we lost a friend in the field. "If I was blown up then nobody would know who I was without them. I haven't taken them off in over two years." She flinched away from my words.

"I don't want to think about you being blown up, thank you." I smirked slightly and pulled her hand to my mouth, I kissed every fingertip and watched her smile. Her bottom lip caught between her teeth. "Can I stay here tonight?" She tilted her head up so that she met my gaze. I nodded instantly. I was hoping she wouldn't want to move.

"Stay here forever if you like..." I grinned as she giggled and flushed red. I pulled her close so that her neck was against my lips. I nibbled her softly as she chuckled.

"That's probably the best offer you've ever given me," she whispered. I laughed softly and pulled her so that she was now laying on top of me. My eyes wandered over her delicate features. She was a beautiful woman. "Do you really not know how long you're back for?" I shook my head.

"No idea," I added. She looked saddened all of a sudden. I placed her head down on my chest and stroked the top of her hair. "Don't worry about it yet." I tried to comfort myself by telling her not to worry. "Cross that bridge when we come to it." She laughed softly and glanced up at me. "I'll stay here, if you want me to?" She planted a kiss against my mouth. I melted again.

"We're going to have fun hiding this now, hey?" She reminded me of everyone else involved in this situation, and I nodded. That part wasn't so nice to think about. For one, I was absolutely certain her brother would want my balls on a platter, and my brother would never let me live this down.

"I suppose so." I ran my nose over hers and shook my head. "Should have had a plan." She smirked and put her head back against my chest where my heart was still pounding. I had never felt this comfortable with any other human in my life.

"I didn't really plan on sleeping with you." She smirked as she ran her lips over my chest. My eyes rolled internally as I ran my fingers over her shoulder. Her breathing was mellow as I lay with her for a while. This was a little surreal.

"Get some sleep, baby." I wasn't sure why I'd given her that pet name. I shook my head as I held in my own laugh. *How fucking fitting.*

CHLO

He'd slept soundly. He didn't writhe around like Haz, and he certainly wasn't mumbling to himself tonight. I ran my fingers over his shoulder muscles and then his jaw. I took my time to examine him. His handsome face. His cheeks weren't as chubby as his brothers but still slightly puffy. I couldn't help but smile to myself as I touched him. He looked so much younger than what he actually was. I sighed and wished that was true for a time. Trust it to be me who ended up in this situation. I'd known this brute since I was fifteen. He had always been so big brotherly in his actions back then. He was always the one to hold the line between friends and me pushing to flirt every now and then. And now here we were. I moved my leg from over his hip and felt his hand catch it. A small groan left his lips, my heart fluttered at the sexy sound, and I smiled as I leant to kiss him slowly. My lips lingered against his and his grip on my leg tightened. The sun was rising, and it was low in the sky, shining through the cracks in the curtains, and it caught his mousey hair. I chuckled and felt his weight against me. Even laying down, he was so much bigger than I was.

"Juve?" I called his name in a whisper.

"Yes, Chloe?" he whispered back. His eyes were still closed. I was relieved that he knew who I was. I ran my nose over his and felt my stomach flip.

"Do you remember last night?" I asked with caution, praying that he wasn't high on something.

"Every second of it." His smile broke across his mouth and the sight made my breathing falter. It was the best thing I'd ever seen. I found myself smiling like an idiot as his lips traced mine and then my chin. He pulled me closer towards him and his eyes opened. He stared at me for a while. "God, Chlo, you're stunning." His words were breathy, and my cheeks were stained with blood as I rolled my eyes.

"Stop trying to sweet talk me," I teased. He grinned a wide grin and I watched him examine me. "What you thinking about?" I traced lines around his chest with my finger slowly.

"Not sure how we ended up here." He half laughed and my gut twisted slightly. "I've always looked at you like you were... I dunno..." He paused a little, as though he was trying to think about his next words carefully. "Like a distant cousin or something. Like family." I pushed his shoulder slightly.

"Oh God, Juve, that's disgusting!" I exclaimed. "Wrong." He laughed at my disgust.

"You haven't let me finish." He raised his brow upwards, and I smirked as I kissed his lips softly. His mouth parted slightly as I deepened our kiss, and he pulled away slowly. "When you walked through that front door and I realised it was you, I nearly died." He shook his head and then moved my hair from my eyes. "I was not expecting you to look like you do." I felt my cheeks fill with blood and smiled to myself. "Or be so..." He struggled to find his words.

"Brash?" He shook his head slowly and ran his hands from my thighs towards my arse.

"No, just you." He closed his eyes for a minute as he held me still against him. My breathing was uneven. "I remembered you crystal clear. You were all little and pretty and fragile. Then when you walked through the door looking like your twenty-odd and a completely different person. I just wasn't prepared to feel like this." He ran his mouth over mine and I froze. "I still want to protect you, Chlo. That feeling has never gone away." I rolled my eyes and pushed him slightly.

"I don't need protection." He nodded a little and ran his nose over mine again.

"Doesn't stop me from wanting to give it to you though." I smiled at him and flushed in colour.

"I'll let you do whatever makes you happy." I pushed

him slightly so that he was now pinned beneath me. His eyes wandered over my assets, and I felt the colour in my cheeks rise again.

"Whatever makes me happy you say?" He grinned as he winked at me—that panty-melting fucking wink that had always set my world on fire.

CHAPTER SIX
HIDING THE TRUTH

CHLO

I was an absolute moron for thinking I could switch my feelings off around others. He hid his for me pretty well, for the most part. The house was pretty quiet today, Carol was at a yoga class, Henry was working, Harry wasn't back from wherever he'd pissed off too yet, and Aimee was with her friends at their house. I was making pancakes, my absolute favourite thing to eat. His hands pressed against my stomach, and I smiled as I ran my hand over his cheek.

"What are you cooking?" He nosed over my shoulder, and I pointed towards the plate with three on already.

"Fancy some?" I asked. He wriggled his brows, and I rolled my eyes. He was so incredibly dirty-minded.

"Always." He got to work next to me, dressing pancakes with ease. Lemon and then sugar. My favourite. "You like them like this?" He raised his brow and I nodded.

"Perfect." I offered him a smile as I flipped the next

one. I watched him, he was dancing awkwardly and singing to the radio as he whizzed around the kitchen. I laughed a little as he sang the words out loud and spun me around. I chuckled as he caught me in his arms and kissed the side of my head. It was a Script song that he was singing. We were laughing so loud we hadn't realised his two younger brothers were staring at us. I instantly blushed as I spotted them. Juve grinned and released me from his grip. I cleared my throat and pointed towards the pancakes.

"Cooking." I spoke, Buddy was laughing, and Warren was grumbling. Juve just winked at me and snook another kiss when neither of them were looking, before he left with his pancakes. Warren was pushing his brother's arm and I frowned as I followed them towards the dining room. I had no bra on and was dressed in just a crop top and grey joggers.

"Isn't she a little young for you?" Warren asked him innocently.

"Oh, I'm way too young," I added as I sat with them all at the table and heard Juve scoff, almost choking on his pancake. I bit down on my lip and watched him frown. "Aren't you an old man?" I teased as I smirked and then pouted. Buddy laughed loudly and high fived me. The front door banged, and keys were placed down against the side.

"Co?" It was Haz, his voice echoed in the hallway. He was back and that meant he was safe. Instinctively, I was giddy with relief that he hadn't just abandoned me, and I ran towards the sound of his voice and wrapped my arms and legs around him the second I got near him. He gripped me tightly before he dropped me to my feet. "Jay's out in a couple of weeks." He smiled widely at me.

"That's ace!" I watched as he looked at my lips and I moved instantly as he tried to kiss them. He frowned as I put space between us. I shook my head softly and tapped his chest. My short sense of relief was gone. "I'm glad he'll be out soon." My voice was cold as I turned away from him and automatically climbed the stairs to my room. He was high. He'd been gone for nearly two weeks. He'd ditched me to go and check on business, and the second he was home he wanted affection I could no longer give him.

JUVE

It had been quiet in the house since Haz had returned. Mum and Dad had avoided being around him—Mum was bitter and cold, and Dad had no interest in him laying around and working for the enemy. He was here because of Mum's maternal instincts for Chlo. She was spread out on the sofa of the formal living room, Haz was at her feet, and I felt jealousy pulse through me. Neither of them had said it but I *knew* he'd had her. My only thanks was that he didn't gloat about it. His face twisted up into a smirk as he placed his hands on her feet. She flinched away from him and looked towards me. Her delicate features hardened.

"Can you stop," she barked at him. I placed my foot against my knee in the chair and heard Haz chuckle at her request. "You know I hate having my feet messed with." She added to her earlier comment and proceeded to kick him slightly in the bollocks which made me grin from ear to ear. I knew he was her best friend, but they had shared more than just that intimacy, and I hated it.

"Fuck's sake, Chlo, you're gonna make sure I don't have any kids!" He scoffed out in pain as he leant forwards. Her eyes lit up.

"Don't need another one of you anyway, you arse." She relaxed back as she continued to watch the television. Aimee appeared in the doorway, she beamed at Chlo as she legged it towards her and then threw herself on her lap. Her blonde hair swished behind her. Chlo giggled with her. My two favourite girls, my heart was bursting.

"Please paint my nails?" Aimee's voice was high pitched and Chlo reached forwards and began tickling her; huge laughter escaped my sister's mouth. "You promised!" she managed to choke out. Chlo glanced towards me and smiled softly, her eyes were full of an emotion I couldn't read.

"Maybe we could paint Juve and Haz's nails?" Chloe suggested as Aimee clapped her tiny hands together in joy.

She was pulling on Chlo's arm.

"I think that's a great idea!" Aimee stood to her feet and skipped towards me.

"Come, Juve! Chloe can paint yours pink!" she exclaimed, her blue eyes sparkling.

"Oh, I think I'd like them red." I wiggled my brows at her and heard her chuckle. Haz groaned as Aimee was now pulling his arm.

"I'll have blue." He didn't protest having them painted. He went along with it, and I smiled—only Aimee could bring the hardest men to their knees.

"Purple!" Her arms folded as she disagreed with his colour choice. Her lip curled downwards, a sigh left his mouth and he nodded.

"Okay, okay, you win." Chlo left the room and made her way to find some sort of nail polish.

SNEAKING

For as long as I could remember, Dad had charity balls annually, and this year Chlo and Haz were home for one, and so was I, which made a change. Tonight would be the first time I'd be in a room filled with people since I was in Afghan. There would be loud booms and lots of people. I shuddered the memories of the war zone from out of my head. I had pushed them aside. Mum was smiling softly at Buddy and Warren as she leant down to place Aimee's bow back in her hair properly.

"Are you ready, Juve?" she called.

"Yup," I shouted down the stairs towards her, pulling on my dicky bow.

"Will you make sure Chlo is okay, please?" My chest fluttered at the thought of her, and I smiled to myself.

"Sure!" I called back to her. I knocked against her door. "Only me." I pushed down the handle and opened her door. This was the room she had been staying in. It had even begun to smell like her. The smell of her sweet perfume clouded my senses. She flushed as she looked at me standing in her doorway. "Jesus Christ." I gasped as I took her in. She was wearing a form-fitting dress—my mum had clearly chosen it. It looked like it cost as much as one of the cars on the driveway. I fought with myself to breathe. Her dainty olive-skinned shoulders were exposed as the golden glittery dress shimmered underneath the lights of her bedroom. "Fuck me." I spoke again. She flushed a deep red as she shook her head.

"Somebody is gonna hear you," she scolded me as she placed her hand against my chest softly. It was pounding away underneath her hand like a small band. I glanced at the back of her dress and looked at the way it pooled behind her. It looked like a prom gown. Black tie was a very serious dress code at these events. "Your mum chose it," she mumbled as she forced her eyes to look at me. She didn't look one bit under eighteen. I'd have placed her at my age at the very least. I shook my head in disbelief almost. Shock. I swallowed and fought the urge to re-adjust myself in my boxers.

"You look stunning." I tripped on my words and watched her warm eyes look at my lips.

"What's keeping you?" Buddy was shouting up from the stairway. She pushed her curled hair behind her ear and smiled shyly at me.

"I'm coming. Sorry, Bud!" She called out, her posh accent ringing around the house. "Shoe problem. Juve saved the day," she lied. Though it sounded like nothing but the truth. I clutched her hand in mine and shook my head as I continued to look at the stunning young woman in front of me.

"I'm gonna have a heart attack." I laughed at my admission. She smiled sweetly and shrugged her shoulders.

"I thought you might." Her eyes lingered on my bow tie as she pulled it straight. "Old man," she whispered in my ear and planted a kiss against my ear. My dick grew in my pants, and I growled as I followed her down the stairs.

The venue was full of men and women I'd never seen before–well, some of them. Most of them were Dad's group of cronies and some were legitimate business partners of the 'legal' business he ran. The British Heart Foundation was the charity of choice for this year's charity event. Aimee was dancing with my younger brothers, and she had dragged Chlo up too. Chlo was smiling as the song *my girl* played. She was singing with Aimee, dancing with her in her arms, Aimee's powder pink dress was all puffy and adorable. My mum and dad were grinning as they watched them both. Mum had grown to really love having Chlo around, and so had Dad. She was like some sort of extension to our family. Haz nudged my arm as he handed me another shot of alcohol and took his seat beside me.

"Pick your jaw up off the floor, kid," he slurred. "It's embarrassing." He teased me as I downed the shot of apple sours. I winced as it burned my pipe on the way down to my stomach. I needed the drink this evening.

"You can talk, all you've done all night is gawp," I added. He shrugged at me and smirked.

"Name one young lad in here that hasn't looked at her." He raised his brow my way and I rolled my eyes. The song changed and the dance floor flooded with people dancing in couples. Haz tilted his head towards her. "Go on then, Juve, go stake your claim." He laughed and I wiggled my brows. I would recognise the sound of Frank Sinatra's voice anywhere. I moonwalked towards the dance floor and watched as my dad held Aimee in his arms and danced. She looked overjoyed. The words of the song echoed around the room. I grinned as I wrapped my hand behind her back. She gasped and laughed all at once.

"Fuck, Juve, your hands are freezing!" she screamed. I fought the urge to place my head in her neck and kiss her. This would be the hardest thing I'd ever done. All I had done all night was admire her from a distance, try my hardest not to stare at her in an inappropriate manner, and now I was battling furiously with my inhibitions.

"You never usually complain," I muttered in her ear. A small innocent laugh left her mouth as we swayed to the sound of the upbeat music. She cleared her throat as we placed some space between us. I raised my brow at her, and she flushed.

"Stop looking at me like that," she growled, and I flushed.

"Like what?" I snapped a little.

"Like you want to rip my clothes off." She frowned at me, and I smirked as I shrugged.

"But I do." She shook her head and then threw it backwards with laughter. I sang the words of the song as we danced, and I spun her around gently. She fell in my arms, and I watched her roll her eyes at me. She was laughing as we continued to dance.

"You're gonna get us found out," she warned me quietly. I shrugged as we continued to dance and listen to his voice play throughout the huge venue. The song ended and people were whistling and clapping from all around the venue. The voice of the speaker came over the speakers to announce that prize bidding would start shortly, and everyone should take their seats. She smiled and nodded at my mum, and then we both did exactly as we were told.

Haz had been home for less than a week and the dynamic of our relationship had changed so drastically. Somehow, seven weeks with her didn't seem long enough. I glanced down at my watch and grabbed my gym bag. Haz's red eyes raised at me. I frowned.

"Going out?" I nodded at his questioning tone.

"Yup." I placed it over my shoulder and made my way towards the car before he could question me further. There was no getting anything past his eyes. He wasn't born yesterday. Chlo had made her way up to the top of the hill a while ago. This had become our only time together. My gym bag was filled with a bottle of wine and food. I laughed to myself as I drove and parked at the bottom of the hill. I'd never really felt the way I felt about her with anybody else. I spotted her on the top of the hill and smiled widely to myself. She looked tiny on the hill. I jogged up behind her and kissed her cheek. She smiled widely and kissed my lips as I dropped my bag on the floor next to her.

"You brought the wine?" She raised her brow and then wriggled it as she asked the question. I laughed and nodded as I leant down and kissed her lips softly.

"Yes, Ma'am." She grinned and rolled her eyes as she opened the bag.

"You're such a hopeless romantic," she teased as she pulled the wine and blanket from the bag. I grinned and pulled her on my lap. Her giggle exploded from her mouth.

"Hey, if a picnic on this hill is the only time I get to act like this with you, then I am romantic." I nibbled her neck and listened to her chuckle before she ran her fingers through the front of my hair.

"Juve Vens, stop being so needy." She teased me again and I groaned outwards as I sniffed her hair that was in my face. She smelt like a mixture of vanilla and a strong scent of her perfume.

"My brother isn't fooled easily, is he?" I asked her, and her shoulders rose and fell.

"He knows me very well." She ran her nose against mine. "I think he knew something was wrong when he got home." I frowned as she pulled on the back of my hair slowly. My chest fluttered at her subtle sign of affection. "I refused to kiss him." I scoffed my laugh as her face turned serious. My stomach twisted. *Was this her admitting they had once been intimate*? "Honestly, I've never said no to him." She laughed as though it didn't bother her, and I frowned deeply. The green-eyed monster in me appeared. I couldn't picture my little brother and her in that way.

"It makes my blood boil." I spoke through gritted teeth.

"Oh, don't be a baby about it." She kissed my cheek and climbed off my lap. "I'm supposed to be the baby." She placed the blanket on the ground and threw the bag of Doritos my way. "Cheer up." She smiled at me softly and I rolled my eyes. I knew eventually the nickname I'd given her would grow tiresome. I just wasn't expecting it to be so soon after I'd given it to her.

CHLO

I was tucked up in the snug, Haz had left me to 'fend for myself' whilst he went out for the afternoon. He'd never really said where he was going. My only assumption was that he was going to get high. Part of me ached to go with him. I frowned deeply. I hated being alone in this house. Aimee was in bed. She had left me hours ago when Carol had told her she had somewhere to be the next morning which thrilled her. I'd noticed she loved to dance, ever since that night at the charity ball when we danced all night long. She was forever stretching or dressing up in her ballet attire and dragging her brothers to dance with her. She was the sweetest little thing in the universe. I couldn't remember a time when I'd felt so free as a child. I sighed as I closed my eyes and pushed memories to the back of my mind.

"Hey, baby." Juve's voice made me jump a little as it pulled me from my daydream. My eyes shot open, he smiled widely at me, and then his expression saddened. "What's on your mind?" he asked innocently. I held out my hand for him to take and watched as he took it and flopped down next to me on the sofa, all the time his eyes never left mine. I placed my hand over his face and smiled a little.

"Just reliving childhood trauma." I was sure he shuddered.

"Oh, Chlo," he breathed as he pulled me in to cuddle him. "Talk to me." I shook my head slowly as I placed my head against his chest. I noticed that he smelt fresh and clean and glanced up at him.

"I'm okay," I lied. His brow furrowed as he placed himself spread out next to me. I loved this room. I'd spent lots of time in here over the last few weeks. It was well hidden away from all the other rooms, the older red in colour fabric sofa was soft against my skin, and I leant to kiss his cheek as I glanced at the film playing on the television. His fingers trailed through my hair. "You smell clean," I added to try and divert the conversation. My voice was quiet, and I felt his chest move as his deep laughter escaped him.

"I've been in the shower, finished training late." He peppered kisses against my hair, and I tilted my head up to look at him. My hand was resting softly against his chest. My stomach released the butterflies. I just adored being like this with him.

"Did your mum ever mention us dancing at the ball?" I asked him. He grinned and shrugged.

"Sorta." My eyes widened. I'd been worried about that. It had played on my mind.

"What did she say?" He raised his brow and then smirked.

"She said she has never seen you laugh that much before." His eyes glistened as though he knew that he had made me smile that much.

"You bring out my big smile," I reminded him and felt his heart beat unevenly beneath my hand.

"She didn't say anything else, our secret's safe." He chuckled and I smiled to myself. I'd wanted it that way. When we were just us, I allowed myself to hold him for hours, to kiss his soft lips, to stare at him, but the fear of that getting out crippled all the happy thoughts.

"Fancy watching this film with me?" I again changed the direction of conversation. His dark pools of blue met mine and a genuine smile slipped from my mouth.

"Do you want hot chocolate and a cry too?" he teased as he used my own words against me, words I'd used years ago to coax him into being near me. I remembered when my teenage dream was being like this with him. I smirked to myself and placed myself on top of his lap, and I could feel him growing beneath me almost instantly. "Chlo," he warned softly as his eyes looked towards the entrance to the snug. I shrugged my shoulders. His hands traced the outline of them before he gripped softly. "You're such a thrill-seeker," he joked, and I chuckled softly as I felt myself blushing.

"I am not!" He puckered up his lips in the most juvenile way and my heart was swelling.

"Don't leave me hanging, Miss Conway," he protested, and I smirked before I leant forwards and landed one on his mouth. He instantly deepened it and then smirked against my mouth. "I think I like you," he muttered as our kiss became more intense.

"I think I like you too," I whispered back. I feared I was beginning to like him more and more and that I wouldn't be able to pull myself back.

LEAVE

I'd fucked up. I had been the one to push for a relationship, and now I couldn't stop it. I didn't want it to stop either. Ever. Jay was out in two days and Juve was being deployed too, so that forever I'd dreamed about was about to stop. Ever so abruptly. I frowned as the memory of that phone call coming through appeared.

***

His eyes fell from mine as he wandered away from the living room with the phone attached to his ear. By the look on his face, I knew it was going to be something I didn't want to hear. I frowned as I looked at the television and heard Warren chuckle.

"What's up with you, mardy bum?" He threw the remote my way and I threw it back with more force.

"Nothing. Would you all just get off my back!" I bellowed his way. I'd been moody and miserable for the last couple of days. More so than normal, but I was blaming it on the fact my brother was home soon and then I'd have to leave him. I stood to my feet and began to climb the stairs, hearing Haz laughing with his younger brothers. I wandered past the kitchen and heard Juve's mumbles with his mum and dad. I tried my best not to overhear anything, but I just knew. I placed myself in the spare room that I barely ever spent any time in and threw myself back on the bed. My head was spinning. I took a long deep breath and heard the door handle creak.

"Haz, I'm really not in the mo..." My sentence was cut short when lips trailed mine. I frowned softly and pushed him away as my eyes opened. Juve's dark pools were staring through me. I ran my fingers through his hair and then pulled him closer towards me. He didn't pull away, instead he embraced my efforts and kissed me deeply. My nose ran his once he'd pulled away and he smiled.

"I've been called." My heart stopped. Just four weeks ago we said we would cross the bridge when we came to it, and now it was here.

"But you've only been back for a month." He nodded. My voice

sounded desperate. Like a plea. He traced his fingers over my jaw as he looked at my lips.

"I know, but they need me." I frowned deeply at him.

"I need you," I whispered as my eyes filled with salty tears. I opened my eyes as I pulled away from him and watched his face twist. I placed space between us and crossed my arms.

"Chloe…" He called my name so seriously that I didn't know what else to say. "Please don't make this hard." I scoffed a laugh and shook my head as my tears dropped from my eyes.

"How is this going to work?" I questioned him. "You barely have any signal. You can only call family." I reminded him of all of the little things he'd probably forgotten about.

"We'll make it work." I shook my head and felt him pull me towards him again. "I swear it will work, Chloe." He held my face between his hands and my heart stopped. I couldn't picture him not being around. This hurt.

"Just promise me you're coming back." He nodded softly and ran his thumbs over my cheeks.

"Promise."

***

I frowned at my memory and reached to push Haz's shoulder. I watched his reddened eyes open. His face fell towards my boobs, and I slapped him hard across his chest. We'd been here for eight weeks already. He'd hated every second of it, even though he'd pissed off for the majority of it. I think he'd guessed what was going on between his eldest brother and I, but he never asked. Which I found weird in itself. He'd never been a jealous guy when it came to us and that was something I was always thankful for. He smiled at me and shrugged. I felt sick and I was tired, so I placed my head against the pillow.

"I'm tired," I admitted to him. His eyes ran over me like he was examining me with intent.

"Not surprised. Weren't you up all night?" He teased a little, and I bobbed out my tongue.

"Shut up." I rolled my eyes and sat upright, placing the

pillow against my stomach.

"I need to go and see if Darky needs anything. Behave while I'm gone." He placed his feet over his side of the bed and left the room as quickly as he'd woken up. I glanced down at my stomach which was a little more rounded than normal and shook my head. This wasn't happening. Not to me. Not now. Not ever.

I DON'T LOVE YOU

The house was deathly silent and had been all day. Somehow, even when it was so silent it was the closest thing I had ever had to a home. We had all made arrangements for our return to Devon. *Alfie.* I wasn't sure who he was, but apparently, he was a nice guy. The sad thing was, we had no other option, and I would rather be staying somewhere warm than spend the night on the street. Or in a hostel. I ran my hand over the small lump on my stomach and sighed. I was barely old enough to make a decision on what colour knickers I was going to wear let alone make *this* decision. I had fallen head over heels for Juve in the short space of time we'd been together, and I knew if I told a soul about the baby growing in my stomach, he'd be chopped up. I shook my head softly as sick began to rise in my throat. I'd been running through the possibilities of telling him about the really unplanned thing growing in my stomach, but that didn't appeal to me either. I knew he would stay, and he would be wasting his life. Being with me and a brat was a waste of life. The truth was, *I* wasn't ready for this. I was absolutely terrified I'd end up like my own mum. A shiver rolled down my spine and I closed my eyes as tears dripped from my eyes.

"Hey." The bed dipped, and I swallowed the hard lump in my throat, wincing as I did.

"Hey," I whispered. My voice was unstable. His fingers trailed across my jawline, and I frowned a little as I held his fingers in mine.

"Why are you crying?" His eyebrow raised upwards as I opened my eyes. This was his signature confused look. I couldn't help but smile, and I tilted my head to one side as I took in his beauty. "I'm sad that you're leaving me again," I muttered and pulled myself to sit up. I crossed my legs slowly and looked down at his chest where his dog tags were resting. "I hate that you have to go." I forced the words out of my mouth. I couldn't tell him. I wasn't ready for this. I was only a baby myself. That was one thing he hadn't let me forget. He'd made a point of calling me baby at every available opportunity he had. I was seventeen. He placed a soft kiss against my cheek and sighed before he trailed my stomach with his fingers. Bile made its way towards my throat.

"Yeah, I don't really like the idea of leaving you either." I felt him smile and shook my head as I held his face close to mine. "I've been called though, Chlo. I've gotta serve." I nodded and kissed the corner of his mouth that was now turning upwards into a sexy smile.

"Why did I have to fall for the noble soldier?" I heard him scoff and my stomach dropped when I realised I'd just told him I loved him. "I didn't mean..." My eyes sprung open as he placed some space between us. I dropped my grip on him and scrambled to my feet. "Shit, Juve." I gazed at his shock riddled face and felt bile rise in my throat. *Fuck, fuck fuck!* "I don't love you," I blurted and watched his face twist. I had no idea what I was saying or doing, my brain was a complete piece of mush and I hated how I felt. *Fucking stupid hormones.* My hand was now resting against my stomach, and I rushed to move it. I turned quickly and left his room without saying another word. It was my turn to have my experience with turmoil now. Now I'd know why Haz was the way he was. Now I'd understand what having the only ever love you've ever had ripped from underneath you was like. I jogged across their hallway and into Haz's room. He was passed out on the navy sheets in his bedroom surrounded with sticky notes.

"Haz?" I shook him softly before I shook my head. "Fuck's sake, Haz, wake up!" I bellowed and hit his chest with force. I was frowning, crying and shouting all at the same time. I wiped the snot that was falling from my nose with the back of my hand and watched as he shot up. His red eyes examined me.

"Oh, Chlo, what have you done?" He was high–or had been. I wasn't sure which and I didn't care. I needed him now. No matter what state he was in, I needed my best friend.

"You can't tell Jay." He frowned deeply and shook his head. "I mean it, Haz. He can never find out about this." He pulled me softly towards him and pity filled his eyes.

"What the fuck has happened, Chlo?" he quizzed. My stomach dropped to my feet and my mouth became dry all too quickly. His hands held my face softly as confusion swirled on his face.

"I'm pregnant." My voice was raspy as I struggled to tell him the truth. "I need to get rid of it." I breathed. "It needs to go… now," I choked out. "I can't fucking do this." I sobbed and collapsed in front of him in a pile of snotty salty mess. This was real. It was really happening. I'd got myself into this mess and I had to get myself out of it.

"Okay." He spoke softly as he joined me on the floor and wrapped his arms around me tightly. "Okay." He kissed my head softly and rocked me for a time. Just like Jay had done once upon a time, many, many years ago.

I was curled up on the bed, my knees up to my chin and my head resting on Haz's pillow. I felt nothing. I was empty. The door cracked open slightly in this strange house that wasn't home.

"Are you coming out of here today?" Haz's voice was soft, so soft and almost melodic. I just shook my head. I squeezed my eyes together to block him out. I wanted nothing more than to disappear. "Please, Chlo?" he begged, his footsteps echoed around the room and I flinched away from his touch.

"Don't touch me," I snapped as pain ripped through my stomach. It had been two days, just two days and it still stung just as much. My decision. My shitty fucking decision. I was completely alone. Haz's hands wrapped themselves around me from behind and he moved my hair from my face. My blood ran cold. "I mean it, Haz, leave me alone," I begged as my voice broke.

"I'm not leaving you alone. I'm sitting here. With you." He ran his hand over my hair in an effort to comfort me and sighed aloud. "He's asking why we ran, Chlo." He spoke quietly as I closed my eyes again.

"Lie," I barked and squeezed the pillow tighter. "You promised you wouldn't tell him anything." My voice was a whisper as I fought back my tears. It had been such a long time since I'd let myself feel like this since I'd given in to feeling fucking destroyed. Vulnerable.

"And I swear I won't, but you need to know he's asking." I shook my head as my stomach clenched again. The pain was like a knife was being put through it. I gasped as it ricocheted through me.

"I'm so sorry." I released my sob now, remorse hitting me full force as I thought more on what I'd done.

"Hey," he whispered against my hair. "Stop saying sorry, you've done the right thing." I knew he was trying to comfort me by telling me this, but it didn't help. I just felt sick to my core.

"I haven't, Haz." I pulled myself up with force and winced at the dulling ache in my tummy. "I left him with no explanation the night before he was being shipped off to fight in a fucking war zone." My voice became more irate as his brow furrowed. "I made the choice to abort his fucking kid without him having a clue!" I screamed at him and felt him pull me into a hug. He squeezed my head against his chest as I cried harder. The overwhelming feeling of guilt was all-consuming. I would never be the girl I was less than a week ago again. I couldn't even picture being her again after tonight. "It fucking hurts, Haz." I choked and felt him sway slightly.

"It's alright, Co. I got you." I gave in and hugged him tighter. He was the only comfort I had. He was the difference between me being completely alone or having some sort of support.

127

CHAPTER SEVEN
TIME HEELS
** Three Years Later **

JUVE

She didn't return. I was deployed into a war zone the day after. There was never any explanation as to why she left. She just did. I thought my brother would at least ask her why, but he said she just wanted to go home and didn't divulge any further information. I knew they were lying, both of them were lying. I didn't really have time to get my head around it either. I couldn't dwell. If my mind wasn't in the game out here, I'd end up blown to pieces. Mark was dipping the tattoo gun into the ink again and there was a buzzing sound as I was pulled away from my memories of that evening. I glanced at his beard that had flecks of red in it and smiled at him a little.

"You seem so out of it lately." He was an observer and a cracking tattoo artist. I flinched a little as he continued to tattoo my neck. He was wasted over here in the field. My talent was shooting a loaded gun at a moving target, his was shooting a tattoo gun into my skin.

"I am a little." I'd had more and more nightmares that

involved Miss Conway than I dared to think about lately. I wasn't sure if it was to do with the stress of being back here for the next nine months. "Could say I'm being taunted by my past." Garry laughed at my admission, and I frowned at him. His red stubble glistened in the light. Faint sounds of gunfire in the background could still be heard over the tattoo gun. It was so fucking hot here.

"What past could possibly taunt you?" He raised his brow at me, and I winced as the needle hit a sensitive spot on my skin. I decided now to shut up before I spilt my heart out to them both. "Ain't you grown up living a life of luxury?"

"Heard him say some names in his sleep that ain't his sisters or his Mrs lately," Mark added, and I frowned as I pushed his hand off my neck with the gun. Garry and Mark were my best friends out here, and even when we had all been back home, we had kept our bond up.

"What you heard?" I asked him with a harsh tone to my voice. He looked shocked at my reaction. I was their senior, but I never raised my voice. I never had to. "C'mon, Mark, tell me." I asked him again but softer this time. His eyes lowered as he looked towards Garry.

"Chloe." Garry muttered her name and my heart stopped. My jaw tensed and I pushed myself up from the bed. Even my dreams were betraying me. I shook my head and stormed away from my seat. I wanted to be alone, which was nearly impossible in a war zone. I ached for the girl. It didn't matter who I was with, what I did, or where I was. Every single piece of me missed her.

CHLO

The boom of the bass playing throughout the club pulsed in my chest. Flashing strobe lights from above us hit the silhouettes of the people enjoying their night below us. The place was crawling with people, most of them were familiar faces and I'd grown to like some of them over the last few years. This was a regular place we'd come to do business. Music blared from every angle. The lifestyle I'd been accustomed to had started to take its toll. It had all gone pretty downhill since I'd turned eighteen, since I'd made the shitty choice to bale on Juve and abort his fucking kid. I loved the money, the drugs, and the sex. The hot steamy sex with strangers in clubs and bars alike. I frowned at Haz who was leaning against the bar talking to somebody. His physical appearance had changed over the years. He was taller, broader, and more of a man than most men in their thirties. I hid my laughter with my hand and heard the voices of his gang beside me. One of them was a long-standing acquaintance. I wouldn't have gone as far as calling him a friend really, he was mostly just a business ally. His dark skin looked soft, like smooth melted chocolate. He'd always been an attractive young man from when they were younger and he'd grown up right alongside them, taking Haz and Jay's side when things turned bitter between Rava and my brothers. I was watching him flirt with Missy before I looked back at Haz. He had warned Missy and I that this was a business outing and there was no partying to be had. I was pretty pissed off that he wasn't getting high with us but knew that would come later, maybe. He tilted his head towards the bar, and I stood before looking back at Darky and Missy giggling.

"Don't start without me," I demanded as I straightened out my dress and wandered towards Haz who was making his way towards the office.

By the time I'd reached him, he was spinning around in his old Chesterfield leather chair behind his desk. The only light in the room was from the shitty desk lamp next to him on his desk and from the old industrial window behind him. He was sighing.

"Told you not to bring Missy here tonight, Chloe." His blue eyes were redder than normal, and I shrugged.

"No, you said this wasn't a party night." I reminded him of his earlier words. "And anyway, isn't your business deal already done?" He raised his brow upwards, and I heard the office door open, Jay appearing and frowning at us both.

"Leaving Missy and Darky around that much sniff isn't a good idea." He was sort of laughing it off, but I agreed. It would all be gone before I'd get a chance to touch it–well, sniff it. I craved that euphoric feeling. "Why are we gathering anyway?" I examined the concern on my brother's face and sighed. He'd aged, that was for sure, but he looked more stressed than concerned. The truth was, they were in deep with gangs and drugs and the Mafia. My skin tingled at the thought. Rava's father. Bandoni. Rava had gone rogue after destroying Holly's life, which in turn ruined Haz. Bandoni used this as an opportunity, a way in with Haz. He knew Haz would do anything to disobey his own father. *Poor Henry.* I shook my head. At first, it was gifts, expensive gifts, and then it was an eye for an eye, and now it was direct orders that would be obeyed, or heads would roll. Haz and Jay dealt the drugs, moved the women around, organised the shipments and asked no questions. They were just paid. Jay had said he owed Bandoni after the brutal killing of our dad. I frowned as I perched myself against the desk and zoned out of their conversation before it moved onto Haz's dad's affiliates.

"Larry is here tonight." Jay was talking directly to me now.

"Okay." I frowned at him as I was pulled from my own thoughts.

"I'd rather you weren't high as a kite tonight, to be honest." Haz chuckled at my brother's desperate plea. I rolled my eyes and turned towards Haz. He was now standing next to me. I tilted my head upwards to kiss his cheek and placed my hand in his pocket. He just grinned against the skin on my cheek. I pulled the bag of white powder from it and jiggled it in front of my brother's dark, desperate eyes.

"That sounds terribly boring, Conway," I teased as I placed the small bag down my bra and wandered back down the stairs towards the club.

This was Queens. It was one of the best clubs for nightlife in London's Waterloo. This was a regular spot to meet up with business acquaintances but there was the oddest atmosphere in the world here tonight. I could see it all ending in tears later on tonight. Jay had made his way back out from the office and was sitting next to me, examining our surroundings in the dark. People loved it here. They were enjoying themselves and I found myself miserable again.

"I meant it when I said I don't want you incoherent," he warned as my head snapped to face him. His mouth was in a hard line.

"Why?" I spoke loud enough so that he could hear me over the music.

"Because of them." His head tilted towards another table close by. There were older gentlemen gathered. A mixture of dark hair and grey hair. They were so out of place just staring. "They're Larry's lot." I rolled my eyes. Since we moved down to Devon for the last time, Larry had abandoned us. All ties that were safe and involved Henry were destroyed. I knew it was something to do with the huge fallout Haz had with his father, but I never quite understood all of it. We moved in with Alfie and we hadn't left. The thought of my big, blonde Devon surfer boy Alfie made me smile. He was the kindest guy I'd ever met in my life and was probably the most strait-laced guy ever too. Money was no issue for any of us now, but it never had been for Alfie. He had grown up around it and now he made his own the right way. The legal way. I envied him. My way wasn't the right way. My life was falling apart.

"And you think they're going to kidnap me?" I spoke again and watched his brow furrow. His dark eyes closed slowly before he opened them again. He was growing tired of my backchat.

"Can you just trust me for once?" He spoke loudly, and I shrugged. Darky leant forwards and handed me a bank card. I smiled widely at my brother and shrugged.

"No." I heard Darky chuckling with Missy and watched as he winked towards me. I bit down on my lip as I leant down against the table and snorted the line. Euphoria was almost instant.

My head was sore this morning. I could sort of cope with the comedown but not the headaches that came from the alcohol. I'd awoke next to Missy, who was spread across the bed in absolutely no clothes. Her delicate naked body was tangled around the sheets. She was a slim girl–always had been, even when we'd been at school. She was the polar opposite. I chuckled to myself and frowned all at the same time. I wasn't sure when I'd first decided that jumping into bed with girls would be a good idea, but it seemed it was only ever her. I crawled towards her and trailed my lips across her stomach. She moaned a little and I smirked as I moved from her. I knew her head would be throbbing when she woke too. I placed a T-shirt over my head and then a pair of knickers around my arse. I left my room and made my way towards the kitchen. We didn't stay in hotels often. It was always houses, large expensive houses, under names that had absolutely no ties to ours. The boys said it was safer this way. This house was a terraced Victorian house. It was tastefully decorated. I wasn't up for the argument with my brother this morning about how hammered I had been the night before, so I'd eat and then I'd go back to my room where I would sleep off my huge comedown. Or at least try. Alfie was leaning against the kitchen island and pulling the front of his hair. He was sexy. Surfer dude sexy, with light blonde hair that was longer than it should be, tied back in a bun, and his blue eyes were like crystals. I placed my hands on his back and felt him jump as I whispered, "boo," against his shoulder.

"Jesus, Chloe!" He frowned as he moved away from me a little. Fear filled his eyes as I smiled widely at him. He'd joined us here yesterday as he had his own meetings to go to that had nothing to do with us. The truth was, he kept good company and he was hot, which was an added bonus. He'd always made sure he kept his distance from me. I'd assumed Jay and Haz had warned him any foul play he'd be hung. I chuckled to myself at that. He raised his brow and continued to look at my face. He seemed confused today, distracted almost, and that made me a little sad. He was possibly the nicest guy I'd ever met. He was softly spoken, gentle with his touch and genuine. He almost reminded me of Juve. I gulped down the memory of him and looked back at Alfie. The memory of him hurt a little. Even now. All these years on. My eyes trailed Alfie's physic. I'd seen what was under his T-shirt on the odd occasion. I stepped closer towards him and watched him step back again.

"Why don't you ever let your eyes wander south, Alf?" I questioned him lightly as I ran my hand down my stomach. I'd grown curious about this. I wasn't a bad looking young woman. More often than not, men flocked to me. Most men. Except for him. I wondered if my brother and Haz had actually told him to back off? I was twenty. I was well within his age. He chuckled and shook his head before he folded his arms across his chest. The muscles in his biceps flexed and I bit my lip.

"You don't mince your words, do you?" he teased as I shrugged. "I used to fight myself not to, but now it's a habit." His shoulders rose upwards and then fell. "I've looked a couple of times but you're too young for me." He grinned and I pushed him lightly. He was the same age as Juve. Maybe older by a year. Now I was twenty, the gap didn't seem as big at all. I smirked and walked towards the toaster on the white-topped kitchen side. "I think your brother would feed me to the Mafia." I nodded and crossed my arms.

"I think you're right." I thought the latter part of his admission was probably the truth. He laughed and pressed his back against the kitchen island as I placed the bread in the toaster. I turned to face him and acknowledged the smirk set on his handsome face. "So you have looked?" He simply nodded and then shrugged. His eyes lingered on my legs.

"More than once." He pushed himself off the side and grinned at me as he left the kitchen. I laughed after him and shook my head. At least I now knew it wasn't because I wasn't attractive, and it was because my brother would kill him.

MOVE ON

I had grown up a little. I'd gotten my head around my past. Sort of. I'd watched the gang life pay off. My brother and Haz being so heavily involved with Bandoni had landed them some status in a law firm. But it had also landed them in a world of shit. He wanted something nobody had yet been able to find. A girl. None of them knew the real reason why he wanted her so desperately, but they would be utterly foolish to say no. I'd gotten dressed and ready for a night with them at The Top Hat, Alfie's place. He'd worked hard to build his name as a bar owner around here, it was one of the best around for miles.

"I'm guessing you've found your target then?" I eyed up my brother, his brown muddy eyes were sparkling as he grinned and pushed his arm through his blazer.

"She sings, you know. Voice of an angel." I rolled my eyes at his comment and watched as his shoulders rose and fell. He seemed more amused by my response. He'd been weird lately, absent almost, and I could only guess why. The truth was, over the last two years we had grown apart and I blamed my lack of honesty on that. He'd tried but I'd pushed him away, I'd built my walls up slowly and without realising. I was realising I was harder and sharp, and it bothered me just a little. I knew the type of man Bandoni was, I had seen what they had done to people, and I shivered at the thought.

"If there's one person you don't go against, Jay, it's him," I warned him in a lower tone as my brow furrowed at the memory of seeing our dad bound and gagged in an abandoned warehouse surrounded by his own blood many, many years ago. I wouldn't lose my brother over a girl. Not like that. "I am not losing you over a girl, Jay." He laughed out loud, and I pushed him softly.

"You won't." He leaned in to kiss my cheek. "I swear." I just nodded. I had to trust that what he was saying was right and that wouldn't happen.

Lights were dim in the usually upbeat bar. Alfie invited loads of up-and-coming singers and bands to play live gigs here a couple of nights a week. A few of them had been signed from this very pub. I smiled at him and watched him wink. It was a sexy smile that he offered me, and I looked away quickly. I glanced at Missy who was staring at Haz with her big doe eyes, I really wanted to roll my own at her but I stopped myself from being so mean. Part of me pitied her. He had used her for what he wanted, and she knew this, yet she still kept going back for more. I watched the way Haz was moving, he seemed relaxed, he too was dressed smartly. I sighed and looked towards my glass of wine on the bar. *This girl must be special.* Voices from behind me faded in and out as I sipped my wine and focused on Missy's bleak expression. It was pure desperation for Haz. My brother's arm hung over my shoulder, and I turned around to see what he was chuckling about. That sound was a rare sound. The girl standing in front of us looked as though she was about to pass out. Her olive face paled ever so slightly, and her beautiful green eyes widened.

"This is my sister, Chloe." She was clearly struggling to find her words as she paused and then smiled. I recognised her. She was beautiful. She looked almost foreign; her green eyes were the only thing that didn't add up. They were a wonderful sea green. I hoped to God that this wasn't *the* girl. I went to school with her. She was a couple of years below me. *Avaya.* I reached to touch her shoulder as I returned her smile.

"He said you're good. So did Alfie." I pointed across towards him leaning all sexy across the bar. "And he doesn't give compliments often, so you must be good." I winked at him, and blood filled his cheeks. I looked back at her, and she too was flushed.

"Thanks." She glanced towards my brother, and so did I. He was examining her with intent. I'd have to ask him if he was into her or if she was the target. I couldn't tell which of the two it was. I could never tell with him. She then pointed to the stage that had a piano set up and watched my brother nod at her. I watched her scatter away. I frowned deeply as I elbowed my brother in the ribs.

"Fucking hell, Jay!" I gasped at him. "She's younger than me!" He chuckled a little and then smirked. He took his seat at one of the tables and winked my way. A feeling of dread consumed me.

I sat at the table and listened to her. She was stunning. Nothing like I'd remembered her from school. Her hair was long, thick and dark chocolate in colour. Her voice was absolutely out of this world. I could see her appeal—hell, even I was drooling over her. There was the familiar sound of *'This is a Man's World'* flying throughout the room now, which was accompanied by an explosion of cheers and whistling. She sang effortlessly. I couldn't picture why Bandoni would want her of all the girls in Devon. She was the girl in school who was good, quiet, was never in trouble, and it baffled me completely why her. I looked towards the bar at Haz. He was slouched back against the bar, just watching her, and my chest twisted. This would explain his lack of interest in Missy over the last couple of weeks. He winked towards me when he caught me looking, and I smiled to myself. This would be a great scenario to watch unravel. I clapped as she finished her set and watched her hug her friends. The redhead in particular looked as though she was about to burst with pride. I smiled to myself and then watched her walk towards Haz. Her figure was full, not quite as full as mine, but she had curves and she wasn't straight up and down. I watched him pull her towards him, his hand low on her thigh. She was blushing and they were laughing. I wanted to roll my eyes, tell him to stop dragging somebody so innocent into our way of life, but this was the first time in such a long time I'd seen a real, genuine touch of something on his handsome face. And I loved it. If she was *the* girl, then I'd do anything to protect her from being handed to Bandoni, because she made my best friend smile. He looked his age. For once.

CALLING

Bandoni had called on me. I was working as a fucking double agent, or so it seemed. I ran my hands down my black dress that hugged every curve of my body and stood in my heels as my name was called. The honey blonde behind the desks eye's ran over my figure and then she forced a smile.

"Bandoni will see you now, Miss Conway." I swallowed my nerves and nodded.

"Thank you." The grotty old office smelt like a cigar; my senses seemed heightened. I knocked delicately on the door to his office where his men were guarding outside. The plume of smoke hit me in the face. The bald man with the scar opened the door for me the second he spoke. My heart pounded. This had been the first time since that night in the warehouse that I was worried to confront him alone. Bandoni knew when he was being lied to, he knew when he was being betrayed. He spun in the chair. His large stature nodded. His eyes sparkled as he puffed on his cigar.

"Why am I here?" I questioned him as I sat down opposite him. His face softened.

"I wanted to know how the boys are getting on." His eyes lingered over mine and I shrugged softly. I had to lie now. "Have they found her, Chloe?" *Shit.* I shook my head.

"No." I spoke more bravely now. I didn't want her to be dragged anywhere with him. I'd seen how cruel he could be, what he did to people and what he would do to her. My gut twisted. She had seemed like such a sweet, delicate young woman, who didn't need to be dragged down with Haz let alone Bandoni. He puffed again on his cigar.

"Are you lying, Miss Conway?" His eyes narrowed and I smiled widely.

"I feel insulted that you think I'd lie to you, pops." I

tested my bravado and it worked. His lips thinned into a smile.

"I would never think you would lie to me." His green eyes lingered on mine and he smiled a wicked smile. "This girl is important to me; she is a critical part of a plan." I gulped as he stroked his face. "I am going to get Rava involved. I never trusted him with it but needs must." My guts twisted. I wanted to scream but knew that this would raise alarm bells. My eyes met his lagoons, and I falsified a smile. I knew that everything about this man was bad, but he'd always been so kind towards me. So *good* to me. I had never understood why. I couldn't understand how he was so kind to me, yet so horrid to my brother and Haz. This wasn't my fight. I vowed to Haz I would shield Avaya from harm's way for his sake and his sake only. He cared deeply for that girl, and I cared for him, but I hadn't promised to keep Rava out of the picture.

"You know bringing Rava into this will complicate things." I swallowed. He smirked and nodded.

"I have no doubt you can handle my son and your brothers." The hairs on my arms stood on edge and I just nodded. I was frozen. My brain was in complete turmoil. This was a risk I was willing to take for the sake of Haz and Av. I'd got nothing left to lose.

I wasn't quite sure when the penny had dropped about Av being the girl Bandoni had sent the boys for, all I knew was that she had been around more and more, and Missy had been around less and less. I think I'd known Haz loved her when Arlo confronted them at the bar. Arlo and Rava had appeared from nowhere again, just like Bandoni had promised they would. Haz looked tortured and broken as I watched him cocoon the poor girl. I remembered him vividly repeating her name in his sleep after that night. I also remembered the morning when she braved eating breakfast in nothing but his T-shirt. Most of all, I remembered her leaving him.

***

He slammed his keys down against the side in the kitchen, his shoulders were full of tension and his eyes filled with tears. I knew then something had thrown him off course.

"What's happened?" I asked him as I followed him into the kitchen. He just shook his head from side to side. I mimicked his action and my hair swished around my face as I poked his chest.

"I don't want to talk about it, Chlo." His voice was a growl, but he was sad. I cleared my throat and nodded as I dropped my hand from his chest.

"As you wish." I was shaking my head as I moved from him and made my way towards the living room to join Alfie again. He had stormed out and I could hear his footsteps above. Then the raised voices started. Alfie looked across at me from where he was lazing on the sofa, and I smirked.

"What's the betting he's fucked her and now he's telling Jay?" Alfie grinned my way, his boyish devilish grin. It was infectious. I raised my shoulders and pouted.

"Oh, I'd say a good ninety percent chance," I pondered. "Maybe even higher." He rolled his eyes at my words, and I snuggled back into the huge beige corner sofa. Alfie pulled off my shoes and ran his hands over my feet softly. I smiled at him as I yawned. I loved how he made me feel like I wasn't alone.

***

I chuckled at the memory as it leaked into my brain. I nudged her arm gently and watched her wonderful pea-green eyes stare straight back into mine. We had grown close; I was comfortable with her being around. I enjoyed her company; she was kind and soft-hearted and so fucking good for Haz. But she would soon find out what kind of man she was in bed with, and if she decided to leave, I wouldn't blame her. Not one single bit. She had found me lying on the sofa with our friends surrounding us. Buddy, Haz's younger brother, and his friend–Marley–were joining us for dinner with Haz's folks. The dinner

Avaya was dreading. The dinner that I had been dreading. She was lying next to me. I had joked about looking forward to seeing Juve again in front of my brother and Haz, but deep down I was dreading having all of those memories brought back to the surface. I wondered what type of guy he was. Had he changed? Would he still be that soft, kind-hearted, wonderful human being I remembered? Or would he be tortured just like me? Confused and fucked up?

JUVE

Dad had always said that time was a healer. She'd walked out of my room six years ago after telling me she didn't love me and didn't return. She practically ran away from me. I had never been able to wrap my head around why. Maybe she'd had a moment of realisation? The realisation that she had in fact made a mistake. Maybe she decided she picked the wrong brother after all? She had never been a mistake in my eyes. I'd served two more tours since I was twenty-two. I'd seen things that would never leave me. My life had changed dramatically. I glanced at my girlfriend, Hazel, who was running her hands over her rounded stomach and smiled falsely at my mum. It was about to change even further now. My mum's brow furrowed into a hard frown. I knew that all of this would have upset her. I'd only been back for less than nine months, and I'd already got myself all shacked up with her. I grimaced to myself. Hazel was a pretty little thing, dark hair, blue eyes and leggy. Really leggy. I remembered taking her to meet some of the lads I'd served with. I scoffed back my laugh as I realised she was nothing like Chlo. I must have deliberately chosen somebody who didn't remind me of her.

"What on earth do you see in her?" My mum was now at my side, helping to pour the tea.

"Don't ask." I shrugged. I didn't know. I wasn't all that interested in holding the conversation with my mum about her. "I'm not sure."

"You can't just be alone, can you?" Mum barked. Whilst I'd been away it seemed my mum had turned hard. Cold. Like ice. Not her. I shook my head as I made my way towards Hazel and placed a kiss against the side of her head.

"When are you going to see your brother, babe?" She turned her head towards me, and her long sleek dark hair fell behind her back.

"Next week." I glanced at my dad who nodded.

"He's really looking forward to it." She chuckled and I watched as Aimee rolled her eyes. I bit down on my lip to hold in my laughter. This couldn't be any worse if we tried to make it awkward.

"It's been five years since we've seen him," Aimee stood up as she spoke, tucking her mousey blonde hair which was slightly lightened out of her face. "We are all looking forward to seeing him." She walked away from Hazel who stilled on my lap. I shrugged my shoulders and moved her.

"I'll go speak to her, don't worry." I couldn't make her feel any more uncomfortable any longer, so I left her with Mum and Dad whilst I went off to find Aimee. She was folding her arms, leaning against the kitchen island and frowning at me. *She looked just like Haz.*

"Honest to God, Juve, could you not have chosen somebody with more brains to be involved with? She's gonna be the mother of your child!" She groaned outwardly and I shook my head as I smirked at her admission.

"Aim, don't be mean," I scolded her lightly.

"I liked Chlo." She smiled at me widely, her icy blue eyes shone brightly, and I froze. All traces of a smile gone. "She's still single, you know?" I shook my head.

"Stop it, Aim." She laughed and pushed my shoulder. My heart hurt when I heard her name.

"I'm pulling your leg!" She beamed. "Lighten up for Christ's sake." She wrapped her arms around me and sighed. "But I honestly don't like Hazel. I'm sorry. She doesn't get my approval." I chuckled as I cuddled my baby sister. "Don't think Mum does either." I laughed again and rolled my eyes, the thought of visiting my brother still fresh in my mind.

BE MINE BABY

CHAPTER EIGHT
FIRST IMPRESSIONS COUNT

Aimee was next to me in my car as I drove down the motorway. She had flicked through all of the music channels and had now given up and was playing the music off her phone through the car's speakers. I glanced in the back at Mum and Dad. Dad nodded at me.

"Behave tonight," he warned, and I chuckled as Aimee smirked at me. She'd changed so much since I'd been away. She had really grown into her own young woman.

"He never behaves." She placed her head against my shoulder. "Missed you." She spoke very softly. Her mousey hair hid her face for a split second.

"Missed you too, sweetheart." It was nothing but the truth. I had missed her, probably the most out of all of them. Whilst I'd been overseas, she'd left school and was now pursuing her own dreams. She was fucking eighteen. I suddenly felt really bloody old.

"Are you looking forward to seeing Haz?" she questioned as I turned off the motorway.

"Yeah." I paused as I glanced at her. "I suppose I am.

We were close growing up," I reminded her.

"Apparently, he's changed." Her eyes looked hopeful. "Met a girl." She wriggled her brows and I chuckled.

"Probably at a drug meeting." Mum threw her two pence in, and I shook my head.

"Let's save judgement, hey?" I spoke softly as I drove towards the family holiday home down here. The one I had no idea existed. Aimee jumped out giggling and I shook my head. Youth was on her side. I ran my hand over the screen of my phone and tapped it. Time had placed us all in different predicaments in our lives. Some welcome and some not.

The Old Barn Inn was the establishment of choice. My younger brothers, Warren, Josh, Levi and sister Channa had joined us for the occasion. Josh and Levi barely ever came anywhere with us nowadays, so I was shocked when they had turned up. They probably wanted the latest gossip. Warren nodded towards the door. He was my dad's right-hand man now in their empire of illegal activities. I knew that the relationship between Haz and my dad had been strained for many years, but I'd never been back for long enough to find out exactly what had been going on, and the time I had been back I'd been battling my own demons with post-traumatic stress, sex and beer.

"Here they come." He grinned at Dad, and I stood up. I was nervous for some absolutely ridiculous reason. I placed my hands down my shirt. *You can do this, Juve.*

"Bro!" I called towards him. "Long time no see!" I examined him, he looked older now and scrubbed up well. His eyes were clearer than I'd seen them in a long time. I wrapped my arms around him and hugged him. He even smelt expensive. I'd noted the suit he was wearing. It wasn't cheap. Armani possibly. He must have been doing well. Crime really must pay.

"Been a while. How was Afghan?" He pulled away from me and I straightened my white shirt before my eyes landed on Chlo. She was dressed from head to toe in a cherry red dress. *Fuck me.* The dress hugged every curve of her body. I was suddenly finding it difficult to focus. There wasn't an inch that was out of place on her. I knew my eyes had grown a mind of their own. I could see almost instantly she'd had some work done but she was still as breath-taking as I remembered. I fought closing my eyes as I pulled myself back down to earth.

"Oh…" I stumbled on my words. "You know…" I watched him smirk and shook my head. "As good as war can be." My eyes met the pretty little thing on Chlo's arm next. "Who's this?" I pointed towards the dark-haired woman. She was really quite something. Her dark navy dress was longer at the back but deep cut. She blushed as she looked at me. Her skin was olive in colour and her hair was thick and dark but warm in its colour. It was her sea-green eyes that stood out.

"Avaya. My name's Avaya." I smiled at her and ran my hand under her chin.

"It's lovely to meet you, sweetheart." I smirked at her reaction and Harry stiffened as I touched her. *This must be the girl.* The girl Aimee was talking about. I released her and watched Chlo lean towards me. Her lips landed on my chin, and I stopped breathing.

"It's been a while," she whispered against my cheek. I could feel my mouth twisting into a smile. I nodded and placed my hand behind her back as I pulled her slightly closer towards me. *How did it feel like no time had passed at all? Like she didn't just walk out and leave.* She fit there against me just right. I fought my groan as I took a breath inward, her fragrance all-consuming, a sweet but strong scent that set me on fire. I felt myself growing hard.

"Juve, put her down." Jay was snapping instructions my way. I was sure I heard her moan as I released her. Jay relaxed and then continued to talk to Avaya.

"Sit by me at dinner," she whispered towards me. I frowned as I glanced towards her. Her face was painted with makeup. Makeup that I just wanted to wipe off. Haz was taking the small brunette towards Mum and Dad. I tilted my head towards them.

"Fill me in on that whole thing." She smiled and nodded before she examined me. Her eyes were practically dancing over me. I felt exposed when she looked at me like that. "You look well." She flushed and pushed her hair behind her ear. She hadn't changed it much since she was younger. It was just longer now than it had once been and was shiny. I wanted to run my fingers through it.

"Your tattoo collection has grown," she whispered my way again. I chuckled softly and shrugged.

"You're so observant, Miss Conway." She grinned and shrugged. Her mud-brown eyes sparkled as she looked towards her brother who was deep in conversation with Warren now. I looked at her side profile and smiled to myself. Even with all that makeup on, she still looked youthful. I wanted to reach and grip her fingers in mine. She turned to face me again and then ran her fingers over the tattoos on my neck, and a shiver ran the length of my spine. "Please don't," I croaked. "You'll make me self-destruct." She just chuckled as she shook her head from side to side in disbelief. I'd missed her. I'd missed how everything was this easy. The sound of her laughter made me feel at home. The waitress waved at me and then nodded, and I smiled. "Table's ready!" I announced to anybody who would listen. I instinctively gripped her fingers in mine as I dragged her towards the table. Laughter consumed me. Jay wouldn't be pleased about the way I was touching his sister but what he didn't know wouldn't hurt him.

CHLO

Six years. Six whole years had flown by since I walked away from him. He'd made it all too easy for me. So much had changed in that time. I was no longer a fragile teenager. I'd grown in more ways than one. I was stronger than I gave myself credit for. I glanced at Avaya who looked like a lamb amongst a cage of lions. I almost felt sorry for her. I snapped a picture of her and Harry and smiled to myself. He was leant behind her and his lips were against her ear. She looked flushed. I wondered what he was saying to her. If there was one thing I'd grown to like, it was her. She made my best friend happy and had made him a better man in such a short period of time. Juve leant into me, and I turned my face towards his. I stopped myself from reaching to move the stray hair from his face. He was extremely close as conversations were being held from all around us.

"You still haven't filled me in on how my brother and her came to light." I smiled softly at him and shrugged a little. It was such a long-winded tale to tell. It wasn't really my business either.

"I was hoping that wouldn't be the first thing you'd want to be filled in on." The tone of my voice was brave and teasing, when in reality, I was shaking. I smiled softly at him, and my heart fluttered as he ran his hand over the exposed skin on my thigh underneath the table before he squeezed it gently. My gut twisted and I forced my legs closed when all I wanted to do was the opposite. I hadn't felt a thrill like that in the longest time and my pussy thudded.

"Juve," I warned in a strange sigh that sounded more like a moan. I was sure I heard him growl. Laughter had erupted from around us and I was suddenly thrown back into the real world. The world where him and I didn't exist in the same proximity. I shook my head slowly and pulled my eyes open before I glanced across the table towards

Avaya. Her eyes landed on mine and then flitted over Juve. My heart was pounding as I pressed my legs more tightly together, and his grip released. A sense of relief flooded me, and I watched Avaya smirk. I knew their plan for her tonight, and I was almost certain where they were about to take her would make her change her opinion on all of us forever. And if it didn't then she belonged with us. I ran my hand over his that was resting against his leg now, and my heart sunk for her. She'd be exposed into our way of life. She'd know what we all did and where all the money really came from. She'd find out all she needed to. She'd find out enough to judge us, and that terrified me just the smallest amount.

They had left. My brother looked just as nervous as Haz, if not more so. He had such a soft spot for Avaya and there had been a time when I wondered if he was in love with her too. In fact, I still often wondered that. I shook my head at that thought. I knew when he cared for somebody, and he cared for them both. He wanted to protect Avaya. I was glad of that. So did I. I didn't want her in the hands of the Mafia without knowing why or what for. Every conversation I had ever had with her had been easy, genuine and unforced. I frowned as I thought back on how she came to be involved in my life. I remembered that conversation well.

***

Haz had been wrapped up in himself lately. Jay had been sneaking around too. I knew they had both been pulled into looking for a girl. Bandoni needed them. Bandoni wasn't the type of guy you messed with. If he wanted something doing, you did it. Regardless of what it was. No questions asked. I gulped down thoughts of the huge Italian brute and shook my head. I plonked myself down next to my best friend.

"Do you know where Jay is?" He glanced at his watch and shrugged his broad shoulders. I frowned at him. "Have you forgotten how to use your words, Mr Vens?" I nudged him with my arm and

watched as his small pupils dilated a little.

"I'm not sure where he is." He was raising his eyebrow. "We were supposed to be going to the gym but that's not happened." I rolled my eyes. Their obsession with the gym made me sick. I don't think I've seen abs like theirs other than in magazines. They weren't normal. He stayed quiet for a time. I knew he had something on his mind. He looked troubled. I wanted him to talk to me. Our relationship was strained nowadays. I hated what drugs had turned him into. He was almost a person I didn't recognise. I huffed aloud and watched his eyes fall on mine.

"He found the girl," he mumbled. I nodded and shook my head all at the same time. It took some time for his words to sink in.

"Right." He smirked, his heart-shaped lips thinned, and he looked at his hands.

"So have I." My frown became deeper. There was a pained look across his face. "I can see why he's pursuing her." His lips twisted again, and I punched his arm. Jealousy coursed through me, and I was unsure why. It had been such a long time since he'd been interested in anything other than drugs. Even in me.

"Stop it." He smirked again and stood to his feet.

"I have a wedding reception to attend." He glanced over me, sitting where he'd just left. "I should get ready." He began to walk away from me, and my stomach clenched with fear for the girl.

"You aren't going to hurt her, are you?" I quizzed. My eyes instantly looked towards the floor.

"I don't intend to. No." He spoke a little lower this time. I frowned at his response. I should have been happy that their plan wasn't to harm the girl, but I was confused by his reaction to her. "She seemed very unexpecting." He chuckled as he wandered off to get ready.

***

I was grateful for them dragging her into my life. She'd had such a normal mundane life compared to mine. We were like chalk and cheese. I couldn't quite wrap my head around the appeal Haz oozed to her. She was such a sweet thing. Normal. So sodding normal. Haz's family had left.

Juve and I were last to move. He glanced up towards me and smiled, his deep dark pools of blue made my heart warm through just like they had all those years ago as he tugged on the front of his unruly hair. My chest twinged.

"Don't look at me like that." I was almost begging him.

"Like what?" He tilted his head at me as he sipped on his coffee. I reached for one of the biscuits on his plate.

"Like you can tell what I'm thinking." I bit into the biscuit and smiled widely at him.

"Never been able to tell what you're thinking." His eyes dropped towards the table. I reached for his hand and heard him sigh. "Fancy getting out of here?" He looked up towards me and I shrugged.

"Where are we gonna go?" His shoulders rose upwards and then fell softly.

"For a walk?" I rolled my eyes and nodded.

"I'll show you the beach." I threw his keys towards him and watched as he turned the bill over. *Ever the gentleman.* We climbed in his car and the smell of Aimee's perfume on the seat belt made me sneeze. "God, she wears way too much." I coughed and watched him grin.

"That she does." He agreed with me on something at least. "You haven't changed your perfume," he added, and my heart twisted. *Did he remember my perfume?* I felt my cheeks flushing with blood and nodded.

"I haven't, no." I cleared my throat and listened as the radio played in the background. It lulled the awkward silence. "It was Jay's fault that he met Avaya," I blurted, partly to try and avoid him bringing up the fact I ran away from him six years ago. He just continued to drive the car in a straight line. "She's really good for him actually." I glanced down in my lap at my hands. There was silence between us again as he didn't acknowledge my words.

"Are you seeing anybody?" The question left his mouth so effortlessly and stopped my train of thought. I shook my head.

"No." I tilted my head and looked at him. His profile

was breath-taking. "Are you?" I asked quietly, and I watched as he shrugged.

"I suppose." My stomach twisted. I wasn't entirely sure of the feeling that consumed me. Jealousy? Sadness? Heartbreak? I just nodded and looked out of the window as I watched the lights from the road ahead whizz by. The truth was, I didn't do long term relationships. I did flings and sex. That was it. I didn't like being tied down. Clearly, he liked the comfort of being with somebody.

"I hope she's nice," was the sliver of words that left my mouth. I crossed my arms, almost in protest.

"Does it bother you?" I shrugged as I frowned.

"You're old enough and wise enough to make your own choices." I paused. "Who am I to judge?" A smirk rolled across his lips. His hair was less wild than it once had been. It was no longer curly and unkempt. It was much shorter and styled.

"That didn't answer my question." He stopped the car on the side of the road, and I froze. I frowned at him. He gazed at me for a time and my heart took off on its own direction.

"Why do you want to know if it bothers me?" I snapped towards him. His eyes grew dark as they glistened under the lights of the road we had stopped on, and he leaned in towards me slowly and raised his hand towards my face. I stopped breathing as he pulled me closer towards his lips. They landed on my earlobe.

"Tell me if it bothers you, baby." My heart twisted and then landed in my stomach as he called me baby. I closed my eyes as his lips grazed my ear and then my jaw.

"It bothers me," I gulped out as I took a breath. "Fuck's sake, Juve." I breathed out and his lips moved away from me. He cleared his throat, and he shook his head. He turned the engine back on. It was as though he was fighting with himself over something, like he wanted to touch me but couldn't bear to. I frowned as I looked towards him. I wanted to know what his game was. It was clearer to me now that the hold he once had over me many years ago was still very much intact. He could still get my pulse rising. I pushed his shoulder softly as he pulled back onto the road and placed his foot further down on the accelerator pedal.

"Good." He mumbled the word as he drove. I gasped and laughed all at once. Why was it such a good thing that him having a girlfriend bothered me? I couldn't wrap my head around it. "So…" He paused. "The lovely Avaya…" I shook my head and placed my hand against my head on the car's window. I was a little confused and then angry with him for wanting to upset me.

"I'm not talking to you." I frowned. He sighed, held his hand out for me to take, and I looked the opposite way.

"Please?" There was a softer tone to his voice, and I gave in almost instantly. I wanted nothing more than to tell him to fuck off, that nobody ever spoke to me like a piece of shit, but his hand trailed against mine, which he clutched between his, our fingers laced around one another.

"She's just a normal kid. A nice normal person, with a normal life, and then she met us." I shrugged. "She'll be running for the hills tonight when she realises where all their money comes from," I blabbed. "Well, most of their money." He sighed.

"True that they're in the law firm with Rava's dad?" He was raising his brow now as he turned the wheel towards the beach car park.

"Yup." I sighed and looked at his hand still held in the middle of the centre console. "Jay's actually really good at it." He laughed a small chuckle as I spoke. I wasn't sure how he knew about the law firm. It was actually quite a successful legitimate business. Apparently, this was normal for illegal activities to be covered by lawful ones, and what was more lawful than a law firm?

"I can picture that." I grinned to myself. Seeing him with authority made me chuckle. Every day he worked hard in that firm. He was good at it. He suited that lifestyle, so much more than he suited the life of crime. Haz didn't. He was much more at ease when dealing the drugs and cleaning up the messes. I flinched for Avaya. I wish she'd open her eyes to it all a little more. "She seems like a nice kid." I scoffed at his use of the word kid. I shook my head as he stopped the car where it overlooked the cliff. It was dark, pitch-black outside and would probably be absolutely freezing. I watched him move his seat back and undo his window. My eyes trailed over the exposed tattoos on his neck, and I allowed myself to peek at his exposed chest. It was just about visible because of a few buttons that weren't done up. He had undone them when we had left the restaurant. I bit down on my lip. He had gotten better with age. I knew I had absolutely no right to eyeball him, but I couldn't help myself. He ran his hand through his hair and took a breath. It was deep. I pressed down against the seat belt that was strapping me in and turned to face him. His eyes were just wandering over my face and then my dress. I gulped and felt the colour rise in my cheeks.

"Stop it," I whispered as I squirmed under his watchful eyes. He sat back and continued to stare my way. His eyes spoke for him, he was peeling my dress from me, and I swallowed. Hard.

"I'm just getting my memory of you right." His words confused me.

"Excuse me?" A smirk rolled across his heart-shaped mouth, and I frowned.

"I won't be around much after Christmas, so I'm getting my fill of you now." Anger coursed through me. I wasn't a piece of meat.

"Fuck you, Juve." I rolled my eyes and climbed from his car, slamming the door behind me. I walked towards the beach, hearing the sound of the car door being shut behind me. I continued to walk with some pace. I wasn't sure why he wanted to upset me or make me feel uncomfortable. I didn't remember him ever being cruel when we were younger. He was always the opposite. His hand reached for mine and I flinched away. My eyes leaked tears. I could cope with any other person making me feel like I was just a fuck or even a slag but not him. "Fuck you." I spat venom as I was pulled closer towards him with some force. He held my face between his hands, and I frowned at him as I tried to pull him away. I caught my breath as I pushed against his chest. It was hard underneath my palms. "Does the army give you a personality transplant?" I barked at him as tears escaped the corners of his eyes now too. He shook his head slowly.

"I didn't mean to make you feel like that, Chlo." His words seemed genuine, but I pulled away from him as his grip became tighter. "It just changes you." My eyes closed as he placed my head against his chest. "I'm sorry for upsetting you, Chloe." He breathed as I wrapped my hands around his back, the warmth of his body pressed against mine distracting me from the brutal British weather. He was large and warm and just how I had remembered him. He smelled like clean laundry and sandalwood. "That was the last thing I ever wanted to do." My heart stopped as he held me. I didn't ever want to let him go. I never had done. "My memory didn't serve you any justice," he croaked out, and I squeezed him tightly.

"I remembered you being the exact same," I whispered as I pulled my eyes to look at his and felt him place a small distance between us.

"I've changed, Chlo. I'm not that boy anymore." His words were so sad. I placed my hand against his cheek and then ran my thumb across his bottom lip. His eyes fluttered closed. I could see he wasn't the boy I'd ran out on, but I was no longer the baby that left him.

"I'm not that little girl anymore either," I assured him as his hands fell towards my waist and then further down my back towards my arse. Desire flooded me.

"I can tell. You're all woman now, baby." I pushed

against his chest slightly as goosebumps flooded my arms.

"Don't, Juve. It will just be a fumble in a car park." I felt his lips curl upwards against my cheek and caught his smile.

"I'm just admiring you." He spoke softly and with an air of innocence that made me chuckle a little.

"Take me home, Juve," I asked quietly as his hands landed against my hips. The cool air blew between us, and he frowned as he placed his lips at the corner of mine. My heart rate spiked almost instantly at how close and intimate we were.

"Just walk with me, once…" he whispered against my mouth. "Please?" He was practically begging me. I simply nodded, traced my hands over my waist and towards my hips before I placed his hands in mine. I couldn't say no to him, no matter how much I wanted to, and if I was being really honest with myself, I didn't want to say no to him. I wanted to be closer to him, I wanted him to hold my hand between his and I wanted him to look at me like I was the only one he'd ever adored. He had always had the most amazing way of making me feel as though I was the only girl in the world.

"Let's walk then." I squeezed his fingers between mine and put some space between us. My senses were overwhelmed with a desire and need for him, and another emotion that I didn't want to acknowledge ever again.

The sea breeze was cool against the skin on my exposed arms and my teeth began to chatter. We had walked in silence for a while, listening to the sound of the freezing waves crash against the shoreline. We were in the car now and he placed his hand over the door handle before I could pull on it. His stance was overwhelming and warm.

"I got it," he muttered, his voice deep and raspy and so Juve like. Just as I had remembered it being. It stirred up an emotion I was convinced I'd buried. I took a deep breath and turned to face him. My eyes met his in the dark, and he placed his hands in mine as he pulled me closer towards his body. "I got you, darlin'." His lips turned upwards, shivers rolled down my spine and somersaults churned my stomach. I was alive. My hands found themselves around his neck as I threw myself at him like some sort of desperate slut. I pressed my lips against his with an overwhelming force and pulled against his blazer. A groan vibrated in the bottom of his throat and liquid heat pooled between my legs as our kiss deepened. Everything about this should have felt wrong, awkward and unwanted, but it was anything but. His hands were fumbling with the handles on the back door of his car.

"Fuck, I want you." He groaned, and the rasp in his voice matched my desperation. I tugged on his shirt and began to tear off his blazer as I pulled myself on the backseat of his car.

"Then have me." I spoke softly as my teeth grazed my bottom lip. He was halfway into the car and staring at me, his eyes burning with a look I hadn't ever seen from another man, a look that made me feel sexy as sin. The straps of my dress dropped from my shoulders, it was bunched up around my waist and my heels were still firmly attached to my feet. His hair was tousled in the most delicious way. I reached forwards and placed his shirt in my hand. "I'll just have to sort myself out if you don't want to help me out." He was suddenly still as his eyes fought to stay on mine and not wander. I traced my free hand over the bud of my already hard nipple beneath the dress. Heat pooled again between my legs, and I caught my breath. His eyes widened as I released him from my clutches and pulled my thong down my legs.

"Chloe." He groaned my name and every hair on my neck stood to his call. "Don't," he panted. My southern region clenched the more he begged me not to touch myself. My fingers trailed the wet slit between my legs, my focus wavered away from him. My thumb circled the most sensitive place between my legs as a subtle wave of pulses consumed my thoughts. My eyes closed briefly, and lips landed against my inner thigh. "You're gonna make me combust." The sound of the car door closing made my eyes open, the overhead light now off and it was dark. The feeling of his stubble edging closer towards my pussy made my breathing hike and I continued to stroke myself. He moved my hand and spread my legs. I gasped from the force and shock of his warm mouth being *there*. Everything pulsed as his tongue slid inside of me, my back arching the more he ate. Teeth grasped my bottom lip to stop uncontrollable noises leaving my mouth. I pulled against the top of his hair as a wave of pleasure threatened to push me over the edge. His mouth was suddenly no longer around my clit but at my thigh as I fought the brink of an orgasm. He sat up, gripping my wrists in his and pulling me on his lap. My hands gripped the hard muscles of his shoulders as he bit the skin of my neck and then kissed it. My orgasm still on the very brink, I pulled down his suit trousers and glanced down at his hard, thick, wonderful dick. I gulped and glanced towards him to see the world's sexiest smirk, and my heart raced. I wrapped my lips around the tip of his glorious cock and heard him moan my name. I smirked as he pulled on my hair so that our faces were now so close I could kiss him. This suddenly felt a little too intimate for me. The buds of my sensitive nipples began to rise hard again as his hand traced them over the fabric of my dress. He pulled my legs so that I was now straddling him in the back of his car. He reached into his trousers and pulled out his wallet. I raised my brow at him and watched him smirk as he dangled the silver foil wrapper at me. I grinned and watched him tear it with his teeth, that sight alone was sexy enough to tip me over the edge. I was desperate for him. His hand slid down it as he covered his glorious cock in the barrier. His hard length was millimetres away from my drenched and leaking pussy. My head arched backwards as I placed myself on it.

"Juve," I moaned as he thrust into me. I rose and fell

against his length, gripping his shoulders to steady myself as my legs trembled. A building feeling growing inside of me made me want to call out for Jesus himself. I saw stars as he pumped himself inside of me. I had just had sex with my ex. In the back of his Range Rover. And I fucking loved it.

CHAPTER NINE
IGNORANCE IS BLISS

JUVE

Beads of sweat fell from her face and I struggled to catch my breath. I couldn't help but kiss her lips again. She pushed against my chest softly and fought a smile of her own.

"Oops," I mumbled in her mouth, and she shook her head and bit my lip. A slight moan escaped my mouth as I squeezed her arse that was still in my lap.

"Juve!" She gasped. I grinned and placed her hair behind her ear. She was blushing, and oh boy it was the sexiest thing I'd ever seen. She rolled her eyes and moved from my lap. I caught her wrist in my hand and smiled.

"Where are you going?" I raised my brow and watched her smile.

"In the front. Get dressed, Juve." Her eyes ran the length of me before she winked. "Take me home." That fucking wink sent pulses to places that hadn't felt alive in years.

"Is this going to be a fuck 'em and leave 'em date?" I joked as I pulled my trousers back up my legs and she placed her dress back on properly. She was straightening out her hair. Her shoulder rose upwards and fell softly. She gave me a shy smile.

"This wasn't a date." She frowned. "It was a mistake." Suddenly, I felt like I'd been punched in the chest by Mike Tyson himself. I placed my hand over my heart as I frowned at her.

"That's brutal," I mumbled to her. She glanced out the window and pushed open the car door. She slipped out without even looking back at me.

"It's the truth," she murmured as she climbed into the front passenger seat. She threw the car keys at me. My mouth was open as I watched her. I wasn't entirely sure how I was supposed to win this girl back. Or what I'd done that was so bad that she had left me in the first place. But it was game on now. I'd win her heart back if it fucking killed me.

She left my car and as I dropped down against the pebbles beneath my feet, I caught her hand in mine. Half pulling her towards me, she stopped and her eyes widened. She pressed her hand against my chest, and I tilted my head to one side.

"Let me take you out somewhere." I felt pathetic but I had to try. She flushed again as she shook her head. She tried to pull away from me, but my grip tightened. "Please, Miss Conway…" I paused as I eyed her. "Don't make me beg." I was sure she shuddered as I ran my thumb over her cheek softly. Her eyes closed momentarily.

"We can go to the shack at the beach, if you'd like?" she suggested. I just nodded, knowing full well I had no idea where this place was. She laced her fingers through mine and walked silently next to me.

"So…" I cleared my throat as her head snapped up to mine. "Is this a date?" I teased as she rolled her eyes. I smiled at her and watched her fight her smile too.

"We've never been on a date." She shot me down. I ran my fingers over my chin, pondering that thought.

"We have," I added. "We used to pack a picnic and sit at the top of the hills in the summer. I'd steal Mum's wine." I wiggled my brows at her and heard laughter leave her. It was melodic. Beautiful. It sent shivers through me.

"It amazes me that you remember those little things." Her eyes lingered on mine and I smiled sweetly back to her. We walked quietly with each other towards the cliffs and then down them. She pointed towards an old run-down beach house, and I smiled down at her as she squeezed my fingers in hers. "No idea what it's like inside. I haven't been in it for years." I simply nodded.

"I'm not judging, looks cool." She smiled up at me and that stopped my drumming heartbeat. "You're so fucking stunning, you know?" She pushed my chest softly and made her way towards it. I looked on as she moved. Her figure turned my thoughts from innocent to anything but.

CHLO

I hadn't stepped foot in the shack for years. I had tried to shut him down after I had fucked up in the car. My heart wasn't ready to admit that I could fall for him so quickly, but I was bringing him to this cabin to have some sort of date. I laughed to myself. I pulled him through the door and watched him smile at me.

"Chlo…" He called my name softly. I was looking around the hut. It had been cleaned and there were sheets on the bed. Somebody had been in it. "Doesn't look all that run down," he added. I placed myself down on the little sofa in front of the log burner. He reached to light it and I smiled to myself.

"Somebody has been in it," I told him. He just nodded as he successfully set the fire up. I watched as the embers burned. The fire gave the dark room a wonderful orange glow. He looked wonderful. His shirt wasn't all the way done up.

"I wanna know why you left, baby?" He placed his hand over his chin and turned towards me. My heart stopped. I shook my head.

"I ran scared." I croaked out my lie. He scrunched up his face.

"Are you gonna run scared again?" His eyes searched for mine and I was lost in them, my stomach flipping inside out.

"That depends on how hard you push," I whispered as he edged closer to me. He was holding his foot on his lap. "I'm not the girl I was, Juve, things have changed." I tried to justify running. "I'm living a double life." He shook his head.

"Tell me what's going on, it might make you feel better." I scoffed at his kindness. "I'll tell you mine if you tell me yours?" His big boyish grin made my heart flutter.

"Will it make me feel better telling somebody that my brother, Haz and I are hiding something really important from Av?" I couldn't help but tell him how I was feeling. "That I've been feeding information back to Bandoni for years?" His face twisted.

"Why have you been doing that?" His tone was inquisitive and not angry, though he had every right to be. His dad was his worst enemy and I'd been telling him all sorts. I'd never admitted why I felt like I owed him anything. I shook my head, but he ran his hand over my face, moving my hair gently from it. I caught my breathing at his kindness. "Why?" He pushed again.

"Because he helped me get over my dad." My words felt like they were silent, but I could tell from his expression he was confused. "He caught him and ended me looking over my shoulder for the rest of my life." Relief filled me as I spoke. "He's looked out for me." I shrugged and watched as he pulled me closer. "You're right, I do feel better." He smiled and ran his mouth over mine.

"You think any of that makes you a bad person?" I pushed my hand against his chest but kept his mouth against mine. My eyes fluttered closed, and I suppressed the warmth escaping my slit. *Fuck's sake.* "I've been calling your name in my sleep for the last six years." His admission made my skin prickle and my heart pound. "In a war zone, you've never left my dreams, baby." He ran his mouth against the corner of my lips, and I shivered.

"Juve…" I whispered his name in a warning as I pulled on the back of his hair. I was certain a groan escaped his mouth. It was the hottest sound.

"Tell me how after six years you still set my world on fire?" he asked in a low grumble.

"Tell me how after six years you still make me feel like I'm special?" I mumbled my response back to him.

He laughed a little. "Because you are, baby." He pulled me on his lap as the fire popped and crackled. "You're so fucking special it hurts." I couldn't help but grin like a Cheshire cat.

"Stop smooth talking me." I ran my hands to either side of his shoulders. "I've met many guys like you." I raised my brow and heard his laughter leave his body.

"Riiggghhttt." His word was elongated, and I giggled at him. "Any as memorable?" he asked with a devilish, dazzling smile attached to his mouth.

"Hmm." I heard the fire burning away behind us and shrugged. "Maybe." I felt him release me gently and smiled as I wandered across the kitchen towards the fridge. "Nothing can change, Juve. You're my best friend's older brother," I reminded him lightly as I threw a bottle his way.

"That should have stopped us years ago and never did." I frowned and bit the lid off the top of my bottle.

"I mean it, Juve. Tonight didn't happen." I watched his shoulders rise and then slump as he looked in the fire.

"You keep telling yourself that," he snapped. "Because it did. And you can't deny you still feel that spark." He was right. I couldn't deny it because it was still in the room as we spoke, pulsing between us. Making me want to crawl back onto his lap.

JUVE

I'd witnessed first-hand now that *that love* existed. The love that stops everything and consumes a person. The love that's depicted in movies. My brother had *that* love. It was almost sickening. I smiled at Avaya who was sprawled across the sofa at Alfie's. She was laughing with Chlo and her redhead friend, Nance. I didn't quite catch what was being spoken about. Haz appeared at my shoulder and nudged me softly.

"You perving on my Mrs?" I laughed and shook my head.

"Not quite." I turned my head to look at him. "She's a pretty thing though, isn't she?" His lips pursed into a smirk as he folded his arms across his chest. I watched her with intent. She was small in her frame, delicate almost, but she was still curved in all of the right places. Her hair was the colour of dark melted chocolate, long and thick down the small of her back, but it was her soft icy eyes that had me when I first met her. Piercing sea-green eyes. Beautiful. I could see how she would be attractive to him.

"Christmas was good this year." He spoke softly and I smiled as I placed my arm around his shoulders. I was glad he'd found some joy in the festive period for once.

"Christmas is a good time," I reminded him. He huffed and laughed all at the same time. Chlo was looking at both of us. I cringed internally and my eyes landed back on my younger brother. "Buddy is besotted with Avaya, isn't he?" I tried to make light conversation and he nodded.

"Haven't come across somebody who isn't yet." He rolled his eyes. "Chlo is more in love with her than I am I think." I chuckled and shook my head. I knew that was a big lie. I'd never seen a bloke more loved up in my life. It was almost sickening. His bad-boy persona, gone. Without a fucking trace.

"I don't think that's possible," I added as he grinned, and his blue eyes twinkled. He looked more full of life now than he had in years. The music had been turned up in the living room as the girls cleaned up the plates and cups. Avaya began to sing the soul music that was playing, and I felt the hairs on my arms stand up. She really did have the most magical voice. I smiled at her, and she grinned back. Haz made his way to help them, dancing around like a little bit of an idiot, and I rolled my eyes. Chlo made her way past me, hands full of cups and didn't even glance my way. I knew I'd upset her that night by the beach. I had known when we slept together in the back of the Range Rover that she would go back to pretending like we didn't happen. I was still pissed that she could leave us like we never happened. The smell in the air changed when she brushed past me. I frowned as I took a breath inward and I followed her out of the room with my eyes. I glanced down at my phone ringing and saw Hazel's name flashing. I groaned as I placed the phone to my ear.

"Heeeyyyy." I hung out the word for longer than I should have. There was a small giggle from the other end.

"Hey, handsome." I frowned and rolled my eyes as I watched my brother and his girlfriend laughing like kids in front of me. I couldn't ever picture that with her, but I could with Chlo. "What's all that noise? Who's singing?" she questioned innocently.

"It's my brother's girlfriend." I paused. "She's really good."

"She sounds like an angel." I laughed and my shoulders rose and fell.

"I'd love to meet them at some point. Not sure why you won't take me with you when you visit them." I placed my jaw together gently at first.

"It's just complicated." It wasn't. Haz wasn't interested in meeting her. Haz was wrapped up in his own girl. He was absolutely besotted with her. I didn't want her here because of Chlo.

"So you say." I rolled my eyes as I pictured her lips filled with filler pouting.

"So, are you up to much today?" I tried to change the direction of the conversation. The sweeter I kept her while I was away the easier my life would be when I eventually returned home.

It wasn't often I ventured out anymore. I'd told myself that drinking was bad. In fact, I wasn't the only one who had said alcohol was a bad idea. Dawson had too. I groaned as I thought about filling him in on all of this shit. I was almost certain it wouldn't have a great outcome for my file. Whenever I drank, things got really fucking bad. I ran my hands over the bar at The Top Hat and felt my brother's hand against my shoulder.

"You good, old man?" he teased and flashed me his pearly whites. I rolled my eyes and nodded, and I looked down at my pint of coke.

"Never better." Laughter erupted from next to where we were standing, the dirty little cackle was leaving Avaya's mouth and it was infectious. Chlo glanced at me for a split second, and I held my breath. My eyes grew a mind of their own and ran the length of her. Her dress was cut just above her knee and showed off her thighs. I cleared my throat and shook my head before I sipped on my drink, wishing it was something stronger.

"Look like you've seen a ghost." He was half blocking my view of her now and watched as she dropped her gaze from mine. She'd been better at hiding things between us this time than I had.

"I'm good, bro." I nodded again and looked towards Alfie who had possibly the world's largest smirk across his face. He hopped from the barstool next to me and wrapped his arms around Chlo's waist. She pushed her shoulders up in an uncomfortable motion and laughed with the girls as I watched on. Her eyes didn't meet mine again for a long while. I ached to touch her and gripped my hands together into small fists. I ushered down the barmaid and pointed at the beer.

"Any of those would be good." I flashed my teeth at

the pretty young thing, and she did as I asked speedily. "Cheers." I almost gulped down the alcohol that filled the glass. I'd drown out this shit feeling, even if it sent me off the rails.

I placed my best false bravado on, which was easier now that I'd had a skinful. I placed my arm inside Jay's and Haz's for support as I stumbled towards Alfie's front door. I may have overdone it, just a little. Haz was laughing with Jay as they opened the front door and I laughed with them.

"I'm so fucking sorry," I slurred.

"Don't be, this is the best thing I've seen since I was like seventeen." Haz laughed again as they helped me towards the stairs, and the girls followed in their own drunken states not far behind us. They both let go at the same time and I chuckled as I stumbled towards the stairs.

"I can get up there myself, cheers." I gave them a thumbs up and huffed as I looked up the steps to see the rivers of stairs flowing back down them and groaned. My head would ache terribly tomorrow.

Just as I thought, my head did not thank me for the copious amounts of alcohol I had let slip past my lips the night before. My mouth was as dry as the desert and every sense stood on end. Sickness swirled in my stomach as I ran my hand over it. Dawson had been the one who had suggested having a break from the military and I had thought for a time that it was the right thing to do. I had lost one of my squaddies less than a year ago, and yet, it all seemed like years ago. That had felt like my fault, but this situation seemed somewhat more torturous. Being around her was an addiction. One that I couldn't get my entire fill of because she legged it away from me constantly. Dawson had told me point blank to get over it. Coming here was supposed to be closure. I was supposed to move on from this. The door knocked and it was Jay, all fresh-faced. I groaned as his eyes lingered on my chest.

"You getting up, big lad?" He was resting his bed head against the door frame.

"How do you look so alive?" I pulled on the covers and threw them over my head.

"Because I didn't get smashed out of my face." The taste of whiskey lingered along with a faint hint of cigar.

"Did I smoke last night?" I heard laughter as the question left my lips.

"Yeah." He was laughing again, and I groaned. "My bad." I threw a pillow from off the bed I was laying in and watched him enter my room further. "Can you do me a favour?" He looked towards the door, and I nodded as I looked at him. His eyes that were the image of his sisters saddened. "Chlo's been a bit weird." Guilt threatened to tip me over the edge. I was already feeling far too fragile for this conversation. "She's always opened up to you." I was sure I gasped as he spoke, but he was too busy playing with his hair to notice. I watched him move awkwardly and sat up in the bed.

"What do you want me to do?" His shoulders lifted and he scrunched his face up.

"Just dig around. See what's going on." I felt the anxiety of my lies rising, and so I nodded. I would 'dig' for him. I would dig to find out that the reason she may have been off was something to do with me.

"I'll dig." I just smiled and watched as he nodded and pointed towards the door, backing out slowly.

"Thanks, mate." He winked and left. I groaned and flopped forwards on my bed.

CHLO

Ignoring him was becoming increasingly more difficult. Especially when he got himself into states like last night. I pushed the thoughts of the blithering drunken fool from the forefront of my mind. I hadn't touched a drop of alcohol last night; I'd made a conscious effort to stay away from beer because part of me thought I'd be the one carrying him up the stairs and tucking him into bed. Pain teased his eyes last night, I longed to soothe him, and as I looked across the room at Avaya and Nance, they were grinning like Cheshire cats. We had spent the afternoon watching Fifty Shades of Grey and another I'd never heard of before now. Av was humming *'I Put A Spell On You'* and I smiled at her softly, tilting my head towards the piano.

"Make me a happy girl and sing Av." I grinned at her as I placed my glasses back up my nose. She grinned and placed herself behind it, colour flooded her usual level skin-toned cheeks and I listened to the piano playing. Her voice was absolutely beautiful. The tones of it were perfect and she made my skin prickle with goosebumps. Nance winked towards the door where the boys were standing. Jay looked like a proud big brother and Haz looked like he was about to combust. Juve… my heart stopped. His eyes were looking at me but through me, still filled with pain. I gulped and tried to focus on Avaya. She was laughing as she realised she had an audience and stopped playing.

"Guys!" she exclaimed. "Please don't just stand around staring at me." I smirked and watched Haz sit next to her. He leant into her, and I rolled my eyes. I knew him. He'd be whispering dirty things in her ear. I laughed as I wandered away from their intimate embrace at the piano and into the kitchen. I fought the urge to look for Juve. I poured myself a glass of orange juice and listened to the piano again. She was singing softly to a familiar lighter tune, and I hummed it to myself. It was a Nora Jones song.

She began to sing along with the words, and I smiled as I listened to her. Her voice was absolutely out of this world, the low husk and sweet tone made the skin on my arms prickle in the best way. Fingers traced my arm before they trailed my palm. Juve's smell clouded my senses, and I caught my breath. Every inch of my skin felt like fire and it wasn't because of my best friend's voice.

"She's got a wonderful voice, hey?" He twisted me to him, and I flushed.

"Juve," I warned him as he began to sway from side to side, and I couldn't help but laugh as I rolled my eyes and followed him, swaying softly. "She has a wonderful voice," I added as he smiled back at me. His eyes were playful and endearing.

"You joining them tonight?" he quizzed me.

"Yeah, are you coming?" He shrugged.

"If it's all right with you?" I frowned at him as my mouth twisted into a smile.

"Ooo, I'm not sure about that…" He chuckled and spun me around in his arms. I pushed against this chest softly and shook my head. "Of course it's fine with me." My little glass like heart was cracking its coating of ice the more he gazed at me. I was melting.

"Will you drive with me?" I could feel his breath against my mouth as he asked yet more questions. My eyes closed involuntarily, and I swallowed hard.

"That's pushing it a little." His sideways grin made me want to press my mouth against his. I fought with myself internally.

"What's the worst that could happen, baby?" His lips were lingering against the corner of my mouth and as I gripped his T-shirt between my hands, I felt how hard his pecks were.

"I could end up in the back." I spoke innocently as my eyes fluttered closed again, his hands pressing me against him. I hadn't got a clue why I'd decided to bring up our rendezvous in the back of his car. Part of me wanted to draw on the memory of his mouth between my legs, his hands around my waist, and his mouth moaning my name. I cleared my throat as I tried not to combust in his arms.

"I don't see that being a problem." He planted the world's softest kiss against my cheek, and I shivered. I physically shook. "I'll see you later." His lips left my face as heat roared within me. His hand snook around the back of his neck as he placed space between us. He looked all boyish and cute when he did that. His eyes were ripped from mine when Nance appeared in the kitchen. She stumbled through the door and hesitated a little.

"Oh, hey, Juve!" She smiled widely at him and then her eyes fell on mine. He raised his hand towards her so awkwardly it hurt me. I fought my laughter and bit down on my lip to try and contain it. He chuckled as though he knew my thoughts. "Will you come to town with me, please? My mum needs some errands running but she's hung up in meetings." She was asking me. I had no reason to say no. The only reason I'd say no was standing in front of me. I frowned and nodded.

"Yeah. Sure." She nodded and smiled at me.

"Thank you!" She skipped from the room and laughter flooded Alfie's home. I smiled awkwardly at Juve and watched him wink at me. That fucking wink would be the death of me. I shook my head and wandered off to try and at least distract myself.

The Highway Man was another of our favourite spots to eat. We came here often. I had managed to sneak a ride with Jay, much to Nance's dismay. Nance fancied the pants off my brother, and it was apparent. I was glad she was his distraction. Hopefully, he wouldn't have twigged onto my shift in mood. I was as wound up as a spinning top, ready to fucking pounce on Juve, and frustrated that he made me feel something again. Nobody had ever managed to tip me over the edge quite like him. I cleared my throat as I pulled myself from my memory and closed my legs together. Heat already pooled in-between them. I ran my hands over the satin cream fabric against my legs and I shivered. I tucked myself further in and noticed Juve next to me. I groaned outwardly. This wouldn't make my evening any better. I frowned at him and watched his shoulders rise and fall. It was like he understood how fucking difficult it was to be around him. My eyes trailed him, his dark shirt undone a little and buttons against his chest that were slightly taught. He was a sight to behold. His tattoos were visible because his long sleeves were rolled back. I placed my lip between my teeth as I stifled the moan from deep within. He'd clearly set a spark off; I was partially glad that he'd managed to make me feel something again. I was genuinely beginning to think I wasn't attracted to anything anymore. I was wrong. I was. But it was him. I flushed as he reached for the glass of water on the table, the muscles in his forearm flexed and I was sure I squeaked. Av laughed and kicked me from underneath the table. I glared across at her and she winked. She must have known.

"When you due back up North then, Bud?" Jay was quizzing Juve and he tensed a little beside me.

"Not sure, Dawson said it would be good for me to get away for a while," he admitted, and Haz laughed.

"Why would Dawson tell you that? Does he know what your baby brother does for a living?" he joked, and my heart grew sad. I had no idea who Dawson was, but he clearly thought a lot of him. "Also, isn't Dawson going back out on tour with you?" I caught my gasp as it left my mouth, and I crept my hand in his. He ran his thumb over the back of my hand. Hearing that sodding word again brought up some not so nice memories of him being deployed. The thought of him going back out there made me feel physically sick. I had spent years training myself not to dwell on him, but he was sitting next to me. I'd felt his heart pounding against my own as we fucked in the back of his car. He was a real person again.

"No, he's my shrink." The laughter subsided as Juve spoke. Nance looked at him in shock and I squeezed him softly. I wanted to offer him support to be there for him. "I'm not even sure if I'll be allowed back out there," he croaked as he squeezed my fingers now. I smiled to myself and stopped myself from placing my head against his arm—and I mean really fight with myself.

"Maybe you should book in to see him, Haz?" I raised my brow at him. "Sure you could have some of your trauma dealt with." He scoffed at my sarcasm. This was my way of helping Juve divert the attention from off him. His expression changed and he smirked at me.

"We're all experts in trauma, hey?" Haz glared at me, and I bobbed my tongue at him. Avaya laughed along with Jay and the rest of our friends around the table.

"Thanks," Juve muttered towards me and then released my hand.

"No worries." I spoke softly back towards him. He nodded and cleared his throat before he reached for his water and glanced down at the menu.

CHAPTER TEN
ALL IN YOUR HEAD

CHLO

I plonked myself down next to Haz and watched him smile at me. My attention span had grown thin recently. I had a job to protect Av and keep an eye on her when they couldn't. I had completely failed because of Juve being around more often. The very sight of him hurt and brought back a ferocious fire in my gut.

"You found anything else out for me?" Haz asked as he continued to weigh out the white powder on his desk. I had, and it was almost by accident. Rava had grown sloppy in his own affairs and was keeping a little secret which was the complete opposite to what was happening between Avaya and Haz.

"Other than that dark-haired bird leaving his house, no," I assured him and placed my head back on his pillow. I had been on the lookout to try and find his weakness. I'd witnessed first-hand just how deeply Haz and Av's connection went, so I snooped on Rava for my best friend and I would put myself in a ridiculous position if I got caught. It was worth it.

"I should go and see Bandoni really, shouldn't I?" I sighed as I watched him squirm and nod.

"If you wanna keep your cover then yeah, I suppose you should." I sighed aloud and watched him sit up straight as he zipped the clear bag. His blue eyes were crystal clear around the edges for the first time in the longest time. I couldn't even remember him ever being completely drug-free. He was healthy again, and it was now I realised I was probably smiling a little too much.

"I've missed this, Haz," I admitted. He chuckled and shrugged.

"I haven't missed the nightmares." He laughed out his admission.

"Maybe you should call Dawson?" I teased as I drew on our little tiff at the Highway Man. I watched him roll his eyes.

"Oh yeah, and admit my heinous crimes?" I frowned at him. "Like beating Mr Smith to a pulp." I threw the pillow towards him and watched as he caught it. "Somehow, I think that would land me in jail for the rest of my life."

"Why did you have to use him as an example, you fucking idiot?" I screeched at him and watched him shake his head.

"Sorry, that was the worst one." I rolled my eyes as I pushed the memory of my sperm donor being tortured from my mind. "Tell Dawson that I'm terrified of something happening to the love of my life?" He raised his brow, and I threw my hands in the air in surrender.

"Okay, okay," I repeated. "Not a great idea." He nodded.

"I'm actually jealous that Juve can talk to somebody about it." He half-laughed as my gut twisted.

"Yeah, me too," I added. It was true. I'd been so terribly jealous of the fact that he could talk to somebody about his struggles—all whilst I kept my demons locked up in a little box, buried under a mound of other emotional trauma.

"At least his killings have been legal and not personal."
I rolled my eyes as I hauled myself up from his bed. His
eyes lingered at the necklace around my neck, and I
touched it. "Haven't seen that in a long time." He tilted his
head towards it, and I nodded. The precious necklace that
was resting against my neck had been my Aunt Lynne's.
Having Juve around had transported me back in time, and
I had felt more nostalgic than ever. I craved for my past
for the first time in forever. I felt my eyes leak salty
droplets of water and let them fall.

"I can't breathe when Juve's around, Haz." I opened
my eyes and watched him walk towards me.

"Hey, Co…" His tone was soft and mellow, and I felt
him kneel between my legs. "It's all right." I shook my
head as my feelings were on the edge of bursting.

"He's back but not properly, and it's thrown me," I
admitted. He ran his hands over my legs and shook his
head. "He's got a fucking girlfriend." I scoffed and
watched him frown.

"He hates her." His expression was confused. "Why
does it matter anyway? I thought there was no going back
for you two?" I wanted to roll my eyes at him. I hadn't
told a single soul that we'd ended up back in the exact
same position that left me heartbroken in the first place.

"Jesus, Haz, sometimes you're so emotionally detached
it's unbelievable."

"He still wants you, Chlo." I shook my head and
pushed his head as I stood to my feet in an attempt to pull
myself together. "He might be my brother, but I know the
look he gives you. I've seen it time and time again." I
frowned at him. He wasn't making me feel any better. He
was sighing. "What will make you feel better?" he asked
me. I shook my head as I glanced around his dark
bedroom.

"I dunno." He placed his arm in mine and pulled me
down the stairs with him. I frowned up at him and
watched him take me into the main living room and

towards the piano.

"Sit there." He tilted his head towards the seat, and I crossed my arms. He hadn't played the piano in years. He'd shut off from music, dance and singing when he lost Holly, and since Avaya had fallen into his life, he'd suddenly found his passion for it again. I huffed and placed myself down on the stool. He joined me and began to play the chords of a familiar song. It had been a favourite of mine at the worst point in my life, but it had made me feel so much better. His fingers flowed over the keys and my heart instantly dropped. I was transported back in time as my best mate sang the all too familiar sad song. I could feel the tears streaming down my cheeks as I listened to his lovely voice echo through the room. It portrayed exactly how I felt. I was jealous of everything and everyone who was near him or got to touch him. I placed my head against his arm, closed my eyes and just listened to him play and sing. This would fix me for a little bit. This is why he was my very best friend.

JUVE

Nightmares were regular and more frequent since coming back to Shropshire from my visit to Devon. Part of me wished I'd have ended my relationship with Hazel the second I got back home, but I didn't. Sweat dripped down my chest and I glanced in the mirror at my appearance. I looked fucked. I glanced down at my phone and began to type out a message.

Juve: Think I need to talk to you.

I hit send and waited for a reply from my shrink, Dawson. I tried to breathe deeply and pull on every bit of advice he'd ever given me. My phone buzzed.

Doc: How bad are you?

Juve: Sweating in my bathroom bad.

Doc: I'm free for an hour at twelve, get to the office.

For some reason, I felt slightly better now I'd got that off my chest. I patted the sweat from my forehead with my towel and scrambled to get ready, pulling my hoodie over my head and placing a pair of boots on my feet before I grabbed my car keys. I jogged down the stairs and Aimee was standing in the hallway with my dad, they both looked towards me.

"Goin' to see Dawson," I called towards them before I left the house. I knew my little sister well and I had known that she had been worried since I had returned from Afghan this time around. I stepped on the acceleration pedal and drove as quickly as I could to Dawson's office before I broke down.

His office was a fancy looking place, in a nice part of town. He'd been a good friend of mine for many, many years–he too had served one tour back in our early twenties, but he retired and sought after his current career path. The army used his services regularly, but this wouldn't be down on my record. He was doing this as my friend. I glanced at the pretty dark blonde poised behind the desk and smiled. She grinned at me.

"What are you doing here, Mister?" She raised her eyebrow at me, and I smiled falsely at her. Jenna had been the receptionist here for years, I always assumed they had a thing going on, but he'd never admit it. Somehow, we both had a thing for blondes that were younger than us. I scoffed at my internal thoughts.

"Need Dawson's services again, don't I?" I watched her eyes roll before I knocked against the door a couple of times before I pushed it open. He was sitting with his leg across his lap, facing the window.

"Come as you like, Juve." He sounded exhausted and I hovered by the door.

"Thought you were only free from twelve?" He rubbed his temples and shook his head.

"What can I help you with?" His eyes looked sad, and I sat down opposite him. He looked like the one who needed the counselling.

"You told me to go and build bridges, right?" I spoke and watched his eyes widen.

"Right." He ran his hand over his chin and sighed. "Juve–" He called my name, and I shook my head.

"Bad nightmares," I cut him off and took a large breath because I knew what he was going to say next, he would ask me to go into detail. "Sorta like flashbacks but not because they involve Chlo…" My voice trailed off.

"Is Chlo in the field with you?" His question was not one I was expecting. I nodded and shook my head all at once.

"Yeah, like right next to me, when I'm shooting people and she doesn't flinch but then she just bolts and I can't get to her quick enough." I swallowed the lump and pushed away tears as I looked back towards Dawson. He had been there when I had first been deployed; it was where our friendship blossomed. He had seen first-hand how deeply I adored Chlo, even as a kid, how her legging it back down South with my brother had fucked me up. I appreciated everything Dawson had ever done for me both in and out of the field. I placed my head in my hands and shook it.

"So, similar situation to when we lost Green?" He had also been there on the second tour when we lost one of our best friends to an IED. I shuddered as sweat dripped from my forehead.

***

It was hot. Not muggy but baking hot. The air scorched my windpipe as I took a breath inward. I yawned as I pushed Green's shoulder. He was laughing with Dawson over something trivial, about one of the girls in the squad putting out for him. I rolled my eyes as I swapped the bullets around in the gun in my hand.

"Lilly said you've got a good aim," Green teased me as he snatched the gun from my hands. His hazel eyes matched the colour of his hair. His bicep flexed as he shot towards a glass bottle.

"Lilly wouldn't know how good my aim was." Dawson began to laugh as he sucked in his breath. "I don't fuck everything that moves." I knew my words were a little harsh, but he needed to hear it. That he was acting like a bellend.

"Oh, lighten up." Dawson nudged me softly, his brown eyes glistened as he winked at me.

"I'm light," I snapped as he rolled his eyes. "Can we not scrap like little boys?" I groaned and watched as Dawson and Green lay back on the camps bedding—they were almost cuddling. I smiled to myself as I watched them take the piss out of each other. They were kissing each other on the cheek. "Hey, people will start to talk about you lot if you carry on." I laughed as I spoke. Green winked at me and then placed his hand behind his head.

"I don't mind, every hole's a goal." Green spoke with confidence, and we all laughed out loud.

186

***

I was pulled from the flashback of Green by Dawson's voice. "You've been around her a lot lately though, haven't you?" I nodded because I knew he was talking about Chlo.

"Do you remember how gutted I was on that first tour?" I asked in a low voice. He didn't respond. "I thought that by taking your advice to build the bridge it would bury that part of my life." I shrugged. His eyes were sad as he watched me. "I should have known that me and her can't just be friends." I shook my head. "You told me to build bridges," I reminded him.

"Yes, Juve, build bridges," he repeated his advice. "Not fuck her into next week." He stood to his feet and cracked his neck from side to side.

"Not very professional language." I tried to make light of our conversation, but he just shot me a cold look.

"How the fuck am I supposed to get you back out in the field if being near her has brought all of this back up for you?" His question was a valid one. "I just still can't believe she plays on your mind this much after six years." He raised his brow at me, and I folded my arms. There was now silence between us two old friends.

"Hazel keeps talking about kids," I blurted it out. I watched his mouth drop open. "I don't want them, and I think that's why I'm having nightmares."

"Shit, Juve." I frowned, and I hated myself for saying it. It was the truth though, and if I couldn't tell him, I couldn't tell anybody. He simply nodded and reached to scribble in his book as he sat back down. He was quiet as he wrote his notes down.

"I'm having all sorts of fucked up nightmares. Nightmares about being out in Afghan, having her ripped from me, Green, my fucking kids." I placed my head in my hands and groaned aloud. Still silence from him. I looked back up and he was just paused, looking down at his book.

"Juve, I don't think you can go back out to Afghan in

187

the state you're in." I opened my mouth to defy him, to push his opinion, but I couldn't. "As much as I know how much you probably wanna go back to escape but, dude, I think it'll fucking kill you." He placed the pen down on the table and frowned at me. "You need some time out. I think we might need to look at medical discharge."

"No!" My voice boomed around the room, and I watched him jump. "For fuck's sake, please don't say anything to them yet." I felt myself shaking, trying desperately to justify why I would even want to go back to a place where all I did was kill people. I bunched my hands into fists. "Just give me a couple of months, sign me out sick. I'll sort it out." I stood to my feet and watched as he mimicked my actions and reached for me.

"Juve…" His voice was low, and I shook my head.

"For me, Dawson, please?" He just nodded slowly and then released my arm. I made my way from his office; this was the first time I had left there feeling worse than when I'd gone in. I wanted to scream. Instead, I ran. Fucking medical discharge, my arse.

The breath from my lungs made the air around it warm which was causing smoke. I placed my phone between my fingers and placed my back against the wet grass of the Shropshire hills. It was pouring down with rain, but it didn't matter to me. I was dithering but consumed with confusion and regret.

Juve: Come up to Mum's for a bit?

I begged in the form of a text. I lay in the freezing rain.

Chlo: I've told you before about drinking in the day, it's bad for you. X

Juve: Not drunk, baby, just desperate to see you. xx

Chlo: Can I eye-roll through a text?

Juve: Come up, Chlo.

There was silence again for a while before it buzzed again.

Chlo: There's a lot going on down here at the minute, Juve, take care of yourself. x

My heart dropped to my stomach again as I fought with the feeling of rejection. She had made it clear time and time again that me and her weren't supposed to be.

Juve: what type of stuff is going on? x

I couldn't stop myself from asking her more questions. My phone rang. It was her.

"You don't give up, do you?" She didn't sound mad at all. In fact, she seemed more amused than anything else.

"Not one to let it drop," I confirmed to her. Her small giggles flooded my ears and my chest fluttered.

"It would be really great to get away, but I can't leave Av." Her breath caught in her throat. "Your brother and my brother are gonna end up getting her or themselves in trouble." I was so glad she was still able to talk so openly. "I shouldn't even be telling you about this." I could hear the strain in her voice. Birds tweeted from around me. "Juve, are you outside!?" She gasped; her voice raised an octave. I half laughed.

"Maybe…" I could tell from her silence she was trying not to laugh.

"You'll catch a cold," she warned as my mouth twisted into a smirk.

"Do you care if I catch a cold?" I was winding her up all again.

"Why are you outside in the rain, alone?" she questioned me. "And if you're not drunk, why are you texting me? What's happened?" I'd always loved the way she spoke her mind. I smiled as I breathed outwards again.

"I miss you," were the only words I let leave my mouth.

"I'm eye-rolling, Mr Vens." I laughed and glanced at the grey skies. They were releasing their own tears.

"I've had bad dreams lately, that's all, mainly about being back out there." I admitted that part. I wouldn't tell her that they were about her or anything else. "Lost a man on the last one, he was a good bloke." I paused. "You would have really liked him." I thought about Green again. His cheeky grin stained my mind. She was silent.

"I wish I could come up, Juve, but I can't," she breathed, her tone full of guilt. I just smiled to myself.

"Probably best anyway, hey?" I gulped down the lump that was growing in my throat and closed my eyes. My mouth began to chatter from the cold.

"Go back home, Juve, please." She was begging.

"See you later, beautiful. Look after yourself," I whispered and placed the phone down. I threw it next to me and let the tears from my eyes mix with the rain that was falling onto my face. I just needed a minute.

JANUARY

I had joined some of our old friends for a meal, they had all been called for deployment in the next six months. Dawson had signed me out, and I wasn't sure if I was grateful or pissed that he'd done this for me. Hazel was smiling with Mark's wife, Whitney. I liked Whitney and I valued her opinion. She wasn't a huge fan of Hazel, but she tolerated her for me. Mark sipped on his pint glass and looked at me.

"How'd you pull her?" He tilted his head towards Hazel, and I took a deep breath.

"I dunno." I frowned and then looked into the coke glass that was bubbling. Her blue eyes glanced at me, and I nodded at her. She looked away almost instantly and I felt pain twist in the pit of my stomach.

"You never seem very touchy-feely with her." He spoke again, and I frowned. I looked at Mark again, his slightly ginger beard caught the light around the quaint little country restaurant, and I leaned into him.

"You don't touch your wife much either," I teased him and heard him burst with laughter.

"I didn't scream another girl's name in a war zone." I hissed at his words and pushed him away from me. "How hot is the other one?" I shook my head and placed my head in my hand.

"Unreal you are, mate." He just laughed and wiggled his brows at me.

"You love it."

CHAPTER ELEVEN
PASSING US BY

CHLO

No amount of time away from him made it easier. He'd been back for a while last year and he'd really given it a go. He'd reached out to me, and I'd shot him down. I was kicking myself. I was almost convinced I was going to be lonely for the rest of my life. I rolled my eyes as I glanced down at my phone. Avaya and Haz had ran away too, and I didn't blame them at all after the rumour mill that was circulated. I wouldn't be at all surprised if neither of them returned back to the UK again. I ran my hands over the back of my neck and sighed aloud. How much longer could I be alone and happy? I had my brother and Alfie with me, but somehow, that wasn't enough. I placed my phone to my ear as I dialled Carol's number–it rang a few times. I wanted to hear her wise words of comfort. She had been the closest thing to a mum I'd ever had.

"Hello, sweetheart!" She was so pleased when she answered the call.

"Hey, Carol, just checking in, making sure all is okay

with you?" I asked with genuine interest. I wanted to hear about her shopping trips with her girlfriends, her date nights with Henry, what Aimee was getting up to, and how Warren was losing the will to live with his dad. I wanted to know it all and she didn't disappoint.

"We are fine. Do you remember Larissa?" She opened her mouth and what followed was wonderful, she had taken me through a scandal in her friendship group that had rocked the boat, she had divulged the fact that Juve was still with her—which had shocked me. I had assumed he was back on tour. I hadn't heard from him in a long time. Not a text, a like on an Instagram post, nothing. Radio silence. I gulped.

"So, he's still home?" I asked.

"Oh, sweetheart, I thought you knew?" I shook my head and frowned deeply.

"Haz and Avaya are travelling." I changed the subject, as difficult as that was, and she again took me on a journey of when she travelled last year with Henry for work. It sounded just blissful. I smiled at my phone, and I was warm again.

JUVE

Hazel's stomach was growing day by day. I should have been overjoyed, but truth be told, I was fucking gutted. I placed my hand on her stomach and then my ear. I smiled and kissed it. She giggled and I sat up in our bed. She brushed her dark hair from her face and fluttered her lashes my way. I felt like a complete dickhead. I'd slept next to her every night since I'd been back living with Mum and Dad and even slept *with* her, but the whole time I pictured *Chlo's* face. I swore that I'd buried my feelings for the girl years ago. I wasn't expecting that zing to still be there. I wasn't expecting to feel so jealous when somebody else touched her. I climbed out of our bed and stretched upwards before I placed a loose T-shirt over my head. Hazel's eyes danced as she fucked me with her eyes.

"Dawson signed you back to being fit yet?" I frowned and shrugged.

"Not yet, no." I flinched at the memory of my hands around her neck one morning when I'd woken up. That hadn't left me yet, and this was apparently something new. "I'm gonna have to speak to him about what happened last week." Her eyes dropped from mine, and she nodded when she touched her neck.

"Your bad dream?" I bit down on my bottom lip at the naive words from her mouth. I nodded instead of correcting her. She looked beautiful sitting in our bed with a large stomach, pitch-black, long, sleek, dark hair cascading down her chest, and gleaming blue eyes, and yet, I hardly had any emotion at all for her. Dawson had reminded me how fucked it was that I wanted to put myself in the position of battling a war rather than facing my own demons at home.

Mum was washing up plates in the sink, the usual sound of the Beatles played throughout the large open plan kitchen as I grabbed a tea towel and began to dry up everything she was washing. The sun was up, and the light worktop was reflecting it into my face from the skylight above us. Her eyes ran over me. She could tell I was stressed.

"You should really go and speak to Dr Dawson if you're having nightmares again, son." Mum's tone was soft and gentle, but she didn't look at me as she spoke. I shook my head.

"I'm not having nightmares." I continued to wipe the plates. "Not unless you can have them when you're awake?" I forced a smile and watched her smile too before she nudged my arm.

"I had a call from the Conway's this morning." She glanced towards the kitchen door where Hazel was standing, watching us. She knew that this would completely confuse Hazel and she knew that any mention of their names would throw me into turmoil.

"Which Conway?" I whispered softly and I watched her grin.

"Miss." My heart thudded. Chlo didn't call my mum. *Not unless…*

"Are they all right?" I placed the plate down on the side and I watched her nod slowly.

"She was just checking in. Said Haz and his new girlfriend had gone away for a while." I raised my brow. I instantly knew it was a bad sign. She placed her hand on my shoulder. "I think you may want to check in on them, son." Her eyes searched mine. "You know how closed she can be." I nodded at my mum and looked back at a confused Hazel hovering by the door. Her face looked pained as she moved a little. Her large belly was unnatural on her slender frame.

"You're leaving again, aren't you?" She looked at my mum who was smiling. She loved that I was jumping for Chlo and Jay. I nodded.

"Yeah. Not sure when I'll be back." I grabbed my keys and climbed in my car. I wondered what the fuck had happened for her to call my mum. What shit had they really got into now? I huffed and slipped behind the wheel of my car. I recalled a conversation from sometime last year when I'd had a minor breakdown and text her again. I swallowed as I drew on the memory of her saying things were a bit of a mess down there.

Alfie's house was pretty quiet. I'd gotten from the Shropshire Hills to Devon in record timing. Just over two hours. I glanced at Jay sitting with his foot resting on his knee. He looked like he'd aged more in the last month than I had. He was sipping a coffee. The sofa he was sat on was in the kitchen. This sofa had the best views from the bifold doors. It was just the sea. Huge waves. Stormy skies.

"Jay?" I called him and watched as his dark head of hair spun around at my voice. "What's happened?" He shook his head and closed his eyes as he breathed a sigh.

"You really ready?" My gut twisted.

"They're alive, aren't they?" Fear twirled in my stomach, and he nodded.

"Just about." My eyes widened as I placed myself next to him. He placed his black coffee down on the table in front of us. "They are on the run, Juve." I focused on the words leaving his mouth, but they didn't make much sense.

"How much trouble are they in?" He shrugged softly.

"Rava is hurt, I couldn't bring myself to finish the job." I flinched away from the words that left his mouth. "Chlo is being questioned." I shook my head slowly.

"What? Why?" I barked at him as he placed his hand on my shoulder.

"Because there was so much noise the neighbours were called." His frown became deeper. "It comes with the territory of being involved in crime. You get good at lying." I pushed his shoulder as I stood to my feet. Anger bubbled through me. They spoke so fluently about the life of crime, and it made me sick.

"She's never asked to be in that life though, has she,

Jay?" His brow furrowed as he stood to his feet too. His hand pushed my shoulder.

"Don't start me on the debate on what is best for *my* sister." I rolled my eyes as the dangling of keys made us stop in our tracks. Chlo was standing, staring at the both of us.

"Will you both just stop?" She looked exhausted. Pity filled my stomach and another emotion. It had been a year since I'd last seen her. A whole year that I'd managed to get myself into yet more trouble without her. "I'm going to bed." She turned around and stuck her finger up towards us. "Be nice to know what I was covering for though, Jay!" she snapped as she walked away from us both. *Did anything phase this woman?*

CHLO

I placed myself on my bed and sighed loudly. I thought about getting my phone out to text Haz to see what the fuck was going on and why I'd just been brutally laid into by the police. I frowned as my bedroom door cracked open. I was too tired for an argument with my brother. I'd already had this argument with him previously. From what I had taken from our earlier conversation, Av had fucked up, and now we were just holding the fort. They were travelling. I rolled my eyes at the lame excuse. I knew that this is how it had to be. The less I know the better. I wouldn't be able to trip myself up in a web of lies this way. I would be telling them all I knew. I closed my eyes again and turned over in my bed. He'd leave me alone if I ignored him for long enough. The bed dipped, the duvet went with it, and I frowned. It wasn't my brother's expensive aftershave that clouded my nose. His stubble tickled my shoulder and his hand wrapped itself around my waist. My heart boomed and my stomach twisted as butterflies released.

"You're not great with boundaries, are you?" I teased him in a whisper and heard him chuckle lightly as he squeezed me softly. It was low. He placed his lips against my shoulder. My chest twisted as I closed my eyes. As much as I hated to admit it, I fucking loved having him touch me.

"If you want me to leave, baby, then tell me to go and I'll go," he whispered against the skin on my shoulder, and I rolled my eyes internally at his words. I stayed quiet for a long time. Quiet and still. He was draped around me like the blanket that was resting against our skin. I sighed and turned to face him before I frowned.

"Why are you here?" I snapped his way. I was pissed with him for coming and even more pissed with his mum for letting him know that I'd called and asked for him. And yet, I was sort of overjoyed that he'd decided to drive for two hours or more to come and cuddle me like nothing had changed between us at all. My eyes wandered over his so that I could gage his reaction.

"You called my mum." He raised his eyebrow and my heart thudded. It was like a bang in my chest, an explosion of TNT. I took a breath.

"I was just calling to make sure you were all right." I scoffed out my words as I lied. No matter how much I lied to myself, I wanted this to be the outcome.

"Why were you checking up on me?" I stumbled through my own thoughts. I wasn't sure why I'd called. I never called for him, but today, I did. It could have been the fact that I thought I was going to get locked up for covering a fucking attempted murder. I shook my head and placed my hand in his face as I pushed him away from me softly. He pulled me closer towards him instantly and there was no room between us again. "Why, Chlo?" I shrugged and frowned all at the same time. The spark between us was back with a vengeance. I stared at him, and time stood still.

"Why don't you ever call to check on me?" This was probably too close in proximity to me. I held my hands against his chest, his heart beating steadily against my hands, his facial expression twisted.

"I check up on you often," he muttered.

"I don't believe you." His hands were resting against my back. He moved his one hand slowly and traced it down the exposed skin on my back, and I fought a moan. I frowned deeply and sat up quickly to try and escape him. I was in a T-shirt that had ridden up. I flushed. "Also, this is highly inappropriate." I stumbled on my words and gestured between us at the tiny gap. He rolled his deep pools of blue. "Juve!" I watched him sit up and frown as he sat with his head against my headboard.

"I've seen you in less than this." I slapped his chest and watched his lips curl into a smile. He reached for me, and I placed my hand in the air.

"Absolutely not." I stopped him and he groaned.

"You're no fun." I gasped and held my chest as he spoke the words. His head tilted back as he laughed. I smiled watching him. There were little wrinkles by his eyes that weren't there before. I ran my fingers over them and watched him frown. I smirked and shook my head.

"You are an old man now." He gasped now and I cackled as I stood on the bed to climb over him. He pulled me down on his lap and I stopped breathing. My heart fluttered and my stomach clenched with desire. I shook my head and watched his eyes warm. There was silence between us for a while. A long while. He just gazed at me and held me still.

"I'm gonna be a dad, Chlo." The words left his mouth in slow motion. My little heart shattered a little more. Shock flooded me. I wasn't entirely sure how I was supposed to feel, how he was expecting me to react. A year was all it had taken for him to get his shit together. For him to really move on.

"Oh."

Breathe.

My legs were like jelly and my chest constricted the longer I thought about the confession that had just left him. "Wow," I whispered. I was numb.

"I wanted to be the one to tell you." I just nodded, still sat on his lap where he'd placed me only minutes before, and I patted his shoulder. What I really wanted to do was to slap him in the face. I wanted to scream at him, but I had absolutely no right. I hadn't stopped him from ever finding love with somebody else, of course he was allowed to move on. He had every right to.

"Congratulations." I forced the word from my mouth. I didn't mean it, not even a little bit. A mixture of jealous rage and overwhelming sadness lingered in my chest. I needed my best friend. I needed Haz now more than I ever had. My brain was an absolute piece of mush. "Well done, old man." I forced my smile, pushed myself up off his lap and gathered up my laundry from the floor. The information he'd given me thirty seconds prior hadn't quite sunk in yet. Part of me was terrified that when they did that would be it. I would be teleported back in time to when I was alone and seventeen. Miserable and seventeen. Guilt consumed me as I left the room and closed my bedroom door behind where I was standing. Little droplets of salty water escaped my eyes.

CHAPTER TWELVE
ENOUGH

CHLO

I had sort of grown to appreciate Avaya's friends whilst they were in hiding, running around different countries, away from the Mafia. Soph had really been struggling with something lately and neither myself nor Nance could put our fingers on what was going on, until she ended up in a hospital bed, having her stomach pumped, because of her decision to get rid of her baby. The same choice I'd made years ago. The decision I had tried to bury. I watched as my brother weighed out bags of coke alone at his desk and scrunched my face up. It had been a while since I had craved the white stuff, but recent events had me feeling a certain way. He looked up to where I was perched in his doorway, and I crossed my arms. He looked exhausted and my chest constricted.

"You're missing him?" It was a question I already knew the answer to, but both the Vens boys I missed. I knew that Jay was talking about Haz. I sighed.

"I wasn't counting on him being gone for this long." He paused and opened yet another bag before he reset the scales. "Dunno how much longer I can keep this lot up." He gestured towards the drugs on the desk. "Bandoni is sniffing around, and he fucking knows what I did, Chlo." I closed my eyes and took a breath. I refused to believe that. "He wasn't born yesterday," he added. I shook my head and placed my hand on his shoulder.

"C'mon, move." I tilted my head and pushed him off his chair. "I'll help." He moved and I placed powder on the scales. He had tried and failed to seriously injure Rava, and if Bandoni didn't know what had happened already, he was right, it wouldn't take long for him to find out. And when he did find out... I cringed and sealed the small plastic zip-locked bag. "He won't find out what you did. Let's just concentrate on getting them back home." He leaned against his desk and ran his hands over his face, the stress had aged him beyond his years and there was nothing I could say or do to make any of this easier on him.

"They're on their way back, Chlo." He shrugged off his blazer and sighed. "Av knows about Soph." He shook his head and pushed against the desk. "I need to make some calls. Can you count the rest of that out?" I just nodded as I looked back at the white powder.

"Sure." He planted a kiss on top of my head and placed his phone in his hand before he left me alone with my old friend. The thought of what had happened to Soph made me feel physically sick. I shook my head and continued to weigh out the bags of white powder.

Nance was laying on my bed. I watched her frown as she looked at her phone. I had known that she was missing Avaya possibly as much as I was missing Haz. She had kept me pretty sane while they had been away. She had kept me busy; she had dragged me to a couple of her dance classes, she had been in fairly high spirits, and I had never once witnessed her cry. She was crying today. The corners of her eyes matched her dyed red hair. I reached to hold her hand in mine softly to comfort her. I was both sad and furious that Soph hadn't come to either of us—or even Avaya—to go through her options properly. Instead, she'd made a rash decision because she had been talked into it by her fucking nonce of a boyfriend, and now she was having her stomach pumped. I shook my head.

"Why didn't she say anything to me?" Her voice was weak as she asked the question out loud. She was kicking herself for her friend's selfish actions, and I shrugged.

"Maybe she was embarrassed?" I suggested innocently. She looked my way, a bleak, sad look etched in her facial expression, and I reached to touch her hand. "Look, sometimes shitty things happen to good people, stop kicking yourself, Nancy." I used her full name so that she knew I was being serious. "It was her choice." I gulped. "Nobody else's." Her usual smiling face was hard and her mouth in a straight line. She sighed. I was speaking from experience, I had been that selfish friend once, only I hadn't really intended to top myself; I had chosen to go on benders fuelled with alcohol and drugs to fill my void. I took a deep breath inward.

"I just wish Avaya was home." She sniffed as she placed her head against my shoulder. My chest ached as my own turmoil rose to the forefront of my mind.

"Me too," I breathed.

"Think she'll come back soon?" I shrugged and nodded all at once.

"Hope so." I swallowed the hard lump that was growing painfully large in my throat and closed my eyes. She needed her best friend almost as much as I needed mine.

It seemed like no matter what I did, Jay wouldn't relax. He was rarely home, and I was lost. Jamane had popped around again to pick up Nance. He was taking her to another dance class. I smiled widely at my stunning friend. He flashed his devilishly handsome smile my way.

"Are you coming to The Top Hat later or are you staying here?" He raised his brow at me, and I shrugged. I could have done with staying home, behaving a bit. It was something I wasn't very good at lately. I'd been partying. Hard.

"I've told Nance I'm gonna stay in. I've got some accounts to balance."

"For Alf?" I knew that this question was to avoid awkward conversation, but somehow, it made me laugh.

"Jay." I breathed his name and watched him smirk. He was leaning against the white door frame, his smaller toned arms flexing as he crossed them across his chest.

"Is he still running with Daryl?" I bit my lip at the use of Darky's real name. They had been friends growing up. I nodded.

"I suppose you could say that." Nance appeared behind him and pecked his cheek.

"Ready?" she asked him as she hooked her arm in his.

"Yes, let's go." I smiled at them both, she was stunning even in loose joggers.

"I'll be back in the early hours of the morning." She laughed as she spoke towards me. I nodded.

"Enjoy, babe." I winked at them both as they left.

I had balanced the books; I had even read books which was something I rarely did, and then I'd placed myself in the bath before ending up in bed. Fresh and clean, surrounded in light pink bed sheets and sparkled glitter scatter cushions. I was missing Avaya. The door thudded and I jumped out of my daydream. I instantly lowered the television sound and looked at my door. Juve's face appeared, lingering. His body was hidden behind my door. A floating head.

"Knock knock," he teased, and I frowned at him. The fury of his new unborn kid was still as fresh as when he told me.

"What are you doing down here again?" I bit at him. Sadness flooded me. "I haven't called your mum again." My scowl was evident on my face as I stared at him. "I promise." I watched his eyes examine me for a while. His expression was soft and warm and mine was cold and hostile. He entered my room.

"Dad has sent me down. Apparently, I'm not so strait-laced anymore." I could tell by the look on his handsome face that this had made him sad. I frowned as my gut twisted. "Thought I'd check in on you while I was here, but I'll go." His eyes lifted off the floor as he pushed a false smile my way and my entire being ached to comfort him.

"Hey, no." I swallowed as I reached for him, scrambling from my bed. "Come and watch a shit film with me?" He cocked his full brow at me, and I shook my head. "Your pick." I swallowed my own feelings of hatred towards him because all I cared about was finding out what his dad had sent him down for and why he wasn't strait-laced anymore. I watched him smile a little.

"Am I forgiven then?" I watched as he smiled at me and entered my room a little more.

"I wouldn't say forgiven, no, but I can forget about your child for a while." The lump that I had swallowed weeks ago came back and I twisted the remote in my fingers as he placed himself on my bed. It dipped and his aftershave flooded my proximity. He reached for the remote that was in my hand, and I gave it to him quickly. I wouldn't touch him, I couldn't, because every time I touched him it ended in disaster. I watched him smile, kick his shoes off and lay back on my bed. He flicked through the movies on the Netflix account before he landed on the film Up. My head jerked towards him.

"Absolutely no way." I scoffed as I tried to reach to

snatch the remote. He laughed and shook his head.

"Hey, you said my choice!" He held the remote higher in the air with his hand so that I'd have to stand to grab it, and then if he stood, we would be too close. I scoffed at him and rolled my eyes. Disney's Up made me cry. It had been my favourite film and he knew it. I pushed his large arm away from me and heard him laugh, a genuine booming laughter.

"You know it makes me all sad!" I was still protesting, and he smirked. My chest fluttered uncomfortably at the sight of the delicious shape of his mouth.

"I'm here if you need a cuddle." I couldn't help but laugh, and I rolled my eyes as soon as he pressed play.

"So why are you working for your dad?" I quizzed him on the more pressing matters at hand. He stayed quiet and then spoke after some time.

"Need some money." He cleared his throat softly and then rolled his eyes. "For the baby." My heart stopped again, and as the music for the film began, my eyes leaked. *That fucking baby.* I almost growled.

"Still can't believe you're gonna be a dad," I whispered as my heart was shattering inside the constraints of my chest.

"Neither can I." He breathed softly and I bit down on my lip. "Mum isn't impressed." I simply nodded. I couldn't talk about it any longer without wanting to scream and cry, so I didn't speak. Instead, I placed my hand in his and squeezed gently. His head turned towards me as he looked at our interlocking fingers.

"You know, at one point I really thought I was going to be with you forever," I mumbled towards him. He opened his mouth to speak but I pushed my hand against his mouth and shook my head. I didn't want to hear it— whatever it was. I closed my eyes and placed my head against his shoulder. His lips landed a light kiss on my head as he exhaled heavily.

FEBRUARY

I'd never been more overjoyed to lay eyes on either of them. Avaya looked older and really tired but well all at the same time. I wrapped my arms around her and kissed her cheek. I'd missed her. She ran her hand over my back, and I took a breath as I watched Haz enter the room too. The news of his brother's baby had hurt. Actually, it had almost nearly killed me again. Especially as he was born not long ago and was joining us all here really fucking soon. My gut twisted as I held Haz in my arms for a longer period of time than was necessary. He moved my hair from my neck and sighed.

"What's happened?" he questioned. There had been so much going on. Almost too much. "Oh, you know"–I paused–"trauma." I breathed outwards. "I think I may have a breakdown." I squeezed him. He held me at arm's length again and I realised I'd been hugging him for so long that Av and Jay had now disappeared.

"Has the Soph thing brought it all up for you?" His eyes looked sympathetic as I nodded.

"He told me himself about it but knowing he's going to bring him here..." He just nodded.

"Yeah, it's bringing up bad memories for me too, Chlo." I nodded and placed my head against his hard shoulder and hooked my arm in his. "Just pretend you hate him." I laughed a little and shook my head.

"I really wish I hated him, Haz, but I don't." He pushed me away from him slightly as we wandered towards the living room in Alfie's home.

"Missed you, Co." He offered me a sincere smile and I returned it. I had missed him too.

BE MINE BABY

CHAPTER THIRTEEN
HURT

I was sitting alone in Alfie's bar, wallowing in self-pity. I wasn't particularly bothered by the fact that I was alone this evening. It was fairly normal for me–or had been as of late. Alfie leant across the bar towards me and grinned, his classic signature grin that set the hearts of most women on fire, and yet, it stirred nothing from inside of me. I was utterly miserable and had been for months. He handed me another glass of wine.

"Thanks," I muttered and watched his eyes dance. The glimmer in them made me smile a little. It was late, and time was ticking along, evening had turned to night. I was lonely in a room full of people, and I craved a familiar touch. I wanted to feel something, anything other than complete emptiness. My eyes wandered over him. I was examining him. He was such a good-looking human being and I shifted in my seat.

"Your wallowing?" he accused me, and I simply nodded at his attempt to figure out what was going on with me. The numb feeling the alcohol had given me had made life easier. I giggled into my wine glass and glanced back up at him. His brows pulled together into a frown.

"Think you could help a girl out?" I spoke a little lower

than was probably necessary. My eyes were now fixed on his lips. I watched his Adam's apple rise and fall.

"How?" he asked. I didn't look up to meet his eyes. I just started to unbutton my shirt. "Chloe!" he scolded me and held my hand to stop me from going any lower.

"Oh, Alf, please?" I begged as I frowned at him deeply. His eyes were wide and confused. He shook his head slowly from side to side and his blonde hair swished. I was sure he was blushing. The bar had closed a while ago and staff were starting to leave. I sipped the wine again and watched him stand up a little straighter. One of the barmaids–Sandy–made her way closer towards us. Her eyes lit up when they landed on Alf. She was a young pretty thing with legs longer than a supermodel and wonderful dark hair. What I imagined Alfie's type to be. He smiled politely at her.

"I've locked everything up, are you both heading out the back?" She smiled at us both and I watched him nod.

"Yeah." He paused and looked back towards me, but this time, his eyes struggled to leave my chest. I held my glass and pointed it towards him. He frowned at me. "When she's finished, I'll be out. Thanks for tonight, Sandy." He was so polite in his tone that it almost made me sick. She looked towards me and frowned a little. She seemed pretty pissed that we were going to be here alone. I knew the look that she was giving me. She was jealous. I knew because I'd given that look myself.

"Sure, no problem." Her eyes left mine and she forced a smile Alfie's way. "I'll see you tomorrow." I stood up and watched her leave the Top Hat. I giggled as I stood with my head against the door. Alfie was frowning.

"What's so funny?" He was still at the side of the bar which served the drinks.

"She wants to fuck you." I giggled again as I examined his expression. His large arms were folded across his chest, and he was rolling his eyes. He looked so youthful.

"She's younger than you!" He scoffed and I frowned as

I wandered towards the bar. I climbed on it and sat with my legs dangling off the edge, facing him.

"And age was the issue for you, wasn't it?" I teased him about the time he said I was too young for him and watched his smirk twist.

"Yes, it's the age gap." I rolled my eyes and undid the buttons on my shirt again. His eyes stayed on my face. I grinned at him and sighed as I ran my hands over my tits, down my stomach and towards the top of my jeans. His eyes widened a little and I watched him swallow. He still didn't speak. I'd get the distraction I so desperately needed from him at some point tonight. I just wondered how long it would take him to give in. I had wondered for years how good he was in the bedroom, or against a wooden bar. I smirked to myself as I undid the buttons on my jeans and shimmied them down my legs. His eyes left mine and then trailed down my body. He was still holding his arms against his body as I slid my fingers into my knickers and a growl left his mouth.

"Fuck's sake, Chloe." He frowned and stepped closer towards me, ripping my hand from my knickers and landing his mouth on mine. I moaned as his tongue invaded my mouth. Hot, passionate, lustful kisses followed as I fumbled with his jeans. I didn't want the intimate kisses, the foreplay. I just needed the sex. He sprung free from the constraints of his boxers, and after a quick fumble with a condom, he was inside me. The pace was fast as he dived in and out of me. I threw my head backwards as I gripped his shoulders tightly. His pace didn't slow, he was relentless, and it was fucking thrilling. I released a moan as his pulses became harder and deeper. My back was now against the bar as he held my hips and thrust a couple of times in his own climax. It was quite a sight. *Quick and dirty.* I watched him flush as he pulled out of me, and I bit down on my bottom lip before I sat back up on the bar. Nothing about that was awkward. But this would be. Tiny beads of sweat dripped down the side of his face and I leaned against my forearms.

"Happy now?" He raised his brow as he pulled himself back into his boxers before he buttoned up his trousers. He was blushing and it was the cutest thing I'd ever seen. I chuckled and nodded while we caught our breath.

"Oh, very." He shook his head in disbelief almost and held his hand out for mine.

"Get dressed." He laughed as he pulled against my hand, his eyes made a slow assault over my exposed stomach and pussy. I rolled my eyes as I pulled him towards me. His eyes landed on my mouth.

"Not even a departing kiss?" I teased him and watched him hesitate.

"Are you taking the piss?" I laughed as I started to button up my shirt and watched as he handed me my jeans. I leant forwards and wrapped my legs around him again so I could get down from the high bar. He didn't push me away but held me around his waist with his hands on my arse and cleared his throat as he placed me on my feet. I leant down, shimming up my jeans before I placed my heels on, which made me a few inches taller again. I was now chest height. Alfie flushed again as he looked at me. "Fuck's sake, I can't believe we've just done that." He placed his hand over his face, and I chuckled. "Please don't tell your brother." I laughed louder now as I pulled on his hand.

"Oh, I won't tell a soul." I kissed his cheek and felt his hand against the hollow of my back.

"I'm sorry, Chlo." He flushed again. I shook my head. There was absolutely no reason why he should have been apologising to me. I had been the one to instigate the whole thing. I needed him. I craved feeling wanted.

"I'm sorry too, Alf." He just gave me a weak smile and nodded. "It won't happen again." I was sure I heard him sigh with relief as I took his hand in mine. He squeezed it a little and then pulled me to him before I got to the exit of the Top Hat. His lips landed on mine and he kissed me softly. I moved from him a little and stood staring at him.

"I knew I avoided you for good reason." His voice was low. "It was never your age, Chloe. It was who your brother is." I smiled and kissed him back. He ran his hand over my face.

"I knew it." He laughed a little and then pushed me away from him. My hand landed on the door, and we made our way out. I was slightly soberer than I had been before. But still just as empty.

JUVE

Ethan. Tiny baby Ethan. It suddenly seemed so very real that I was a dad. I couldn't really wrap my head around it all. It had happened a little faster than I thought it would. I'd missed his birth. I had taken Mum to visit her sister in Gloucester, and by the time I'd arrived, he had already made an appearance. He lay in my arms all tiny and wonderful. I smiled to myself as he stretched out and sighed.

"I'm sorry your mummy is a nut job." I placed my lips against his cheek and kissed it softly. I was fucked. Well and truly. Hazel had seemed to have lost the plot a little since she'd birthed him. Mum had agreed we could stay in the annexe for a little while. She hadn't gotten dressed in a week, but today, she did. I was by no means going to make this situation any worse for her, so I put on my brave face and smiled at her. She looked tired too, but her eyes smiled a little when she looked at us. She was sitting next to me, and she looked down at the tiny new-born human.

"My mum said he looks like you." I nodded at her softly spoken words and felt her place her head against my arm. I ran my spare hand over her hair and sighed.

"My mum said the same." I watched her place her false nail against his nose and watched him wriggle. "Wanna hold him?" I looked her way and watched her tense. Every part of her went rigid.

"No." She spoke, and I frowned. I couldn't get my head around why she didn't want to hold her son. Our son. I shook my head and stood up, cradling him and turned my back towards her. She needed to snap out of this, and quickly.

"Your mum is staying for the weekend. We have a ball to attend." My words were sharp. She croaked a little before she answered.

"I know. Have fun." She looked weak and sad, but I didn't feel sad with her. I was angry that I had a son with a woman I didn't feel anything for. I was angry with her for letting this happen. I was angry that she wasn't the woman I wanted her to be. I growled and left our room.

We'd arrived at Alfie's house early morning, and I couldn't wait to see if the rumours about Haz being clean were true. I couldn't wait to see this. I bounced up the large staircase and across the hallway towards his room. I knocked on the door before I entered. I caught the tail end of a brunette's hair dart through the bathroom door and grinned.

"Shit, sorry, I always forget you share your room now." I grinned at Haz and he wiggled his brows before I glanced towards his naked chest. "She's got a cracking arse," I admitted and watched him roll his eyes.

"That she has." He was smiling at me. His blue eyes weren't tinged with red around the edges, he was more built than I'd seen him be before. It must have been true. He was clean.

"I came up here for a valid reason." I smirked.

"Right." Haz half laughed.

"Dad's ball this weekend. What's your plan? You gonna walk in there with her on your arm?" I watched his face twist and watched him glance at the bathroom door where the shower had been turned on. He'd forgotten that was the whole reason we were here.

"Maybe. She doesn't know about it yet." I laughed in disbelief and shook my head slowly.

"Well, I think you might wanna warn her, and of the baby." I reminded him gently of his new nephew, hoping that part of him would have changed too. He just nodded and pulled himself to sit up straight in the bed. I pointed towards the bathroom door and smiled. "You have a good one there, Haz." The shower switched off and he just nodded.

"I know." He smiled—it was closed and guarded.

"Don't fuck it up." I nudged his arm and he nodded. He wasn't smiling now. I frowned and placed myself on the bed next to him. I needed a catch up with him. Talking was good for the soul. Or at least it was good for me. For my soul.

I filled him in on some of the guest's that Dad had invited to the charity ball. I'd told him all about the charity Dad had chosen to donate to and the reasons why. It was the CRY foundation in memory of somebody at the firm who passed earlier on in the year of a heart attack. *Poor bloke.* Avaya was now standing against the door frame. Her dark hair was voluminous, it framed her face and was long and curled down her chest. I whistled at her. She was a really beautiful woman. He'd bagged a really good one. Haz was frowning and Avaya had rolled her eyes.

"I like the hair," I said. She flushed crimson in colour, and I laughed as Harry pulled her towards him on the bed.

"The sun suites you, Avaya." She was darker in colour. She must have gone away with him. I wanted to ask where they had been and how long for, but I didn't want to seem like I was prying in their business. She was smiling softly at me now, her sea-green eyes were warm almost, and I patted my brother's shoulder as I stood up. This was my cue to leave.

"Remember, Hazel will be down later with the baby," I reminded him.

"You have a baby?" Avaya spoke quietly and her eyes widened as though she was in shock and was trying to hide it. I heard Haz half laugh and then watched her frown at him.

"Yeah, he's about a week old." He hadn't told her about him? I shot him a look of disappointment and I watched him smile a false smile.

"Kids, who'd have them?" Haz blurted and rolled his eyes.

"Not you." I poked him hard in the arm and left the bedroom quickly before I turned back and punched him in the face. Being clean was an achievement but not telling the girl he was in love with that I had a baby? Fucking arsehole.

CHLO

I'd spent the afternoon discussing plans with Harry about how we were going to introduce Av to everyone at the ball. His family were well off and had friends in high places. Those friends would surely report back to the Bandoni's. None of us were stupid after all, we had been living this life since we were kids. His mum would definitely have an opinion on it. Juve had been this morning and left pretty much straight away. Not that I was surprised by it. It had been a while since I'd seen him properly. I frowned as I watched Av sleeping the day away peacefully on the sofa. I envied how content she was. I reached and pulled her from the sofa.

"C'mon, you've gotta start getting ready. It's the ball tonight." I tried to sound enthusiastic about it. She groaned as she stood to her feet and followed me up the stairs. The difference in time zones must have really thrown her. The poor swine. I opened my door and presented the dresses to her. "Step right in…" I joked and placed my hands against my hips, and I flicked my hair. I'd missed making her over.

"I have no idea what the hell I'm gonna wear." She was staring blankly at the bed that was scattered with clothes and huffed aloud as she traced her hand over the green dress, and I winced.

"You love a green or pink dress, don't you?" I chuckled and nudged her softly.

"Oh, shush you." I wiggled my brow and gestured towards the mirror.

"Why don't you start putting your face on and decide on a gown later." I grinned widely and flicked on the straighteners. I was now in getting ready mode. I pulled my short hair from out of my face and placed it in a bun on the top of my head. I wanted to blow his socks off. I wanted him to want me. I couldn't help but pity myself. I sounded fucking tragic. I glanced over at Av who was

219

clearly struggling to find anything to match her new skin tone and laughed as I threw a Marc Jacobs foundation her way. She scrambled to catch it.

"Fucking hell, Chlo, that must have cost a fortune." She exhaled as she pumped it on the back of her hand. I shrugged. I had never really taken much notice of how much things cost. I'd become accustomed to wealth since my brother and Haz got involved in the law firm and the gangs. It was a far cry from the life I'd grown up living.

"Ninety quid, I think… I brought the bronzer too, look." I went to throw the large white package her way and she shook her head frantically before she winced and placed her hands on either side of her head.

"I believe you! I'll try it, just please don't throw it." She breathed as her hands were still placed out in front of her in a guard stance. I burst with laughter and admired her sitting cross-legged in front of a mirror on my bedroom floor. I simply placed the bronzer on the bed next to me and ran the straighteners through my hair. I was lost in my own thoughts of my childhood and the fact that all of Harry's family would be in that room again. He'd ignore me.

"What sort of ball is this?" She was grinning as she placed makeup on her face.

"His dad does it every year. It's fancy, hence the nice gowns." I placed a false smile on my face. "I wish we'd have met you years ago." My admission left my mouth, and I watched her nod. Maybe life would have been different for all of us if she'd have appeared sooner. If the lads would have been tasked with finding her sooner. I shook my head and continued to sort out my mop and face.

We spent the next hour or so chatting. I'd helped her paint her face and do her hair. I'd managed to wrap it all up in a low bun. She was staring now at the dresses placed on the bed. After she'd chosen hers, I picked up the black one that was long and had spaghetti straps.

"It's black bow tie, so I'm going in black too. A bit like my soul." Laughter left her mouth as we both proceeded to get dressed. She looked absolutely beautiful. The dress was long but not enough to drown her–the slit up the thigh was going to wind Harry up to no end. I had no doubt about it.

"Ready, Av?" I leant down to pick up the designer clutch bag off the bed and watched her nod.

"Yeah, I'll just put shoes on, and I'll be down." She needed five minutes, so I left her for a while. My feet pulled me down the stairs and I frowned as all the important men in my life were congregating. Haz and Jay were laughing with each other, and Juve was now staring at me. I cleared my throat as my eyes ran the length of his tux. His jaw clenched as I stood next to him.

"You're all woman now, hey?" He didn't look towards me as he muttered his comment my way. Instead, he was looking at Jay and Haz, and I shrugged my shoulders.

"I've always been all woman," I barked at him and moved from next to him. I was acutely aware I was glaring at Haz.

"You'll die when you see her." I needed to talk about her. I needed my mind off Juve. "You both will." I teased my brother who shook his head.

"How many more times do I have to tell you?" He paused.

"I'm not in love with her," we both said in unison.

"Yeah, yeah, I know." His lips thinned as he smirked, and Harry hit him hard. "I've worked wonders with her but you're all gonna have to tell her the plan." I grinned widely and heard Haz groan.

"Don't think I like the idea of her being on your arm," he admitted, and my heart fluttered.

"Aww! Haz!" I couldn't help it. His admission was cute. He frowned directly at me.

"Oh, fuck off, Chlo." I smirked and glanced at Juve whose face had hardened. He was looking upwards at the stairway.

"Here she is," he muttered. I smiled widely at her as she made her way downstairs. I glanced at Haz who was in awe of her. I longed to be looked at the way he looked at her. She'd changed him beyond words. In the best way. She had saved my best friend from a life worse than death. A life where he just existed. They were now wrapped up in each other and I couldn't help but smile like a Cheshire cat. Juve nudged my arm softly and my eyes met his deep blue lagoons.

"What?" I snapped. He just grinned.

"Fucking hell." He laughed. "You can't act like that while we're there, kid. She'll be assassinated midway through dinner." Juve spoke the warning to his brother, and Av's eyes darted from Juve to Harry who was rolling his eyes. "Mum will kill you," he added and looked towards me. I flushed a little under his gaze. "Don't worry, we've got a plan." Jay smirked at Juve and I watched as Juve's eyes snapped away from mine and landed back on Haz and Av. Juve grinned at her and she frowned as he pointed towards Jay.

"Act like you like me at least, sweetheart." Jay offered his arms out towards Av before he pulled her body closer towards his and pressed his lips against her cheek. I watched her cringe.

"Oh, fuck off. Is this the plan?" He released his lips from her chin and laughed before he shrugged.

"Oh, Av, don't spoil my fun." He raised his eyebrow at her, and she laughed. "Just be my dinner date." She pushed against his chest to place some space between them both.

"I don't like being that close to you. Your hands should be higher." She was reminding him that she wasn't his to touch, and I loved her for that.

"Yeah," Haz added as she turned around. "They fucking should." His eyes ran over her and he was clearly staking his claim.

I held his arm in mine and painted a smile on my face. This felt natural. I'd spent years acting like his partner, his lover and closest friend. However, tonight I hated it. He should have been able to walk in here and hold her hand. He was like a puppy pining after his mum. I nudged him gently with my elbow as he followed her out of the room with his eyes.

"Fuck's sake, Haz, get a grip," I barked. His blue eyes landed on mine.

"What's up with you, stroppy?" he teased as we moved forwards in the line.

"You're supposed to be in love with me. You're not making that very believable." I placed my head against his hard shoulder and heard him chuckle.

"I love you, Chlo, but I can't help it." I frowned. "I hate that your brother's hands are on her." I laughed a little and shook my head.

"Oh, I bet he's loving every second of it." I pressed yet another button of his and smirked as he shook hands with Dave.

"Hello, Miss Conway, a pleasure to see you again." He took his hand in mine and kissed the back of it. He was the biggest creep in the world. I'd always disliked him. "You didn't say your brother had a new lady friend?" I smiled politely and squeezed Haz to offer him some comfort.

"She's been a friend of the family for a while." He nodded at us.

"Well, she has a handshake, that's for sure." Haz pulled against my arm, and we were free from him and other prying eyes. I hovered to spot Av and Jay and noticed she was looking extremely uncomfortable next to my brother. We made our way towards them, and I plonked myself down next to her.

"I fucking hate that they all think we're banging." I rolled my eyes and glared at Haz. I pulled on my dress's train and placed it up in my lap. "And now everyone is going to assume that Jay's banging your Mrs." Av frowned.

"Kinda the plan, Chlo." He rolled his eyes and I smirked towards Avaya whose mouth was now on the floor.

"Has anybody cleared this plan with Av?" I gestured towards her, and her face must have told them all they needed to know. "Are you happy to act like you're shagging my brother?" She shook her head slowly. Jay cleared his throat before he leant into me.

"Chloe Conway, please refrain from swearing here." He was talking to me like he always did when I was misbehaving as a child. I smirked and heard Avaya holding in a giggle. It was infectious.

"Also, I didn't introduce her as my girlfriend, just a friend." Jay was blabbering now because he felt uncomfortable. It was adorable. I knew he had a soft spot for her, and I knew he didn't want to bang her but winding him up about it was so much fun. I glanced around the room and my eyes landed on Robert's widow. She was cradling their little boy. She looked so lost, and even though there was a room full of people, she seemed alone. I remembered Jay saying that the whole reason Henry had organised the ball this year was because of Rob dying. It had shocked everyone. He was so bloody young. I glanced at Aimee chatting with Avaya and her brother and then looked back towards the young girl who was probably no older than me, holding onto her little boy. My arms ached. For the first time in a long time, my arms were aching for the child I never knew. I caught the tail end of Aimee talking as I pulled myself from my thoughts.

These balls had always made me uneasy. I'd remembered dancing with Aimee as just a tiny blonde little girl at one much smaller than this one as a kid. My heart fluttered as I placed my head on my big brother's shoulder. If I danced with him, Haz would stop having a fucking heart attack over Av being in his arms. I sighed aloud and felt him move to look at me.

"Sup, Coco?" He raised his perfectly dark brow at me. "Too old to dance with your big brother?" he teased me, and I smiled before I shrugged at him. It had been a while since we had actually got close, I hadn't danced with him for years. I hadn't hugged him either. It took me back to being a kid, young and vulnerable, and I didn't need to feel any more exposed.

"You can't dance." I watched his eyes twinkle as he grinned a wide perfect smile at me. He pushed me softly and I laughed with him.

"Hey!" he exclaimed. "I'm not awful." He defended himself.

"When you haven't had a drink, you're all right, I suppose." I grinned as he winked at me, and we continued to dance. There was a slow song playing and I looked towards Aimee swaying with Juve–they were laughing together. He loved that kid. I wondered if that was how Jay looked at me. Like I was the apple of his eye. "Have you always protected me?" I asked him. He cleared his throat. There were obviously scenarios of our childhood that I would never forget, that would never leave, but I always remember him being there. No matter what. He had always fought my corner for as long as I could remember.

"I mean…" He faltered. "I tried, Chlo." I shook my head softly and looked up towards my handsome big brother.

"No, you always looked out for me." He simply nodded as we parted. "Don't think you failed, Jay." I gulped as I squeezed his hands in mine. He offered a false smile and I looked back towards Juve and Aimee. He followed my line of sight and watched them too. We had stopped moving now. We were just still.

"I bet she's feeling the exact same as you." He paused. "Embarrassed." I laughed and nudged him.

"No, she loves her brother." I smiled a wide smile at

him. Tonight had stirred some memories for both of us. He would get my subliminal message. I was sure of it.

I was running, and I wasn't entirely sure what I was running from. I had now made my way from the treadmills towards the bench press machine. I never worked out alone. In fact, I hated going to the gym, but I was avoiding meeting Juve's tiny human being. My gut wrenched at the thought, and I felt physically sick. Since he'd mentioned her being pregnant, I'd been dreading this day. My arms felt heavy, and it wasn't the weight I was lifting. I glanced behind me and noticed two very familiar piercing green eyes and dark locks of hair. It was Avaya. I frowned deeply as I placed the bar back in the holds.

"Why are you here and not cuddling the new-born?" My words were hostile. She just shrugged her shoulders.

"I'm pissed off." I wanted to roll my eyes, but instead, I sat up.

"Oh shit, what's he done?" It was her turn to eye roll now. I knew this conversation wouldn't have been about any other thing in her life.

"His reaction to the baby just threw me." Her eyes followed everyone in the room, but she didn't look at me. I draped my arm around her shoulder. I wasn't sure how much he'd told her about his aversion to babies. I wasn't going to be the one to tell her. He needed to do that. I would comfort her, but I wouldn't tell.

"He just doesn't like them, Av." I spoke the words very confidently.

"Well, I do." Her eyes looked to mine for comfort. I knew that was what she needed but I was struggling to give this to her.

"Look, don't take it personally, I'm sure he'll come around. He just…" I closed my mouth and she gulped. It took everything in me not to tell this girl everything.

"I know why, Chlo." She almost whispered my way. I opened my eyes widely and nodded. *She knew?* "Rava told

226

me that night he nicked me. He told me all about Holly and the baby. Just seeing that reaction has upset me more than I thought it would." I glanced away from her, staring at her sports bra, and my gut clenched. Rava had probably told her the mild version. I knew what really happened. I moved my arm from off her shoulder.

"I swore I'd never tell anybody about what happened with Holly and the baby. He needs to tell you in his own time." I gulped and watched Av take a breath inward.

"He looked at that baby like he wanted to kill him." I shook my head from side to side. Her words left me horrified.

"Fuck, Av, no, he would never. He doesn't like them, but he'd never hurt a child." I could tell her that with confidence as I gripped her hand in mine and squeezed them tightly. "Ever." I spoke softly and watched her blush. Her phone began to flash, and I noticed his name on the screen. I desperately wished he'd tell her what had happened so that she could start to wrap her head around it a little better. His pain was justified, but then so was her anger.

I watched the lads play Fifa for most of the night. Av had handled Harry just right. As she always did. I watched Juve with his son. The tiny little human placed delicately in his large arms like glass. I felt my eyes fill with tears and struggled to push them away.

"Where is Hazel?" I let the question slip from my mouth and instantly regretted asking about her. I didn't care. Not really. My eyes widened. "I mean, if you're here..." Juve's head snapped up. His attention shifted from Ethan to me.

"She isn't coping well." His face twisted as he answered my question. "Mum said she needed to be alone and away from it for a while." He shrugged at me, and I watched as he glanced down at the baby in his arms. I tried to keep my expression still, though part of me was splitting into two. I had been that woman. Only my pain wasn't because

I had a baby to look after, it was because I had made the horrible decision to take that away from myself. I ached to hold the tiny human. My arms ached for him a little. I had never held a baby. I had never let myself hold a baby. I had never wanted to. But now. Now I *needed* to.

"Can I hold him?" I questioned Juve and heard a gasp leave Haz's mouth, and I frowned deeply at him. He needed to shut up.

"Sure." He placed Ethan in my arms and as I held him, he wriggled. I wasn't sure whether I loved the weight of him in my arms and that they were full or if I was terrified of him and how warm he made me feel. "It suits you," Juve muttered. My heart stopped and my eyes instantly filled. I was about to burst into tears. I let myself look him in the eyes. I wished now more than ever that I could just tell him about it all, but I knew I couldn't, so I looked down at the baby in my arms.

"He looks just like you." I tried to keep my voice level as I whispered. This conversation I could do. I could examine the small baby and tell Juve how much they looked alike because that wasn't a lie. I looked down at him wriggling and smiled a little. He made funny noises, like a small puppy. I was lost in him. In awe of him. My arms felt full and so did my heart that was still like glass.

He had fallen asleep not long after Av had taken Ethan. He was sprawled out, snoring softly on the large cream corner sofa. I couldn't help but stare at him. He was just bloody perfect. Seeing him with Ethan hurt more than I thought it would have. It had been a while since I'd last spoken to him properly. Alone. Us alone was dangerous. I frowned as I placed his head on my lap as I sat down. I couldn't help but run my fingers through his soft hair that was so much shorter now. He groaned a little as I touched him, and I smiled as I shook my head. I loved watching him sleep. I always had. Av appeared in the doorway and glanced at me. Her icy green eyes warmed, and I watched her. She was a natural with babies.

"I'm taking him up for a kip." I just nodded.

"Thanks, Av." She lingered and her eyes darted between Juve and I. I began to get the feeling she knew something. She disappeared shortly after.

I sat there for a while, watching shit television and listening to him snore. His stubble ran against the skin on my thigh and my heart fluttered. His lips grazed my thigh, and I gasped a small moan. My pussy clenched. His eyes opened and he smiled. It was a weak smile. His dark blue eyes looked red with tiredness.

"It's been a long time since I've heard that sound from your mouth." He chuckled and I punched his muscular shoulder playfully.

"Shut up." I frowned and watched as he sat up, stretching upwards, revealing his perfectly chiselled abdomen. I bit down on my lip and frowned. I was about to combust. "Avaya has your baby." He stilled and then nodded. His eyes didn't meet mine as he turned his head in my direction.

"I thought you'd have him." I shook my head.

"I can't cope with babies." I tried to sound light-hearted, but it hurt. He shook his head.

"I thought you looked like a natural." His words were so softly spoken. My chest pounded. I wondered when I'd have the bollocks to tell him how I felt. That my world didn't quite turn when he wasn't around. I broke eye contact with him, and his hand touched my face." Come here, baby." He tilted his head towards me, and I frowned but I climbed onto his lap anyway.

"I miss you; you know?" His voice was a whisper. I smiled to myself.

"What… the hot sex we used to have?" I teased and heard him chuckle.

"I suppose that too."

"You get that with Hazel." I reminded him of his girlfriend, the mother of his child, and I watched him wince.

"I wish it was you." I scoffed my laughter out and raised my brow as his hand dropped to my thigh. "I do." He seemed serious and my heart decided to thud loudly.

"If you wish she was somebody else then I think you're with the wrong woman." He smirked at my sassy words and then shrugged.

"The woman I want doesn't want me." I shook my head slowly. The sentence that had just left his lips was so far from the truth that it was painful. I wanted to reach and stroke the soft skin of his cheek that was just above his stubble but stopped myself the second the thought popped into my head.

"The woman you want thinks you're insane," I lied.

"The woman I want left me." He leaned over me softly, the muscles in his shoulder flexing underneath his T-shirt. I could see them clearly in my mind's eye. I took in a sharp breath. "And didn't speak to me for six years." He ran his mouth over mine and I fought the wildest urge to grab his hair and pull him closer. "Yet, she's still the woman I want." My gut twisted as silence fell between us. I leaned in towards his mouth and closed my eyes. His hands wrapped themselves around my waist as he pulled me over him. My legs were spread either side of him and I didn't recognise the sound that left my lips.

"That woman was scared and fragile." I spoke in a whisper as my heart drummed in my chest and my stomach swirled with fear and desire. "That woman wasn't even a woman, Juve." I whispered again as my eyes closed and my throat constricted. "She was just a girl." He traced the exposed skin on my back with his fingertips then reached for the hair that was dangling in my face.

"I know," he muttered as he tucked it behind my ear. Tears threatened to drip from the corners of my eyes the longer we stayed like that. He didn't move any closer towards me. My stomach was still twisting uncomfortably as we shared such close proximity. "I wish things were different." I nodded and sat up softly, forcing my eyes open and inhaling loudly. The memories of being like this with him, in his mum's snug, flashed in my mind.

"Me too." Pain in my chest stopped me from speaking any more words. In that moment, I wished that Ethan was our little bundle, I wished that I didn't have to make that shitty decision all those years ago, and I wished more than anything that I'd have just fucking told him instead of running away from him. I started to wonder if I had caused myself unnecessary torment, confusion and heartache for all those years. I ran my thumbs over his cheeks and felt tears fill my eyes. I glanced down at his dark pools of blue and my heart flurried. I absolutely and completely adored him. I was still in love with him, and I wasn't sure that I'd ever get over him. I was almost certain I'd spend the rest of my life alone because of my feelings towards him.

"Let me take you somewhere." He was so still underneath me as he spoke, breaking our silence. I fought my tears and nodded.

"Okay." I'd have followed him anywhere. I wasn't strong enough to turn him away tonight, and if I was being honest with myself, I never had been, which is why I had run away and hid from him.

"Haz can watch his nephew for an hour or two. It won't kill him." My stomach clenched as he reminded me of his son. I stood off his lap and straightened myself out.

"Where are we going?" I asked him quietly and followed him towards the front door which was where I placed my coat over the exposed skin on my arms.

"Just for a drink." I rolled my eyes and walked with him. I wasn't sure I was ready to be alone and drunk with him. Alone and sober was bad enough.

The car ride to the Top Hat was quiet. I now had the added awkwardness with Alfie. I cringed as I remembered being spread-eagled against the bar. I shook my head and jumped from the car. He didn't offer me his hand and as I looked up at him, and I realised how much older he looked. His face wasn't as youthful as it had been the last time we were here together. Clearly, the stress of the new-born had gotten to him. I fought laughter. I examined him underneath the dimly lit car park lights as we walked closer towards the bar.

"Where did your curls go?" I raised my brow and watched his lips thin into a smile.

"They disappear when it's shorter." Our silence wasn't awkward, it was comfortable. It had always been comfortable really. Alfie waved at us as we made our way in, walking towards the bar, and I examined Juve intently. I wished I could hear his thoughts. His brow furrowed when he looked at Alfie. I tilted my head towards some chairs in the corner of the bar. The sounds of the live singer flowed throughout the room. I pressed my coat closer towards my body. The mood in the bar was sombre and I wasn't sure if it was reflecting my own mood or whether it was the vibe of the night. I thought about our fucked-up situation and frowned. I'd had so many one nights stands, fleeting relations with men and nothing had ever stuck. I knew deep down it was because of him. I was watching him laughing with Alfie and a stab of resentment for myself hit me like a ton of bricks.

"Fuck's sake Chlo," I muttered to myself. I'd managed to fuck it up again. I looked back at the table and messed with the bar mat. The drinks were placed down and as I looked up at him, I just stopped breathing. I really needed this to just stop.

JUVE

Her dark eyes warmed as she looked at me. She was still sitting in a huge puffer jacket and her skin looked slightly paler than normal. I smiled a weak smile her way and watched as she looked away. I knew being here with her was a mistake, but I needed to know how she felt. What she wanted. I needed to find out if she felt the same way that I did and had done for the last God knows how many years.

"Are you cold?" I asked and watched her dainty little shoulders rise and fall as she continued to stare into the glass of alcohol that I had placed in front of her just seconds before.

"I'm okay." She didn't sound it. I frowned as I took my coat off and placed it over the back of my chair before I took my seat. Her expression was tortured. "Juve, why are we here?" Her head snapped up, taking me by surprise. Her mouth was puckered up, and I shrugged. Her big brown eyes were wide with sadness, and I swallowed the lump in my throat.

"I…" I couldn't find my words. I wasn't sure really why I'd taken her away from the comfort of Alfie's house, but I just had. I frowned as she sat back in her chair.

"I slept with Alfie." Her admission made my heart stop beating. She sat up straight in her chair and glared at me. My heart fell through the souls of my feet along with my jaw. It clenched together as I looked towards him laughing with the regulars of the bar. I gripped my pint glass and took in a sharp intake of breath. Jealousy and resentment for him flooded me.

"What the fuck, Chlo?" I managed to spit out. Her mouth opened briefly.

"I wanted to make myself feel better." My heart felt like it was shattering. "Now we're even though, right?" I gulped down the lump growing in my throat as I made eye contact with her. "You get to go home knowing I'm fucking somebody that cares about me." I couldn't place my emotions, but salty tears were on the edge of falling from my eyes, and as I glanced at hers growing red, they mimicked mine. "I thought you deserved to know; I need you to know how bad it fucking hurts, Juve." I felt my brow furrowing as she looked towards Alfie laughing and joking at the bar. Fury raged in the depths of my stomach, and I reached to grip her hand. "Don't," she barked out her command. I froze.

"He doesn't know the first thing about you." I scoffed and watched her tears drop from her eyes. "What the fuck can he give you that I couldn't?" I questioned her harshly. She pushed her tears away as I pushed the beer from in front of us.

"You don't get it, do you?" Her pretty face scrunched. "You're killing me, Juve. You're fucking exhausting." She spat her venom my way. "You're so fucking cruel, Juve, you know that, right?" She pressed her arms close to her chest and her brow furrowed. I was about to justify my words, but she didn't give me another chance to speak. "Does she even know about me?" Her tone was harsh and so not like her as she pointed towards her chest. "About us?" I frowned. "Or am I that big of a mistake?" She paused as her voice got louder. "Am I that much of a dirty secret?" I shook my head and reached across the table for her hands to hold. My heart ripped when she referred to herself as a mistake. She crossed her arms after she'd snatched them away from me.

"She doesn't know about you." I spoke truthfully, I had no right lying to her now. "She doesn't know because she doesn't have to know." I frowned and shook my head again because nothing I was saying was coming out the way it was supposed to. I had known since the second I met Hazel that she would be the biggest fuck up of my life, and I was proving this to be the case. "She will know the second she meets you. That *you* are why I can't love her." I gulped out the truth. Hazel was inquisitive to say the very least. If there was one thing she knew about me, it was there was something that tied me to this place, and I knew the second she met Chlo she'd figure out it was her that grounded me here. Not my brother. Her. Chlo scoffed and took a gulp of her wine as she shook her head. The thud from my heart was louder in my ears.

"I deserve more than being a quick fuck when you visit your brother," she choked her words out. "I deserve more than that." Water escaped my eyes and trickled down my cheek. It lingered on my jaw before it dropped. She broke eye contact and stood to her feet. "I'm more than your mistake." She swallowed and I was sure I heard it. That hurt. Her calling herself a mistake hurt. She had never been a mistake to me. "You don't get to touch me like you live for me anymore. I'm letting you go, Juve." She stood to her feet and reached down for my cheek. I grabbed her hand which was now against my face. "You don't have to pretend that I'm the one anymore. I get it and I'm letting you go." My chest twisted, my hand shook a little as I squeezed hers in mine and shook my head.

"Chlo..." I tried to call her name as tears dripped from both our faces. I went to stand, and she leaned in to place her lips against mine.

"You're fucked, Juve Vens, and I'm not going to watch it all unravel." She placed her hands upon the table that kept us apart and gave me a look that she never had before as she moved backwards away from me. She looked at me like she hated me. "I'm not sticking around to watch you live happily ever after." People were watching us, and even Alfie's eyes were on us. She tucked her blonde hair behind her ear and finished her wine. I gripped her arm between my fingers and pulled her towards me.

"My happy ending?" I growled. "Are you fucking kidding?" I was furious with her. Surely to God she could see how miserable I was?

"I hope she's everything you ever wanted, Juve." Tears dripped down her cheeks and I fought the urge to catch them with my fingers. I hated seeing her cry, always had.

"You don't get it, do you?" I muttered as I released her from my grip.

"No, I don't," she whispered. "I don't understand how you"–she pushed my chest hard with her index finger–"can sleep next to her every night and fuck her senseless if you claim that you feel like that about me." She turned on her heel and began to walk away from me. "Be fucking happy…" My chest fluttered uncomfortably. "Baby." She raised her brow. "You don't have to pretend I'm your person anymore." She breathed her words, and I wasn't sure I would cope with watching her walk away.

"Chlo…" I called after her as she walked away from our table. I went to stand, to chase her until I realised that chasing her would do nothing good for either of us. I had never made it clear that I wanted her, I'd fucked her head around for years by just being with Hazel, and I'd added a baby to the situation. I watched as she walked from the bar. I watched as Alfie ran after her and I clenched my fist tightly. If she was done, I'd let her go. I had to. I fell backwards into my chair and took a deep breath. I didn't cry. I hadn't cried for years, but at that moment, I wanted to. Sick settled in the bottom of my throat, and I hit the table before I left The Top Hat.

To be continued…

ABOUT THE AUTHOR

Anna White is a UK based author who writes steamy, dark romance novels. Her love for writing helped her overcome some difficult times within her life and has always been an escape from the constraints of everyday life.

Alongside being a mother, Anna enjoys long hacks during the British countryside on her trusted steed!

Printed in Great Britain
by Amazon

34987322R00134